The Cursed

A DEATH WITCH

L.A. KENNEDY

ENTWINED PUBLISHING

A Death Witch
ISBN # 978-1-80250-242-8
©Copyright L.A. Kennedy 2025
Cover Art by Kelly Martin ©Copyright March 2025
Interior text design by Entwined Publishing
Published by Eternal, an Entwined Publishing imprint

Published in 2025 by Entwined Publishing, United Kingdom.

Entwined Publishing is a division of Totally Entwined Group Limited.

A DEATH WITCH

Dedication

For Van

"A witch never gets caught. Don't forget that she has magic in her fingers and devilry dancing in her blood."
— Roald Dahl

Chapter One

I stared down at the third body of the night. Her blood soaked the cold concrete around her. There was no way I wouldn't be bringing a piece of her home with me. The sharp metallic scent of her blood hung in the air, mixing with the trash strewn about, making her body smell like the end of the day at the meat market. Death was never dignified, whether you were surrounded by your loved ones or tossed away like garbage. We all met our maker the same way, scared and alone.

Her wavy copper hair was styled in such a way as to reveal the startled look on her thin, tense face. It was the only part of her body that hadn't been ruined by the slaughter. Her pale skin was already graying from the cruel hand that had been dealt to her. Speckles of blood mixed with her freckles, and I held back the urge to clean them off with my hand. Her wide green eyes had seen her attacker, her fear forever frozen and staring back at me. The sparkle in her eyes was long gone, leaving a dead and empty gaze. It chilled me to the bone. The clover pin—which hadn't brought her any luck—attached to the collar of her once-white shirt, glinted under the flashes of police cruisers and unnecessary paramedics. She wasn't taking a ride in the bus tonight. Her chauffeur would come with a full-length zipper and handles.

That was the face of Rowan Sage, an earth witch, and it would haunt me until something worse took up her place in my memories. Given my chosen lifestyle, it wouldn't take long before I moved on from Rowan to something or someone new. Little by little, with each new scene I was called to, I created stains that hounded me while I slept and, at times, froze me during my waking hours. Some horrors never left, and until the sun swallowed the earth, there'd always be nights like this, reasons I slept with a gun and a Hellhound in training.

I crouched down, the movement wafting her last moments up to my nose. I swallowed my urge to gag and picked up her bag, standing and taking a few steps back, out of reach from the perfume of the dead. With gloved hands, I dug through her black bat-shaped purse. Nothing stood out as being reason enough to kill her in a dingy back alley. Handmade lip balm from the witches' market, a wallet with three cards and her level-one Coven membership, fifty bucks, house keys, and an uninvoked hex bag.

"Why you, of all people?" I whispered, scanning the victim once again. I took another look at the alley and wondered if there was any significance to the location. Aside from a fresh body, nothing stood out. Was it a case of the wrong place, wrong time? Or was she the target?

Level-one witches, especially earth witches, weren't high on hit lists these days. A couple decades ago, perhaps, but not today. I put her purse into a brown paper evidence bag, her identification in my hand, and jotted down her information for my report. I passed her driver's license and the brown bag to a nearby officer, who would tag it. After two decades and some change, her life was snuffed out. *What a waste.*

Her body had been discovered while I was at the second crime scene. I'd been called in by Mannix after the first body. He had sensed hell but hadn't been able to find traces of a demon or the energy left behind by another magic user. When I'd arrived, I hadn't seen any hints of hell or magic, either. Hope had called me to the scene, but curiosity kept me there once I came up empty of answers. Hope that such carnage was the work of the pits and not man. It was easier to sleep at night, thinking hell was responsible for all of humanity's problems. If we just kept the gates closed, all would be right in the world. *As if things would ever be so simple.* The truth was, mankind did worse to each other than any damned or cursed ever did. Demons didn't rob grocery stores, kill for a wallet with twenty bucks in it, or shoot up schoolyards. People did. But it didn't stop us from blaming the beasts, even in the face of evidence to the contrary. Of every case I'd been called into, where the guilty claimed they were possessed, only one had ever been able to use that as a defense. The fact is, we're more than capable of horror without hell needing to tinker with our morality. The best thing a demon could do to guarantee our demise was to sit back and watch us go to work on each other. We did all the heavy lifting for them.

Sure, hope had brought me to a dank alley, but I knew I'd leave without any of my own. Nights like these took it away and left me with the raw reality of the hell we all had created without the help of the pits.

Some days, I really hated this world. But the alternative was a cage in hell, which wasn't much better.

I stepped back from the body and blurred my vision, seeing through my aura, a witch's sixth sense. Rowan's soul was long gone, but imprints of the night, those who had come and gone, still lingered. Magic in the air prickled my arms and pulled my attention in circles. My eyes roamed the backstreet, picking up hints of emotion and stains so deep and evil they'd take another few decades to fade. I scanned for the strongest imprints, like picking through a trash can for a missing diamond. Bits of magic and old taint floated in the breeze. It snaked along the ground and held onto the walls like chipped paint. The alley was a popular walkthrough, leaving too much of one thing and not enough of why I had been called to the new scene. I frowned when I didn't find what Mannix had been hoping for. I had come here for one reason and came up short. There were two reasons, if I was counting the memories I was making, that I didn't want.

"*Inretio,*" I whispered, using my aura to send a net out into the alley to trap demonic energy. It was a new spell taught to me by my grandfather, Samuel. As a retired guardian, he was a walking, talking book of spells that I'd find nowhere else. The spell was still new enough that it tingled to hold onto. It turned my hands cold and fingertips numb. I could feel every magic and emotion that had walked the alley for the last week, as though they were all here at once. As I suspected, I saw no hints of fresh black taint. The alley would look like spilled ink in water if a demon had been here recently. I would have been able to see his footsteps, as though his taint was burned into the ground. But I hadn't picked up any hellish happenings at the other two sites, either. With a wave of my hand, I dropped the spell to the ground, refocused my eyes and pulled my shields back into place. My soul breathed a sigh of relief, cut off from the night's carnage.

"I'm ready." I motioned for Mannix, who had emptied the area of souls for me. I didn't need everyone clear of me to do the job, but the combined emotions of onlookers and police made my skin crawl when I was using aura magic.

"Please tell me you've got something, Ailis." He sounded as tired as I felt. Seven in the morning was a painful hour to be awake for those of us who hadn't yet been to bed.

"Like the other two scenes, there's something I can't quite put my finger on." I pursed my lips, thinking. I glanced around the scene once more, trying to piece it together. "Zero witnesses at all three scenes. It's not unusual in a city. It's just odd that three scenes didn't turn up a single set of eyes. None of us want to stumble into someone else's business if that business is ending lives, but it was one hell of a busy night downtown for there to be not a single onlooker. Someone had to see or hear something."

"We're canvasing and checking out the neighboring security tapes. See who came and went, but this alley is a void, like most of them. There's nothing down here of value, except the victim, to keep an eye on," he answered. "What are you thinking?"

"Besides there being eyes out there who likely saw this go down but are too scared to open their mouths, I'm thinking about what is missing from this scene," I replied.

"What do you mean, something is missing?"

"Whenever we're dealing with hell, it's common to feel hatred, pleasure, arousal, and absolute delight in the carnage they're causing. But this isn't hell, Mannix.

I can feel the emotions I usually feel from a demon, but it's missing the actual hell part. There's no scent of the pits, no telltale demonic smells, no taint crawling over my skin, no fresh demonic energy. I can feel evil, but it wasn't caused by the pits. The energy is similar, but it isn't quite the same. There were souls attached to whoever did this."

"But I can feel it. I can feel hell," he replied. "I can smell hell. Why can't you?"

"You can feel and smell Rowan, as can I," I corrected him. "She's a level-one earth witch. I'm guessing what you're feeling and smelling is related to the circle she tried to set, and the lingering magic in the air as she pulled on the energy from hell." I led Mannix back to the body and pointed at the blood splatters on the ground. "These drops of blood are inconsistent with her wounds and the rest of the blood patterns. She was stabbed multiple times, and it sprayed as though the stabs were one after the other. I'd be surprised if the medical examiner came back with only one weapon used." I crouched down and lifted her left hand. "She has a fresh slice across her palm. It's too clean and shallow for it to be a defensive wound. I'd bet my cauldron there's a small blade kicking around somewhere, and it'll be hers." I stood and stepped back, walking in a circle around her. "I can feel the lingering power in the air. She set a circle, thinking it would help her. Whatever came for her, she thought her magic would save her. She had enough time to think she could protect herself. If this were a demon with her name on his list, a level-one wouldn't have time to scream, let alone try to set a circle."

"Unless she wasn't his target. If she was a bystander, she may have had time to set her circle and caught his attention when she pulled on energy," Mannix suggested. "We both know a powerful enough demon can take down a circle, especially one set by a level-one."

"True. But if a demon, powerful enough to take down a circle, did this, then where are the rest of the bodies?" I asked. "Mannix, we're downtown. Bealtaine festivals have been raging since noon. Between the festival and the after-parties, there are thousands of souls, ripe for the picking, all over the streets. People from all over the world are visiting for the celebrations. If this was a demon, we'd have found her sooner by simply following the trail of bodies he'd leave on the ground. Demons don't cherry-pick. They don't kill a few randoms and pack it in. They kill everything with a pulse until they're stopped, or they have what they come here for."

"Unless she owed a debt. Demons pop up all the time to collect souls and don't go on a killing spree. This, what happened to her, may have been a message to *her*, nothing more. I've been to plenty of scenes where demons took their sweet-assed time, carving chunks off of their victims, spending hours tormenting them before killing them."

"Three unrelated folks owing debts to the same demon in one night?" I asked. "The odds of that happening are astronomical. Demons don't save up their collections for a one-night grocery shop. They come the moment the soul is due for the taking."

"Fuck," Mannix groaned. The hope for simple answers faded, replaced with the frustration of the unknown. "I'm sorry I called you away from May Day," he said for the third time tonight. "I owe you."

"Don't worry about it. I'll be issuing an invoice for my consult," I replied. "I'm sorry I don't have the answers you were looking for."

"What are your thoughts?" He motioned at the body. "If you had to guess. I need to go back to my captain with something, anything. Empty-handed is not how I want to start my meeting with Holland. I don't get paid the big bucks to be behind the Eightball."

"Hate to say this, but you're not hunting a demon or magic user. My money is on humans doing all three murders," I answered. "A demon would have ravaged the soul completely. It would take days for that kind of torment to fade. Terrified souls stain the very air. We would have felt the residual energy like a slap across the face as soon as we stepped into this alley. But there's nothing here. It doesn't even smell like the pits. The only fresh odors are the trash cans, mossy earth magic, blood, and us. There are hints here and there from odors long past, but nothing recent enough to give me pause. Aside from the dead body, it feels like every other alley in the city."

"I'm not picking up any other unnatural, either," Mannix said, and I glared at the word he used. "What? That's the official name of a magic user. It's better than what some people call us."

"Metaphysical or magic user are the PC terms. Get with the times, witch," I replied. "But I agree. Every magic user I know would leave an imprint of their energy behind, and there's nothing fresh here, just like the first two bodies you found. I can pick up a little of the emotion left behind — hate, anger, arousal, but it's not strong enough to be hell. It's no stronger than a customer service line the day after a Black Friday sale."

Mannix opened his notepad and read his notes. "At the first scene, a young shifter, the only energy was the victim's. He was attacked from behind and stabbed in the heart. The coup de grâce was removing his head. The second scene, an elemental witch still in training, throat slit and stabbed in the heart. No residual energies outside of the victim's."

Mannix had written down the same thing I had, almost verbatim. "My point exactly. What demon does that? They don't stalk prey unless it is the one who called them, and the demon has no choice but to smoke them out, but they still leave a trail of bodies behind them while they are topside. Neither of the witches have knocked on hell's door even once. There is no debt they'd have. We'd smell the taint if that were the case. And the shifter, even if he somehow figured out how to do it, he didn't smell like he's been ringing a demon's doorbell."

"Shit," he groaned. "When I found nothing at the first scene, I hoped you would. I thought it may have been a demon I was unfamiliar with."

"Trust me, Mannix, you'd have known it was a demon even if they were unknown to you. For this, you need a bloodhound, not a witch. Track the smells, not the magic. It'll lead you to those responsible."

"He's not on shift for another week. His wife had twins a couple of weeks ago," Mannix replied.

"Tell Arlow I said congratulations." I smiled at the news. There were so few of Arlow's kind out there. Bloodhounds were naturally born, not cursed or infected. It had been the luck of the Gods when he had found another and married her. "Twin bloodhounds? Mercy, he's in for a fun few years. I went to high school with triplets. They were a nightmare for their parents until they outgrew puberty and could control their tracking impulses."

"Maybe he'll come out for a few hours," Mannix said.

"Bribe him with chocolate tarts from the bakery near Samuel's house. That's how I convinced him to track a troll when no one else would help me. His wife doesn't let him eat sugar," I answered. "It works every time."

"I'll give him a call," he replied. "Thanks for coming out. Send your invoice straight to me. I'll have accounting issue a direct deposit."

At the tape blocking off the scene, I pulled off my gloves and paper booties and tossed them into a biohazard bucket at the end of the alley. Mannix followed me to my car, jotting down a few more notes. I paused before opening my car door. Like spiders dancing down my spine, I felt eyes on me. Onlookers crowded the sidewalk and huddled in front of neighboring businesses. I motioned to the cameras above us.

"We're already on it, Ailis," Mannix said.

I leaned in. "Check these ones against the others. Look at the crowd and see if the same face pops up. You know what they say about the crazies."

"They like to watch," he replied. "I'll let you know what we find."

"Good luck. If you need me, you know where to find me." I got into my car, hoping he wouldn't need me for another crime scene.

I checked my phone and started my car. I missed a dozen text messages from Cisco, who had been at Samuel's Bealtaine celebration with me before I got the call from Mannix. He'd sent me photos of what I was missing out on. A pang of envy laced through me, but it was quickly silenced by a photo of all the cookies Cisco had smuggled out of the party in a Tupperware container. Miguel had texted me once he got home from Pack, saying to wake him when I arrived. That last message soothed my soul. From horror to home. Sometimes, love was enough to chase away the awfulness of the world. I sent him a text saying I was heading back to the house.

The drive was a blur of early morning traffic, but most were coming into the city while I was heading out. The radio played the same rhetoric from the Humans for Humans group as they did daily. Every turn of the dial had the hate group blaring. They were using the brutalization of three people as their soapbox today. The group had been around for years, and it didn't look like they'd be going away any time soon. They were one in a sea of organizations, all aimed at keeping the city clean of monsters. Fear breeds contempt, and contempt is deadly in the wrong hands. HFH members were usually on the news every night, stirring an already boiling pot. It was hard not to hate them with the same ferociousness they showed anyone who wasn't pure human.

I pulled into my vehicle-clogged driveway and smiled. Sofia, Ben, May, Cisco, Philip, and Miguel's vehicles were parked in perfect lines, each depending on who would be leaving first. I parked at the end, behind Cisco. If I was in the way, they'd move it. I grabbed my bag and stepped into the chilled morning air with the first smile of the day. It never got old, having a full house. On days I had my fill of people, I'd go to my office or bedroom, or Miguel and I would go for a walk. Those days were far and few, and they usually revolved around something evil that had come knocking or swallowing up one of my students. More times than not, being close to the others smoothed out the wrinkles of my sadness. I understood now why being a member of Pack was so important to them all, why they gathered in groups at every opportunity. When you fought a holy war every day and touched hell around every corner, having a family reminded you of why you kept going back out to do it again. Even though I only sprouted fur on weeks I didn't shave my legs, they still treated me like I was part of their family and welcomed me with the same care and love they had for each other.

When I opened my front door, I was bombarded with sounds that warmed me to my core. Inside, a chorus of laughter and chatter flowed from the kitchen. The smell of breakfast filled my nose, and my stomach growled instantly. I kicked off my shoes and headed straight for my shower. I smelled like dumpsters and death and half a bottle of perfume. It was not an agreeable scent. I reached the foot of my stairs before Miguel came from the kitchen with two cookies in his hand. He followed me up the stairs and into my bedroom. With the door closed, the emotions I had held in from seeing death up close and personal rolled from my eyes. I sat on the foot of my bed and tucked myself into his arms. Hugs, love and cookies — the trifecta of soul bandages.

"It was awful," I whispered around the tightness in my throat. "My heart hurts for the victim's families. One minute, their loved ones are here, and the next, Mannix is knocking on their doors. Dear god, they removed the head of the first victim. His family won't even be able to see him again while they say goodbye. The last victim, I lost count of how many times she had been stabbed."

Miguel hugged me a little tighter. "Death, whether expected or not, is painful. That it was done in such a horrid way is deplorable. I'm sorry you had to see that."

"It's the needless death that hurts me the most. I don't understand why we do this to each other," I answered. "Some days, I really hate the world we live in. Some of us are stronger than others, and we don't use that strength to protect each other. We conquer, we take, we kill. I don't get it."

"The world is filled with monsters, Lish. It always has been and always will be. I'm sorry you had to experience it up close," he replied.

"Why can't we just help each other?" I asked.

"I really wish it were that simple. In our world, Lish, most often, keeping your head down is how you stay alive."

I sighed. "I don't think I could ever just keep my head down. All too well, I know what it's like to be hunted. I couldn't just watch someone else go through that. I don't know how so many others can."

"I love you for your soft heart, but it's also why you're usually up shit creek and running for your life more often than anyone I know."

I shrugged. "We all need hobbies."

"Let's get you cleaned up," Miguel said, helping me to my feet. "You'll feel better once you can't smell it anymore. We'll get some food into you, and if you're up to it, we'll spend some time with people who care about you."

"I'm sorry. I must stink," I replied. "I sprayed myself with perfume before I came in."

"I've smelled a lot worse," he answered. "You don't have to hose yourself down with fruity scents before coming inside. This is your home. I am here whether you smell like you crawled through a gutter or daisies."

"You can still smell it under my body spray, can't you?" I asked, and he nodded.

"You smell like a dead body walking through the perfume department at the mall," he answered, making me smile. "I can also smell the donuts Mannix always bribes you with, coffee, and the ink you used to make your notes. Not much escapes the nose of a Lycan."

My clothes went into the hamper, and Miguel got my shower ready, climbing in with me. He washed the smell from my hair and body, gentle with every touch. He had this way of knowing exactly what touch I needed. Miguel knew my soul as well as I did. He wrapped his arms around me from behind and kissed my shoulder. He waited for me to respond before going any further. I pushed my back into him, hinting at my need. The memories of tonight would always be there, but I wanted to feel something good that would replace the heaviness in my heart.

Miguel turned me around to face him before pinning me against the shower wall with his hips. He moved my hand to meet his arm behind my back, locking it in place, holding my body open for him. He pressed his knee between my thighs, pushing my legs apart until I was straddling his thigh. Before I could say a word, his mouth was on mine, muffling my warning of being heard by a houseful of people. Miguel never cared, nor did his Pack. He lifted his knee between my legs, inching it up until my breath caught. I closed my mouth to keep my moans to myself.

Miguel leaned into my ear, licking my lobe. "Oh, Lish, you can try to keep quiet, but you'll scream for me today. I promise you that."

My knees buckled, and I jerked when my groin made contact. Miguel's knee kept me standing while I ground myself against him. He kissed my neck, and I bit my lip. He ran his free hand up and down my side, inching closer to the swell of my breast, teasing my nipple, before sliding his hand down to my hips, thighs and finally, my core. His hiss filled my ear. I was ready. I was waiting. Without warning, he dropped my trapped wrist and yanked me to his chest. He pushed his tongue into my mouth as he gripped my thighs and lifted me to his hips. I wrapped my arms and legs around him, bruising my lips on his. He shifted me on his hips, pulling himself back, and lowered me slowly onto his hardness.

Our groans filled the shower as he slid into me. Inch by inch, he entered me. My nails dug into his shoulders as I stretched around him. My mind and body filled with instant need. Miguel leaned me into the wall until my body accepted all of him. I squirmed against his stillness.

"Please," I said into his mouth.

"Please, what?" he asked, pulling from my kiss with a teasing grin, almost malicious in his intent to tease me. He held me tighter, keeping me from moving against his body. He controlled every movement I tried to make. "Say the words. I want to hear you."

"Fuck me," I said, my nails dragging up his back as I struggled to grind against him.

"Hold on, Lish," he said, and I pressed my chest into him, wrapping my arms tightly around his neck.

Miguel worked his hips slowly until he knew I was ready. His pace quickened, and my eyes rolled back. Leaning into me, holding my thighs, he lifted and pressed forward at once. Our rhythm echoed in the shower, skin against skin, moans, and my demands.

"Close," I groaned. "Please, don't stop."

My breaths came out as sharp gasps as the heat built in my stomach. Miguel pressed me into the wall, knowing I'd be lost to my orgasm soon and he'd have to keep me upright.

"Come for me," Miguel said, his pace quickening. "I want to feel you come."

I squeezed my eyes shut as his pace shifted into something frantic. He was as close as I was. His fingernails dug into my thighs, and his teeth bit into my shoulder. I finally screamed as my pleasure smashed down on us both. I worked my hips against his, matching his speed and intensity. Miguel's voice boomed through the bathroom. He drove himself as deep as he could go and pumped his orgasm to the surface. His heart pounded against my chest, but he didn't lose his rhythm until my orgasm had run its full course. He dragged every inch of pleasure from me until I was nothing more than one long and shaking moan.

Miguel grabbed onto the towel bar to keep himself from falling over. He helped me slide down his body to my feet, pressing himself against me to hold me standing. I wrapped my arms around him and settled into the afterglow. Our breathing calmed as we both slowly came back down to earth. He lifted my chin and kissed me softly.

"I love you," I said, tucking myself into his chest, his heart under my ear.

When our limbs could move without feeling like jelly, Miguel helped me out of the shower. I was past the point of exhaustion. My feet shuffled, and my legs heavy like I had been running full speed for an hour. He skipped the usual conversation about his day and mine, knowing I'd have nothing to offer him with my head still in the clouds. Instead, he dried my hair, braided it, and helped me pull on my pajamas. Rather than heading straight to bed, I waited at my bedroom door for him.

"I just want to say good night first," I said, smiling.

"One cup of tea and into bed, or you'll be a zombie for class later." Miguel grabbed a pair of joggers from the foot of the bed and pulled them on before we hit the hallway.

I cringed at the thought of leaving the comfort of home today. "Thankfully, I only have evening class tonight. Ziggy is helping me show my students how to identify taint on objects and isn't willing to come until his shop closes."

"I really wish you'd stop playing with fire. Ziggtmoy is a demon."

"He's in recovery," I answered and chuckled to myself. "He's a card-carrying member of society, Miguel, who happens to have once been a demon."

"Recovery? He's literally wearing a person."

"So are you, wolf," I countered, and he rolled his eyes. "Don't throw stones. The same magic that keeps Ziggy in his meat suit keeps your wolf at bay."

"Apples to oranges," he replied. "I'm not a demon."

"But at one time, you all were considered demons," I reminded him. "When you die, you become a Hellhound. Your soul will live in hell. How many religions out there think Hellhounds are demons? All of them."

Miguel finally put his hands in the air, giving up on an argument neither of us would win. It wasn't a conversation we would see eye to eye on. Miguel, in human form and wolf, hunted demons. It was in his blood to hate them. I wasn't their biggest fan either. But any demon not wanting me dead and willing to help me in exchange for a slab of chocolate from the witches' market and not a chunk of my soul was worth programming into my phone. Ziggy had helped me more times than I could count and had never asked for a payment that came in the form of skinning my soul alive. Sure, he was a demon, and I'd never turn my back to him, but it was hard to be high and mighty when I smelled like a witchy teabag steeped in hell. I was as damned as they come.

We stepped into a full kitchen, and I grinned. The night washed away with a sigh and smiles as I was noticed. The conversation didn't stall. Cisco pushed out a chair, and I was invited into the group as though I had been there my entire life. May, the resident vampire hunter and partner of a Pack member, sat across from me, arguing with Cisco on the benefits of keeping a vampire hunt old school because technology failed more times than the reliable wooden stake. Cisco, on the other hand, thought differently. He was all about the latest tech. One glance around my house said he had upgraded every inch with top-of-the-line security. He had a thing for telling the lights to turn on and off while not moving a muscle. I had made fun of him for a week for it, but secretly, I loved not having to get out of bed to turn off my bedroom lights. I'd never admit it to him, though.

Breakfast came and went with me asleep on the couch. The noise in the background felt as warm as my blanket and as heavy as my cat. They whispered about the murders, speculating on motives while I let myself drop face-first into sleep. Unless the house caught fire or a demon walked through the door, I wasn't getting up for anything outside my alarm. Before the last voice faded, Miguel lifted me off the couch and carried me to bed, my cat in tow.

Chapter Two

I grabbed my lunch and coffee on my way out of the door, having slept until the last possible moment and making a mad dash to get ready. Six hours of sleep had gone by in a blink. I felt like a zombie, with sunken eyes and sandpaper lids. I had slept with the same dead-to-the-world dedication as the newly dead and woke feeling like it had been a blink in time. My head was still in a heavy fog that followed me home from the crime scenes. I wasn't physically tired. I could live off naps and coffee if I had to. My soul was drained. The human spirit could only take so much before it threw its hands in the air and cursed the heavens. I'd cursed several times while I got dressed for work.

Cisco had left earlier with Ben, dropping Sofia off at the Chapel to dig up old graves and bones from the grounds. She was determined to rid the place of ghosts. I didn't bother telling her that some were there to stay. Sofia was stubborn enough that I was sure some would leave just to escape her constant badgering. Sometimes being pigheaded was the only way to get things done, and Sofia had cornered the market on an irritating level of persistence. Miguel left right behind me. He was on training duty, and tore out of the driveway with a grin. He was excited to reshape the local Pack into something they'd never been — true Lycan. According to him, the local Pack was something closer to abused, wild animals, lashing out or cowering. If anything, Miguel found hope where no one else could. Sofia and Cisco had none, and I was of the mind that once a dog bites you, you put it down. But I also thought that about every magic out there. No one ever came back from the dark side.

Pulling into campus was a nightmare of honking horns and the hate group Humans for Humans picketing. Although their argument today was no different than any other day — the complete segregation of humans and nonhumans — their presence in Vancity was becoming harder to ignore. With a bible in one hand and a gas can in the other, they were no different from the bigots of yesterday. Their signs may have had religious symbols, but their absolute hate and annihilation of anything nonhuman didn't make them the good little Christians they pretended to be. They were worse than any monster group they were currently targeting. HFH was a plague, spreading their hatred, cropping up everywhere, and targeting every magic with the same level of revulsion that the demons showed mankind. What a wonderful time to be alive. For every step forward we made as a society, these narrow-minded fools dragged us back two steps.

When two activists approached my car, screaming doom and gloom for my soul, I rolled my eyes and flipped them the finger. They were just another group of crazies to me. Had it not been for them standing in my way, they'd have remained beneath my notice. As security cleared my path, I heard a few calling me a witch, as though it were news to me or anyone else on campus. The *demon lover* chants weren't new, either. Telling me I was going to hell wasn't a threat. It was a very real ending for me, and it had nothing to do with being a witch. My cursed soul had a foot in the pits already, a free pass through the gates, gifted to me after a car accident. There was nothing new to be seen here. No wonder most of us tuned them out. It was regurgitated garbage every time any of them opened their mouths.

When I parked, I texted Ziggy a heads-up. My warning wasn't to keep him safe. It was to remind him there were cameras everywhere, and he'd lose his top side permit if he ate one of the picketers. I grabbed my bag from the backseat and drank half my coffee before I made it to the demon wing. Every few feet, fliers about our damnation were taped to the walls. *The wingnuts made it pretty far this time.* I sent a text to campus security and a few photos of the fliers, letting them know HFH had made it past the gates and were on campus. I pulled down the leaflets along my way. It pissed me off that my students faced this kind of crap while off campus. I wouldn't tolerate it while they were on campus. They deserved a safe space, and these bastards weren't going to take it away from them.

Philip pointed at the clock as I stepped into my office. "Just in the nick of time, Ailis."

"I'm never late," I said, dropping my bag on the table. Philip gave me a look that said I was full of shit and late more times than not. I shrugged. "The HFH crackpots at the gate slowed me down. It took almost fifteen minutes to get through the crowd." I held up a few crumpled papers from the halls and tossed them into the garbage. "They made it all the way to the demon wing this time."

"You just missed Mannix. He said the same thing. He called it in, but it's pretty low on the list compared to murder victims."

"I sent a text to security. What did Mannix want?"

Philip picked up his message pad. "He wanted me to tell you that there are a few people of interest from last night. All three suspects were spotted at all of the crime scenes. He'll let you know if something comes of it. Also, he wanted me to remind you to send your invoice and report by tomorrow."

"I'll work on it after class. The report will be quick. I wrote the draft in between scenes," I answered. When Philip stood, I shook my head and pointed to his seat. "I need to have a word with you before class."

"Sure, what's up?" he asked.

I opened my bag, pulled out a sign-up sheet for a night class I was teaching next month, and slid it to Philip. "Can you explain why you've bumped two students from the class?"

He didn't need to look at the form. "They're not witches, that's why."

"Uh-huh, and it has nothing to do with the fact that they are vampires?" I asked.

"Since when did you start allowing vampires to take your classes?" he asked. "You only let Coven members take those courses."

"It is university policy to only allow registered Coven members in classes that directly teach spelling," I replied. "But this class is on the history of magic. No spells. No magic. Anyone can take it, and I've always kept it that way."

"And? What's your point?"

"My point, Philip, is that I went through the last twenty informal lectures and have noticed an uncomfortable pattern. You have declined access to every vampire who has tried to enroll. But I see you've allowed every other flavor of magic into the classes, especially those of the furry variety. Your stance that I only let witches sit in my lecture hall is bullshit," I answered. Lines formed around his eyes, and a guilty look followed. "Discrimination is an ugly monster, and there is no room for it in my department. If that is how you plan to conduct yourself, there's a whole group of them standing at the gate, calling for our heads. I'm sure they'd welcome you."

He opened his mouth, and I shook my head again. I wasn't finished.

"At one time, I didn't question it. But since my eyes have been opened to several species I didn't even know about, I've noticed a hateful pattern with you. You favor the shifters and Pack over all others." I shook my head. "Unless it is a demon looking for a soul to snack on, you will run every rejection by me first. If you have a question, ask me. If you have a concern, bring it to my attention. But do not ever let your Pack bullshit touch my classroom again. My informal classes are open to all students. End of story. Do I make myself clear?"

He opened his mouth twice before finally nodding. Whatever he had wanted to say, he swallowed it. "Moving forward, I'll run them by you, but I don't understand why Nest would even want to take one of your courses."

"The *why* of it isn't your problem, not while you're on my time and pulling a paycheck. I understand Pack and Nest have a history. Hell, we all have a history riddled with horror from one group or another, but you leave that shit at home. You are not Lycan while you're at this school," I replied. "If you had bothered to look or even ask, you'd have known these students come from a long line of hereditary witches. They emailed me to request approval before signing up, which I granted. We were covering topics that included their ancestors. Their input and firsthand knowledge would benefit the rest of the class. Do not ever make me lie to a student to cover for your hate. The next time, I won't. You won't have a job left for me to lie about. It can be no other way."

His nod was slow, but his embarrassment was quick. "I'm sorry, Ailis. This won't happen again."

"Thank you," I answered, and would leave it at that. If it happened again, Philip would lose his job. There was enough hate in this world. My class would not be another place for it to grow. There were plenty of monsters out there that I'd rather not stand in the same room with, but while I was teaching, I swallowed it. Philip would need to learn to do the same thing. "The matter has been settled. Now, let's get going before Ziggy makes one of the students cry."

"This is the first class they've all shown up to early. Everyone knows who Ziggtmoy is. They're pretty excited to receive a lesson from a top-side demon." Philip picked up a box for class and held open the door for me. "He makes my skin crawl. Let's get this over with. I have to be out of here by nine."

"I hate to say this, but your personal life isn't my problem, Philip. You were given two months notice for tonight's class," I said and stepped into the hall. "I'm not asking a demon to pick up the pace because you have stuff to do."

"I said those exact words to Miguel, and he told me it wasn't his problem, either. He told me to figure it out."

"The friend in me feels bad for you. It's hard to be caught between work and life. Finding that balance can be difficult." I paused outside the lecture hall. "But at the same time, I've moved your schedule around so much that I'm covering most of your lectures for you. When you accepted your promotion, I was supposed to start working less, but I'm working more now than before. If you can't find the balance, you have difficult decisions to make."

Philip released a long breath. "I'm more than Pack."

"I know," I answered. "But if your personal life is invading your ability to do your job, maybe think of taking a leave of absence?"

"And dump it all on you?" he asked, frowning. "I'll figure it out. I'll talk to Miguel."

"If Ziggy isn't done by nine, you can cut out. I'll think of some horrible way for you to make it up to me," I answered, groaning internally for the rock and hard place he stood between. "This needs to stop, though. Talk to Miguel or put in a leave."

"Thank you." He looked relieved. "Things are tense right now. A new Lycaon, enforcement of law, training, new members, new ways of doing things. Things should calm down soon."

"I hope, for your sake, things do."

I made a mental note to ask Miguel about Pack and why it was still so tense. He hadn't mentioned anything aside from things changing, and change was hard for them all, just like it was for everyone else. I could relate. I hated change. It tossed my world into the gutter and felt like a back-alley root canal with rusted equipment. I liked routine, predictability, well-established patterns, and counting on every day looking the same as the last. I liked knowing exactly what would happen, with very few surprises between the minutes. The unknown was a scary place to be, especially in my line of work. Change usually came with death threats and bleeding out.

"So do I. This shit is getting old."

Philip opened the door to the lecture hall. Every student was already in their seats, leaning forward, hanging on every word. Ziggy stood at the front of the room, dressed as some older-than-sin professor, from the round glasses perched on his nose to his patched-elbow tweed jacket. He held a small statue of a nude woman, explaining the history behind the object. I looked at the clock. We were ten minutes late. We took the side route to the front rather than cutting down the middle as usual. Ziggy wouldn't appreciate us interrupting him. For a demon, he was a stickler for manners. He wasn't the first demon I had met who was insistent on receiving common courtesy, but he was the first not to try to kill me over it.

I sat at the front, to the side, Philip beside me, and listened to Ziggy discuss the importance of knowing the history of an object and what it represented. Some relics were designed to absorb taint, whereas others were simply cursed. Knowing which was which could mean the difference between sending the taint back to hell and taking it on unintentionally. From the other side of the room, I could feel the centuries-old taint crawling over the vestiges Ziggy had brought with him. I shivered at the thought of one of my students dropping a statue and loosing the hell-made soul poison into the classroom.

One at a time, with a knotted stomach, I watched my students take turns with Ziggy, learning how to tune their aura into sensing taint before touching the objects. Ziggy had a row of ten items, and each student had to select the tainted ones. Thankfully, Ziggy had the same fear as I did, and kept his hands close enough to snatch a falling item. Where each student showed an eagerness to learn, I wanted to be sick. I cringed at the thought of touching them. After everyone had a try, Ziggy moved on. He held them on the edges of their seats, regaling them with stories from a time we'd only read about in textbooks. Each set of eyes was transfixed on the demon, mouths slightly open, leaning into every word, eager for more. He had this way of stirring excitement in them all, making them crave each drop of information he put forward. Although Ziggy was a demon wearing the fleshy suit of a man from long ago, there were moments like this when he reminded me of a professor I'd once had, and I could almost forget how many souls Ziggy had gobbled down over the years. *Almost.*

Ziggy was all flare and dramatics now, but there had once been a time when he was all darkness, anguish and torment. A soul-eating demon who was never full. He had been a debt collector, and almost as bad as the human collection agencies. In human form, he had never truly lost his crude and cruel ways of the pits. He was blunt almost to the point of brutal. The truth was a weapon, and he welded it with expert precision. *Once a demon, always a demon.* On a good day, Ziggy wasn't exactly fun to deal with, and he tended to make things uncomfortable for those who weren't used to him. He had the combined personality of pouring salt water over a fresh burn and Sunday dinner with disappointed parents. He either grew on you, or you crossed the street whenever you saw him coming. And on a bad day, he reminded us all that the only reason we were still alive was by his good graces alone. But no one is perfect. I've been accused of worse. Grim was my middle name. My social skills were somewhere between a sweat rash on your inner thighs and the blunt end of a shotgun.

A hand shot up, and Ziggy motioned to her. "If we can remove taint from an object, why can we not remove it from our aura?"

"Good question," he replied. "The taint attached to your aura is part of your aura. Do not think of it as gaining something. Think of it as changing what is already there. Using the energy from hell burns your aura, causing it to darken. There is no addition made to your aura. It's simply a change. Removing it is the same as removing a part of your aura. It leaves your aura weak. It opens tiny doors to your soul, making you more susceptible to demons. But over time, without further acts against your soul, your aura will heal, and the taint will fade."

The student nodded. "I can see why familiar objects were so widely used."

"Witches, as far back as I can remember, created objects to hold taint rather than hold the cost on their auras," Ziggy said, motioning to a crumbling relic. "This one, for instance, belonged to a witch so dark, she coined the word black magic when witches were referred to as *hægtes,* or hags. The practice is long dead and outlawed by the Coven, but during its practice, witches were able to spell without cost. They carried no taint and paid very little price for the use of the hell's energy."

"Why would they outlaw that?" Philip whispered to me.

Ziggy's eyes zeroed in on Philip. The man could hear a mouse sneeze from across the room. "Coven outlawed the practice of familiar objects to ensure witches wouldn't use dark spells. Those were deadly days, when witches spelled without consequence.

Witches now think twice about using their magic when they are the ones who pay for it."

"How does that law stop them?" Philip asked. "History is riddled with dark witches."

"A hereditary witch can live well over a hundred years. The oldest one to date lived over two hundred years," Ziggy replied. "But a dark witch's lifespan, once they begin twisting dark magic, is under five years. Would you give up a hundred or so years of life for a few spells? Spells with enough taint to send you directly to hell?"

"As if a dark witch is following that law," Philip said, his voice sounding like he almost regretted opening his mouth to begin with. Yet, it didn't stop him from digging a deeper hole for himself. "The very practice they're doing, that would require a familiar object, is illegal. Dark magic on its own is outlawed. Why would they not break a few more laws to maintain their life? My guess is that they're still using familiar objects."

"They *don't* follow the laws, which is why the Coven has their own *Malleus Maleficarum*, Hammer of Witches," Ziggy explained. "Dark witches are hunted down for breaching the laws that govern their people. The taint they carry and the darkness on their soul is enough to find their guilt. They are burned at the stake, and the case is closed. There is no trial, no defense, just a sampling of their aura. If the taint doesn't kill you, the Hammer will. But that is a lesson for another day. We're not here to debate laws, simply to explain what will happen if you break them. But, if, at the end of class, you still have an issue with the laws, I suggest you take it up with Coven. I have their contact information if you need it. As it stands now, familiar objects are illegal, with a long history as to why they are."

"This law cannot be so blindly applied. There must be a gray area. What if the spell was dark, but it saved a busload of children?" Philip asked.

"This argument has been made hundreds of times, Philip, and each time, it's been shot down," I answered before Ziggy could embarrass Philip with a heated reply. "If you need dark magic to stop something from happening, you're messing with fate. And fate is as unforgiving as Coven. The Coven's stance is simple. The conservation of magic and our people is paramount. The protection of the Coven and its members is a greater priority than any spell used for any reason. Magic should not be used on a whim, and is not the answer to all problems. Which is why many of the current laws are in place. When magic comes with a price, witches are less likely to use it frivolously. When witches rethink the spell they're about to do, the population as a whole is safer."

"Imagine high-level witches doing as they pleased, seeking vengeance without consequence, using magic as easily as a demon? Mankind would be extinguished in days," Ziggy added. "'Hell hath no fury like a witch scorned' is a saying for a reason. It is one of the causes of the original witch trials, the hunts, hangings and burnings. Without order, without law, the trials will begin again. Only now, the Coven is stronger than the church. It would become a war between two great forces, with innocent people in the middle."

Philip's swallow was audible. Some things were black and white and needed to be. People died in the gray areas. For the Coven, as much as I detested any dealings with them, they made it cut and dry for a reason—it kept the majority of us alive. I wouldn't admit it out loud, but their position of protecting the many over the one was one I could agree with. Coven didn't hold a death grip on their stance without reason. No law was arbitrary. Not even the ones I disagreed with. I personally believed in doing whatever it took to keep my ass above the crust and out of hell, but I also understood that I'd pay for how I stayed alive, just like anyone else would.

Ziggy focused his attention back on the class, and Philip kept the rest of his comments to himself. After an hour of practice, each student was able to choose the objects with the most taint and the reason behind the taint. At my turn, we showed the class how to focus and firm our auras at the hands to be able to grip the taint without it latching onto our souls.

"*Reditus*, Latin for return, will send the taint home to hell," I said. "Do not attach it to another object. It may not hold and will fix itself to your aura instead. Do not, under any circumstances, attach it to a person. You're just asking for the thrice rule to slap you. You don't want to end up becoming a walking magnet for taint." I left out the part about being able to attach the taint to a demon and sending him home with a goodie bag. They didn't need any more brilliant ideas.

I focused my aura, thickening it on my hands. The sensation of pins and needles took a moment to get used to. I blurred my vision and ran my hand up the side of the nude statue, cupping the taint as I lifted my hand. I thought the word *Reditus*. The taint rose from my hand and fell to the floor like tossed flour. It was gone in an instant. One by one, students tried with either Ziggy or me to ensure they didn't eat the taint rather than release it. That was all I needed — a student covered in sludge from hell. I doubted the Dean would think kindly on that, or their parents. I'd be packing my bags before I could utter an apology.

"When you're purchasing your crafting supplies," Ziggy said, calling their attention from aura-thickening practice. "You want to make sure you're looking at each item with your sixth sense. Look through your aura and make sure what you're buying is what you're actually receiving, or you risk bringing home tainted or cursed supplies. Your spells could malform, killing rather than healing, for example."

One of the students raised her hand and received a nod from Ziggy. "Is there a way to stop the sensation of falling when I use my sight? Or stop the headache that comes after? I've gotten so dizzy that I've fallen over before."

"Practice," Ziggy replied. "Like any ability, training is the only thing that will help. You should be doing this every evening until it is as natural as balling your fist. Think of it as exercising a muscle. Like all muscles, they tire when they're not used regularly. Repetition and practice is the only way your muscles will learn."

Ziggy answered questions for class, ending his training with time to spare. He collected his things and left a stack of business cards on the table. In the hall, security was yelling at someone to stop. A shriek that could crack glass pulled every eye to the doors. The entire class shifted in their seats. The discomfort in the air rose to a noticeable level. Tensions on campus had been high since I had arrived that evening, and this only deepened the pressure we all felt. Without having to open the door, we all knew who was being chased. The picketers had already been on and off campus with their posters and hate speeches. That they were being chased down was no surprise.

"Dr. K, what do you think will happen to witches if Humans for Humans get their new laws passed?" Calvin, an elemental witch, asked. "They're calling for every single unnatural to require the inspection of their abilities and a license."

Rose, at his side, shook her head. "Nothing. Witches are human."

"Wrong, Rose," I answered. "First, most witches aren't fully human. It's why there is a classification for us, and licenses to practice. Second, once we start removing the rights and dignities of one group, we walk a road that ends with the removal of those same freedoms from us all, regardless of how much human DNA we possess."

"But Humans for Humans are targeting the anomalous only," she said. "Those who aren't human at all."

Ziggy turned from a quiet conversation with Philip about why his questions weren't stupid, only came with too much misplaced hope that Coven would change for the betterment of witches. From the look on his face, the class topic clearly piqued his interest.

"Pardon me for the interruption, but there seems to be a little confusion amongst the class about what the HFH is really attempting here, and how deeply it impacts each and every one of us in this room, those we care about, or friends and neighbors, and those yet to be born," Ziggy said, walking back to the front and clasping his hands over his middle. I sighed, motioning for him to continue, knowing Ziggy was more of a rip of the bandage type demon than easing a person into learning the truth for themselves. "You, Rose, are anomalous. To say differently is to lie to yourself. You can harness energy the average human cannot. Since that energy comes from the pits of hell, that makes you an anomaly. It sets you apart from a full-blooded human. Say you are correct, for the sake of argument, and it's only those without a shred of human DNA being targeted. Do you truly believe witches will not be looked at next, for simply possessing an ability the rest of mankind cannot? To think you are safe from the reaches of hate is foolish. Witches already need to be registered and licensed if they wish to practice. It is an agreement Coven made to ensure you all wouldn't be hunted down and killed. But with these new laws, what will stop them from taking it a step further and requiring every witch born to be subjected to testing and inspection, as they are seeking with other magics? What happens if the witch fails the tests, or they are deemed too powerful?" Ziggy pressed her, and I didn't stop him. Closed minds create the problems we see every day. Lack of knowledge was a breeding ground for hate and prejudice. "You have a younger sister, Lily. She is powerful, even at her young age. Imagine if the laws that be say she is a danger to society. Who will stand between Humans for Humans and your sister? If you remove the only powers in this world who fight for humanity, who will protect you and your family?"

"I didn't say I supported the removal of them," she answered.

"But you are. This is the first step to doing such things. If the HRH laws are passed, those who are considered not human will no longer be people. They will be labeled as something different. HRH is merely wrapping this atrocity up in a pretty bow and calling it something different," Ziggy said. "Nonhumans will no longer have protection under the human rights charter or the laws that protect mankind. They will, for all purposes, be removed from society, as they will not be welcome within it. They can be hunted and killed again without penalty. And if this can be done to them, it can and will be done to you. Imagine a life where your neighbor can enter your home, while you sit with your family eating a meal, and slaughter you all. Imagine a life where you can be sold, abused, murdered, and there is no consequence. Perhaps they will bring back the pyre and burn you as they did the witches who paved the way to your freedoms? I, for one, take no joy in seeing young children marched to fires. There is nothing to be won with these new laws, besides the freedom to skin a shifter and sell their furs as we once did a few dozen years ago."

Rose swallowed hard enough for me to see her throat bob.

"That, my dear Rose, is what others are being faced with. It is not as simple as a license for all unnaturals. It is a license for the rest of us to hate them. It is a piece of paper that says they are less than the rest of us. This isn't a simple law. It is a death sentence," Ziggy said, and the class winced as he made his point. "Unless you are able to see an opinion from all sides, I suggest you keep your narrow-minded words to yourself. They encourage blind following and hate."

"I'm sorry," she answered. "I didn't think of what *could* happen."

"Live and learn. Do better next time. If not for you, for those who are too weak and scared to have a voice," Ziggy said as the buzzer on my desk went off. The class cleared out within minutes, each one appearing excited at the prospect of seeing the picketers being arrested.

Rose stopped in front of Ziggy and offered her hand. "Thank you, Ziggtmoy. It was a pleasure to learn from you."

"The pleasure was mine," he replied. "Get home safe."

I stepped toward Ziggy packing his cursed trinkets. "Thank you, Ziggy."

"Ziggtmoy," he corrected me, as usual. "I expect my chocolate by Monday. Please wait until the market on Sunday, when it will be fresh. I do not like the week-old slabs from the shops."

"Of course." I huffed a laugh. "What are your thoughts on my students? Does anyone stand out as a red flag?"

"I did not sense any *red flags*, as you call them, but they are all so very blind to their true powers. I fear for the days they will need it, and it will not be there for them. The Coven has castrated their people and removed the ways of old. I'm surprised so many of you exist, given you cannot protect yourselves with real magic, not to mention your stunted reproduction rates."

"We'd be hunted once again if the world knew how powerful we really are, or could become," I answered.

"I do hope, for the sake of your life, you are practicing your magic to its fullest extent. One day, your life will depend on it."

"It already does," I replied. "I'll have your chocolate delivered to your shop on Monday. Thanks again."

"When you are done playing games with spelling pots and herbs, you know where I am. You need real magic, not this..." He waved his hand around, finding the word. "*Diluted* version witches use. You are living off of bread and water when you should be eating steak and lobster. You're not simply a witch. You are cursed. Take the power you are owed before you're killed for it."

"I'm not coming to work for you," I replied. Ziggy had asked me more times than I could count to work in his shop. I had said no every time. Without saying another word, he turned on his foot and left Philip and me standing there.

Chapter Three

Philip released a breath that sounded like it had been held in all night. "I don't know about you, but that was fucking intense."

I locked up the doors of the lecture hall and shrugged at the comment. "Ziggy is always that way. He's politely rude and calmly intense. A terrifying puzzle that man is."

Philip grabbed his bag and walked me to the cafeteria. "He makes me uncomfortable and makes my wolf go batshit crazy inside. I don't know how you can be so calm around him."

"Weren't your people created to hunt down demons?" I asked.

"Exactly. Hunt, not hang out with. My wolf was pitching a fit with me just sitting there asking stupid questions," he answered, and I couldn't help but laugh as his face scrunched and his entire body shivered. "You were calm as a cucumber. Come to think of it, so was the rest of the class. You either have balls of steel, or I'm just a chicken."

"Don't worry about it. It's been years, and I still feel uneasy around Ziggy. But I try not to show it. I know what it's like to be hated for who I am."

"I'm glad he's only on the docket twice this year. I'd rather be in a room full of witches than with one demon."

"I'll take a demon over Coven any day," I replied. "Well, Ziggy, anyway."

"Coven has some strange laws, don't they?" he asked, then laughed when I gave him a questioning look. "Okay, so does Pack."

"At least Coven doesn't kill anyone for finding out about them," I said, rolling my eyes.

"What did he mean? He hopes you're practicing your magic to its fullest? Don't you do that already?"

I shook my head. "Not even close. What I did to the last Master of the City, killing his soul, that was close. I have the power of two level-three witches inside me. Destroying half of this city would be me using all of my power. I keep that part of me locked away for fear of what I would do if cornered and what the Coven would do if they found out. They'd either burn me or force me to become a council member. I'd rather be burned alive."

"Remind me never to piss you off," he joked.

"You've pissed me off countless times, and the worst I've done is hide your coffee pot. I don't use magic as freely as most witches. I have a lifetime of taint to get rid of before my time is up and I go to hell. The cleaner my soul, the less time I spend down there."

"Is there no way to remove the taint quicker, like what you all did to the statues?" he asked.

"If only it were that easy, we'd all be sparkling clean," I replied. "With objects, the taint is not ours and is not part of our auras. The hardest part, removing it from an aura, has already been done. For myself, I can remove a little at a time and attach it to a demon to take home, but I can't take it all off at once, or there'd be holes in my aura. When I give a little at a time, my aura is able to heal the hole I created. Too much at once, and I'd be wide open for demonic attacks."

"Couldn't you hang out on holy ground while your aura healed?"

"I suppose I could, if I wanted to live in a church for a few years. It takes a long time to regrow an aura, and I'm not willing to give up my life for that to happen. Not yet, anyway. Ask me again in twenty years."

"I'd take your taint if I could. I'm going to hell, anyway," he replied.

"As a Hellhound, not as a guest in the cages of Fire and Brimstone. If you take my taint, you give up your place at guarding the Gate. Hell needs you more than Heaven needs me."

"Nothing is fair in life or death," he replied, and stopped at the cafeteria doors. "Are you okay here, on your own?"

"I'm good. I'll get security to walk me to my car later in case the crazies are still kicking around," I replied and waved him off.

Philip headed out with ten minutes to spare, and I grabbed a veggie tray and water from the counter and took a seat. There weren't many people left on campus at this hour, which was both unnerving in a haunted sort of way, and great for those of us who wanted to be left alone.

My phone buzzed, and I smiled. "Hello there, this is a pleasant surprise."

Miguel's soft laugh rolled across my skin, tightening my lower stomach. "Hello to you. I'm going to be late tonight, but I wanted to know if you were okay on campus alone? Philip said there was an incident at the school with Humans for Humans? I can send someone if you need an extra set of eyes looking over your shoulder for you? I'm sure Cisco would jump at the opportunity to get the hell out of here."

"I'm okay here, but thank you. I think the school has called in a few more security personnel. I've seen five patrols since I took my seat," I answered and grinned. "Cisco jumps at any opportunity to kick some ass."

"This is true." Miguel laughed again. "Don't take any chances, Lish. Word is that HFH is amping things up, trying to cause issues between groups."

"I'm here for another couple hours, then heading to Samuel's house. If something feels off, I'll call back."

"If someone is following you, do not drive home. You don't want the whack jobs knowing where you live. Go straight to the cop shop and call me from there."

"This isn't my first rodeo, wolf. I've been followed enough times to know the drill," I answered, then softened at his worry. "It's okay, Miguel. Thank you for worrying, but I'm okay. I'll shoot you a text later and let you know I made it to Samuel's house and again when I get home tonight."

"I'll see you when I get home. I love you."

"I love you, too," I answered and hung up.

With an ear-to-ear smile, feeling loved in ways that really mattered to me, I got right to work and started typing out my report for Mannix. I had kept my notes on my phone and transferred them over to the usual document I used for consultations. It took me all of twenty minutes to do. My invoice auto-populated totals after I clicked a few numbers in the dropdown menus. Thirty minutes later, with my documents sent, I opened my book and ate my dinner. No one would be home until well after midnight, and Samuel was expecting me at eleven. He and Mairi, a fellow witch, were going to help me with my shielding and protection, thickening my aura and adding it to a circle of protection. Mairi also had a jar of healing ointment, a new mixture that didn't smell like an outhouse on a hot day. Mairi had gotten a copy of the Mexico Pack's salve, which smelled like lavender, and tweaked it to suit the needs of a witch—me, given I was her main customer and needed it more often than anyone else she knew.

I had only just finished my veggies and dip when my phone buzzed again. Thinking it was Miguel once more, asking if I was still okay, I picked it up. To my surprise, it was Mannix's name that flashed across my display. I groaned at the thought of being called out for another murder scene but answered it anyway. I'd never leave Mannix hanging, whether I was being paid for consulting or not.

"At this hour, either someone is dead, or you need help hiding a body. I'm hoping for the latter."

"I wish it was to hide a body," he answered. "Did you get my message?"

"Yes, you have three people of interest?"

"We found all three, or what's left of them," he replied.

I leaned back in my chair, stunned. "What? How?"

"That isn't why I'm calling. That case has nothing more to do with my team. The suspects were killed by humans. It was likely to end the trail leading back to the source. They were found dead in their beds. Quick kills, one across the throat, and nothing like the victims," he said, the sound of papers shuffling around in the background muffled his voice. "I tried calling you an hour ago. I have a new vic."

"Sorry, Mannix, my ringer was on silent. I had class this evening and haven't listened to my messages yet. Do you need me to come down?" I asked and looked at my watch. "I have a couple of hours before I need to meet Samuel."

"No need. The scene is no different than the others," he answered. "I had a few questions, though, if you have a moment?"

"I'm all ears, but might not have answers for you," I answered.

"I'd be no further behind," he replied. "The victim was found by her friends in the alley behind their apartment building, near the recycle bins, in East Van. Same M.O. as the other victims. Multiple stab wounds, killing blow to the heart. But this one has her hands removed."

"Are the hands still on the scene or taken?"

"Still here," he answered. "Why would that matter if this wasn't an attack from hell or magics?"

"That depends on what type of magic she is. In some cases, it's merely a trophy or a statement. In others, body parts or bodily fluids can be used for spells and curses," I answered. "I ask because it doesn't matter who did the deed. Body parts from witches turn a pretty penny on the black market. Depending on what kind of witch she was, those body parts could bring in a lot of coin."

"Her friends described her as a malevolent witch. This is a new one for me. Kids today and their labels." He flipped through his papers in the background. He, like me, was meticulous about case notes. I had once made the mistake of thinking I'd remember everything when it came time to write my report. I didn't and hadn't made that mistake twice. "Nothing wicked popped when I did a background search on her."

"It's a slur, Mannix. Mankind has the tendency to assign good and bad to every soul. It's in our nature to separate the two. It's how we stay alive. A malevolent witch is considered to be a breath away from dark magic. One nudge, and they're walking the road to hell. In truth, they're neither good nor bad. They're sort of in the middle until something monumental happens," I replied, wincing at how closely that truth touched my own life. "But the same can be said of every witch out there. Sometimes, we're backed into a corner and choose a little taint over death."

"You're a good witch, Ailis. Don't let anyone tell you different," Mannix said, making me smile. I didn't know I needed to hear that until he said the words.

"Thank you," I replied and released the hate I carried that never belonged to me. Words said, names called, all weighed down on me over the years. I refocused my attention on the victim on the ground, rather than the one I had buried inside me. "I'm guessing the vic is a chaos or elemental witch? They typically are the only ones who are called malevolent, usually without proof, I might add."

"Her Coven identification states she's a level one chaos witch."

"Probably why they cut off her hands," I replied. "There's still the belief that chaos witches pull energy with their hands rather than through their auras. Remove the hands, remove their access to power. A decade ago, during a mass killing of witches in Europe, they cut off the hands of the witches, thinking they wouldn't be able to draw the energy they needed. It worked, in a way. The witches bled out, but still managed to do a hell of a lot of damage on their way to their graves."

"How barbaric," he murmured, and I agreed.

I opened up my laptop and scanned the notes I had made at each scene. "Victim one and three, they slit their throats. The first was an elemental witch, and the third was an earth witch. They likely thought the act of cutting their vocal cords would keep them from calling on magic. The shifter had his head removed, the only surefire way of killing a shifter. Someone has been reading old texts on hunting magics and using those practices. I'm certain they would have burned the witch's bodies had they enough time to do it, to punish them."

"Punish them for what?"

"What don't we punish each other for?" It was less a question than a statement. "Originally, witches were punished by fire for practicing devil worship and summoning spirits the church thought to be demons. Under medieval laws, like the Holy Roman Empire's 'Constitutio Criminalis Carolina,' witches found their end with stakes and gibbets, the fire as much a punishment as a purification ritual. There are still countless hate groups that hold true to these laws. You can find their published works online, advocating to bring back the pyre."

"Jesus, explains why I could smell gasoline at this last site," he answered. "I think they were interrupted. The body was still bleeding when they got to her."

"Do you have any leads on why she was targeted?" I asked.

"I saved the best for last," he answered. "I did a quick database search. The victim's name is Coral Davenport. Her mother is the one and only Cordelia Davenport. Her grandmother was the late Ophelia Davenport."

"Necromancers," I whispered through clenched teeth. My groan slipped out before I could stop it.

Cordelia was one of the most highly sought-after chaos witches in the country. She could call on the dead as I could touch souls. It was a rare gift, and likely why her daughter had been tagged with the malevolent slur. An angry necromancer was more dangerous than a demon on the loose. "Has she been notified? Should I be heading for the hills or sheltering in place? Bloody hell, this feels like you just told me someone killed Lucifer's son. Her retribution is going to kick us all in the throat. A lot of people are going to die when she gets her revenge, and she will get it."

"I'm waiting on two level-three Coven members. Cordelia is going to raise every graveyard in the city when I tell her. The last time someone pissed her off, she raised two hundred corpses just to make her point."

"Where is her eldest daughter, Corali?" I asked.

"She's been in Europe for the last decade. She lives on the Davenport estate. She's in university, getting her master's degree," he answered. "Coven already sent members to keep an eye on her and give us a heads-up if she jumps onto a plane."

"Good luck, Mannix, that's all I can say. I hope you aren't calling to ask me to help you with Cordelia because hell no. She scares the shit out of me. I met her once and have done everything I can to never be in the same room with her again. Her aura feels like dead things and tortured souls."

"No. I'm not that mean." Mannix laughed. "I'm trying to find a connection between the victims, and I'm drawing blanks. There's no overlap between any of them, aside from them being unnat...magical people." Mannix corrected his word, knowing I would if he didn't. "I'm wondering if you have any thoughts? Captain Holland has called an emergency meeting, and I have nothing to offer that isn't obvious."

"You could have saved yourself a call if you would have read my report first. Grab a pen. I'll give you the condensed version, but make sure the report gets to Holland before the meeting. It'll save questions asked that I've answered for you," I replied. "I've outlined the similarities between the three scenes I attended. They're all lower-level magics within the same age group. They're young and relatively low on the magic or power scale, including the shifter and this latest victim, Coral. They're all easy pickings for someone hunting metaphysicals. Although they all live in different areas of the city, they all have links to the same networks and neighborhoods and come from families with a lot of pull in the magical community. My guess on the population most at risk is pretty wide and hard to protect. Young magics, those who cannot defend themselves against a blitz attack from multiple pursuers, children of political and powerful nightmares. That covers a few hundred people."

"Any thoughts on who would be targeting them?"

"Hate groups would be my number one guess. They've been known to attack magical people in the past, and they're not as picky about who or what dies in the process," I answered. "There are four that are active in the city, but only two would be able to pull something like this off. Humans for Humans and For the People. For the People aren't known for slaughtering innocent people, but there's a first for them all. The three people of interest, are they tied to any of those groups?"

"We believe they're linked to Humans for Humans but have no concrete proof. All three have records. The young woman, Marshal, had a record for violence against witches and a break-and-enter at a Wiccan church. The two men have a rap sheet longer than I am tall, for violence, threats, attempted arson, tied to a series of unsolved crimes against magics."

"Targeting witches, how unsettling of a thought," I replied.

"That's the second reason I'm calling. Perhaps you should book off some holidays until we can wrap this up?"

"I'm only level one in name, Mannix," I answered. "I won't be a target, not yet. They'll keep picking off the weak before turning their attention to those of us who have a hope in hell of walking away from an altercation with them. Regardless, my door is not a good one to knock on."

"And the last reason I called you. You're good at this, Ailis. Have you thought about contracting with us on a more permanent basis?"

"Your office already has me on retainer. That's about as close to poking at hell as I want to get."

"My department is expanding and could use someone like you. Just think about it."

"I'm good, but thank you for the offer. I enjoy what I do, but if I ever need a change of scenery, you'll be my first call."

"Fair enough. If Holland has questions later, make sure you bill him for your time," Mannix said, and yelled at someone walking by about the emergency meeting. "I have to run. Thanks for your help. If another body turns up, I'll give you a call."

"Well then, I hope I don't hear from you until you solve the case," I answered. "Be safe, Mannix. You have the same target as I have on my back. If you need help, call me. I'll always come."

"I'll keep you in the loop. Good night," he said and disconnected his call.

Tempted to flick through the local news to see what the hate groups were up to, I picked up my book instead. I needed a little reality break. The world was harsh and cruel, but my book was magical and romantic and exactly what my heart and soul needed. Pulling out a receipt I used as a bookmark from a coffee shop in Mexico, I found my place and dove into a world that never had problems like mine.

"Always with her nose in a book," a familiar voice said from a table away.

I glanced up and found myself grinning. Demitri Belov, a once-upon-a-time exchange student, sat a few tables away from me. He had taken several of the same classes as me and joined the same study groups. His returned smile reminded me of every laugh we had shared. He had never once shied away from me being a witch and had always been excited when I had shown him new spells I had learned. He was one of the first who hadn't turned their nose to me. I couldn't help but smile a little bigger. Everything about him was the same. His black hair was the color of ink, and his ice-blue eyes sparkled as they always had. He was dressed in a suit, which made me huff a laugh. It was the first time I had seen him in a suit outside of the one time he had been forced to wear one for the dance after graduation.

"Demi, when did you get to town?" I asked. "Are you here for a class or lecture?"

"I got back a couple months ago," he replied. "I'm not taking classes, but when I heard you were teaching here, I thought I'd pop by to say hello."

My smile faded into a frown. I was suspicious by nature, and his answer had only cemented my mistrust. How had he known I had a night class? My lecture calendar wasn't posted online due to the zealots my classes had always attracted. Only students were aware of my schedule. He stood, graceful as always and with two steps toward me, I felt the energy pouring off him, growing stronger as he moved from his table to mine. My stomach rose into my throat, and I swallowed down my urge to be sick.

"What the fuck?" I whispered.

"You can sense me now because I'm not shielding who I am from you as I did in the past," he replied and held up his hands. "I come in peace. I'm not here to harm you."

"Demetrius." I groaned. The noise resembled more of an angry growl than disappointment. "You're the new Master of the City?"

He took the seat next to me. "In the flesh."

"Holy shit," I replied and put distance between our chairs. "What do you want?"

"I didn't reach out to you sooner because..." He paused and smiled.

It instantly made me uncomfortable. I eyed his mouth, looking for fangs and saw none, but that didn't mean they weren't there. The older vamps were better at hiding them.

"As you know, it's tense between our people."

"*Our* people? Did you piss off the Coven, too?" I asked.

"Miguel and his people," he corrected me.

"I thought you were a Russian exchange student?"

"I took night classes, Ailis." He laughed. It sounded like it always had, but tonight, it felt like he had killed every good memory I had of him. "Didn't that trigger a red flag?"

"I took the same night classes, but I'm not a goddamn vampire," I said, leaning in to whisper, then pulling back, remembering he could chew my throat out. "How the hell are you a Master vampire? You're the same age as me."

"Tack on a century and a bit," he replied.

"How didn't I know?" I asked, more to myself than him.

"Some of us are better at hiding than others," he answered. "I'm sorry I didn't tell you then, but I couldn't risk it. For some of us, flying under the radar is the only way we stay alive."

"Why are you here?" I asked, not caring to hear his life story.

"If you can believe it, I'm in need of a favor," he replied. "Unfortunately, you're the only person I could think of who could help."

"Oh, hell no. I don't do favors. I damn near die every time I do," I answered. "The last time your people asked me to do something for them, I said no. And yet, I still almost died, several times over."

"I'm sorry for that," he said. "Although I played no part, I'm sorry that was your experience."

"I don't work for monsters," I said, skipping the apology I didn't need or want.

"It has nothing to do with Nest or Pack. Well, maybe Pack, if they find out," he said.

"No, thank you. I'm not doing anything for the fangs," I answered. "I didn't want to work for the last psycho of the city, and I won't be working for the new one."

"Wait, before you say no, just hear me out. Please." His eyes begged me. "I've never done anything to you for you to not even listen for a couple of minutes. I've always been respectful and courteous. In the entire four years we attended school together, did I once make you feel uncomfortable? Did I ever do anything inappropriate or make you fear for your safety? We parted ways on excellent terms, and even maintained emails and letters for years after."

"Fine, you have two minutes." My necklace remained quiet against my chest. He wasn't planning to hurt me, for now. I picked it up and shook it around, just to be sure the thing was still paying attention.

He inched in closer, and I put my hand up. He was close enough, any closer, and he'd have my vein in his mouth. He chuckled. "I'm not going to bite you."

"When I start trusting the monsters, I start digging my own grave."

"That's fair and wise," he replied, but still leaned in a little more than I was comfortable with. "I assume you know about shifters, given your chosen group of friends?"

"Yes."

"The weres?" he asked.

"Which ones? There are a lot of shifters out there."

"Wolves."

I blinked. "I'm not sure what you're talking about."

"This isn't going to work unless you're at least a little honest."

"I've heard some things."

"What have you heard?"

I shook my head. "No way. Snitches end up in ditches."

"Indulge me, just a little, please."

"I probably know less than you do." He motioned for me to continue. I thought of the words I was about to use and what could be said. "From what I've...read," I said, and he rolled his eyes. "A curse invades the soul, resulting in an uncontrolled beast needing to be put down and all that jazz. Kind of like a vampire, when you think of it."

"You wound me."

"Lean another inch forward, and I will do more than wound you," I said.

"In front of all these people?"

I nodded. "Do not underestimate my will to live."

"Nor mine," he answered but pulled back an inch.

"You're wasting your minutes, Demetrius. What do you want?"

"Remember the professor we had, Dr. Calvin Bishop?" he asked, and I raised my brows. "Calvin's son, Rome, was attacked almost three years ago."

"By one of the locals?"

"By Nathaniel," he replied.

I cringed at the mention of the man. "Is Rome's father seeking justice for the death of his son?"

"Rome isn't dead. He's alive and well, besides sprouting fur on a full moon."

"He survived?" I couldn't keep the surprise from my voice.

"He's a shifter."

I shook my head, but the look on his face said he was serious. "That's not possible."

"They don't all die, Ailis. And not all need to be, as you say, put down. Others found him and helped him until he could control himself. They got him to holy ground and stayed with him until he made it through the first few weeks. At the start, while the body fights the curse, the individual's body temperature spikes, and they go insane. It's the fever that drives them crazy, mixed with a war inside their body and souls. When they shift for the first time, they have no idea what's going on. They're driven by their wolves but are still human inside. Most go off the deep end. They can't control themselves. It's why they're so unpredictable after their initial shift. It is similar for vampires after they've been bitten. There is an overpowering drive inside them, and without guidance, they can become wild and in need of an afternoon walk in the sun," he explained.

I couldn't help but slink down in my seat, hanging onto every word as if it were a new revelation. I felt like one of my students sitting in front of Ziggy, in awe of what I was hearing.

"From what other shifters have told me, every shifter out there goes through this change. Other groups are ready for it, though. The wolves, unfortunately, are not. And because of this, almost all werewolves are hunted down and killed on sight by Pack."

I shook my head, trying to wrap my head around his words. Did Miguel know some survived? "I need to go. I have to talk to Miguel."

"No, Ailis." Demetrius reached forward and pulled his hand back when I glanced at how close he had gotten. "You cannot tell him. Rome is being hunted by Pack, under the order of Miguel. I need your help."

"Oh, fuck." The reality set in. He had come to me to help him with a creature Pack hunted and killed without question. If Miguel gave the order, me putting my nose into it wasn't going to go over well. "And what do you want from me?"

"Help to get him and his people out of town before Miguel and Pack slaughter them all. Miguel has Pack out, around the clock, hunting Rome and his kind."

"No way. I want no part of this nightmare. Go to Pack yourself, if you're so concerned."

"What world do you live in where I can simply knock on Pack's door?"

"You tried to, the moment you got to town," I answered. "I was there when you called Miguel."

"To extend my apologies for the actions of the previous Master. I have no desire to fight with any species. I volunteered to return to this territory in hopes of improving the relations between our people. What happened under the control of Julian was barbaric."

"Did you not contact Nathaniel as soon as you got to town and ask for the same deal Julian had?" I asked.

"No. It was the other way around. Nathaniel contacted me. I did not speak on anything more than the blood rights to the territory," he replied. "He offered to meet in person to negotiate. Before we could arrange a neutral location for this meeting, he met his justified death."

"I can't get involved in this. I get you're in a bind, but this isn't something I can put my nose into."

"Please, if you're not willing to help me, help Rome. He's barely an adult. He just turned nineteen. He doesn't deserve to die for what he is."

I shook my head. "I can't go to Pack on your behalf."

"I don't want Pack anywhere near Rome. They'd kill him without hesitation," he said, and I couldn't argue his point. They would. "Can you ask your grandfather? I can't approach him unless I want to go up in ashes. Guardians aren't known for hearing the plea of a vampire."

"No way. I'm not risking my grandfather for you, this kid, or anyone else," I answered, a little creeped out that he knew of my ties to Samuel. It was unsettling to realize quite how small the world was and how far information spread. "I'm sorry, but I'm not sticking my neck on the line for someone I don't even know. Demetrius, you're a vampire. Rome could be seven layers of batshit crazy, and you may be so numb to it all that you don't see the same thing as I do."

"All right then, meet him first. I doubt you will pick up anything more than fear from him. But if you feel you can't help him after meeting him, I'll find a different way and will never bother you again." His eyes pleaded though the rest of his face was void of emotion. It was unsettling. "Ailis, if I don't figure out how to get them out of town, Miguel's people will kill them. For weeks, his spies have been sniffing around, watching Rome. Eventually, they started taking out werewolves, one at a time. Rome is so terrified that he's gone into hiding." Demetrius squeezed his hands into fists. "I can't stand back and watch. I won't."

"And why do you care?"

"I know what it's like to be hunted, and so do you. But unlike us, Rome has no way to stay alive. He has no magic, no power, no people at his back. Other shifters won't step forward to help him. They're too scared of Pack."

"You should be scared of them, too. I am."

He smiled. "I've no reason to be. I've broken no laws. I've done nothing to antagonize them."

"Talking to me sure as hell will piss them off," I replied.

"I didn't realize I needed the Lycaon's permission to talk to you. You are Pack only in name, but your blood is all witch. Coven has no such laws. I checked before I came here."

I chewed my bottom lip. What was the worst that could happen if I met with him? Aside from the vampires eating me or kidnapping me, Pack hunting me down for it, Miguel leaving me, hell opening up and swallowing us all whole. I had the same odds most days, with any given decision I made. I was a walking, talking death wish.

Tapping my nails on the table, I weighed my options and what I could live with. Turning my back on someone who actually needed help didn't feel right. I had just finished telling Miguel that the problem with the world was that the strong never helped the weaker. If I walked away, I'd be part of the problem. I'd be part of the reason the kid ended up dead in a ditch.

"Where is he hiding?"

"My house," he answered. "I assume you know the way? Everyone else seems to."

"You've got to be insane if you think I'm coming to your place." I stared at him like he had just made an even dumber suggestion than putting myself between Pack and werewolf. "You remember that you're a vampire, right? I might as well fill out my own toe tag on my way up your driveway."

"You pick any location, and I'll get him there." He offered me an alternative I could live with. "If you wish, I'll come alone. Whatever it takes."

"You remember Ziggy's, down in Blood Square?" I asked, and he nodded. I looked at my watch. "Two hours from now."

He smiled, his fangs hiding. It still bothered me that I'd never once known he was a vampire. "We'll see you there. And please, don't tell Miguel. I don't want to start a war to protect this kid."

"Give me your word. I'm not at risk tonight."

"You're not at risk from me or my people. Those down in Bloody Alley won't touch you. You'll have my protection while you're there with me. I can't say what'll happen if Pack comes. I don't control them or their actions. But if they come, I will do what I can so you can get away."

"I can handle Miguel and his people," I answered, with a world of doubt hanging on the tip of my tongue.

"Demi… Demetrius, why are you doing this? What's in it for you? And spare me the load of crap about being hunted. We're all being hunted by someone or something. There isn't a soul out there that isn't fighting some uphill battle. You're asking me to put myself between Miguel, his people, and those they've hunted since the first werewolf walked the earth. There had better be a damn good reason why I'm about to add my name to their list of hunted."

"Demi." He smiled at the nickname I had given him years ago. "I owe his father. He found out what I was those years ago and helped me. He invited me into his home and gave me a safe place away from Nest. Julian was the Master of the City when I was here, and it wasn't a safe place for anyone," he said, and I shuddered at the thought of being near Julian for any reason. "Dr. Bishop got me blood donations, so I wouldn't have to seek out a food source or be forced to ask Julian for aid." Demetrius flinched at whatever memory Julian's name dredged up. "And before you ask, the blood came in the form of soon-to-expire bags of blood from the bank. I've never hunted people."

I rolled my eyes. "Uh-huh, and every spell I've twisted has been pure as the heavens."

"I didn't say I don't drink from a vein. I said I don't hunt. I buy my food just like everyone else."

"Gross," I replied.

"I thought the same thing when I woke up a hundred and fifty years ago with the thirst. But we all come to terms with who and what we are eventually, or we walk into our own version of the sun." Demetrius stood. "Thank you for this. I won't forget it. Even if you can't help Rome, I'll owe you one."

"I'm not doing this for you. I'm doing this because I know what it's like to have a noose around my neck and nowhere to turn. Just keep your people away from me, and I'll see you at Alchemy Co." I waved him off. I didn't need him hanging around me any more than he already had. Pack would hear he had come to the school, and that was already a conversation I didn't want to have with Miguel. Tack on the werewolf and my helping an enemy of Lycan, and this was going to turn into a bloody nightmare. I could feel it in my bones. Warning flares went up, and I closed my eyes to them. I'd ignore them until they were burning down my house, which would likely happen in the next few days. Pack didn't fuck around any more than I did. Witches were not the only ones known for fury.

I texted Samuel and rescheduled. I didn't lie to him, but didn't tell him I was getting onto my knees and putting my head on a chopping block, either. Because that's exactly what I was doing. Getting between Pack and Nest was not one of my better ideas. Collecting my things felt like the last act a witch did as her pyre was being built. Each step I took toward Rome was one more log on the fire. Never would anyone accuse me of being a smart witch. My headstone would read *Ailis Petronilla Kyteler, a foolish witch to her bitter end. See you in hell.*

Chapter Four

I was the last person to ever volunteer to go down to Blood Square at night. My trips to this part of town were either unwilling or because I was desperate, and even then, after sunset, I had to be near the end of all hope to find my way down these streets. Daytime was terrible enough. There weren't many places in this city that were worse than this little slice of top-side hell. Between the lack of parking and the smell of blood and vampire spice, it was a variable unlocked zoo, and I was fresh meat. During the day, it was a tourist trap. Shops hawking their wares opened their doors and suckered in the excited travelers, pandering to the humans who wanted a photo with a shifter for twenty bucks. Coffee shops, with their five-dollar coffees and ten-dollar cookies, had lineups for an hour. You could buy organic honey, art and a mummified head on the same block.

I could see the appeal when the sun was up, and there wasn't a target on your soul. But the moment the sun went down, it was a different type of trap. The sidewalks filled with those seeking the high that a vampire bite could give or the drugs only the shifters sold, laced with demon blood. Here, between heaven and hell, souls were sold, and futures were bought and auctioned off. Blood Square didn't make many promises, and only one was ever true — every sin was available, and every soul paid equally for them. My skin crawled at the thought of stepping onto the street without the sun overhead. Yet, there I was. Because I didn't have enough problems in my everyday life, I needed to grab the sharpest stick and poke at beasts who bit back.

I pulled up at Ziggy's back door, having called him thirty minutes before arriving. I didn't hide what I was doing from him. He'd have kicked us out the moment he smelled us hiding. He was curious about how this would unfold and welcomed the shitshow to unravel before him. To be honest, I was wondering the same thing. I unrolled my window and breathed in the energy that flowed from one end of Water Street to the next. I felt vampires, shifters, ghosts, a few odds and ends that felt similar to hell but not quite evil enough, an out-of-place harpy, but no Pack. It wouldn't take long. Pack had eyes and ears everywhere. Worse, Miguel was owed more favors than I was, and Sofia lived a few blocks up the road. If favors didn't sell me out, fear of Pack certainly would.

I opened my car door and glanced around. The vampires across the street took a step back and changed their direction. True to his promise, Demetrius had spread the word. *Leave the lone foolish witch alone.* I watched vampires scatter for blocks. What I would give for that kind of power. Everything but my mortal soul, blood and body. I'd make a terrible monster, and an even worse negotiator. I wasn't willing to part with anything of value, at least not the tasty parts that kept me out of hell.

I circled around my car to the back door. The door was painted red, and Alchemy Co. was written in bold letters with a broomstick painted under it. I waved at the camera hidden in the top corner of the building and waited for the door to click. With a clunk of the locks, I pulled it open, jogged down the short alley that smelled of regrets and old blood, and waited at another door. I didn't know why Ziggy's strip of street held the scent of death. I could only imagine, and wasn't brave enough to ask. The light flicked on and off twice, and the door buzzed. The coast was clear for me to go inside. For now, but give it time. I could feel it in my bones, the pending doom I was walking into. My soul warned me, and yet I still chose to pull open the door. To stay out of sight, I went in through the back door of Alchemy Co., as I unfortunately had to do on several occasions. Even in Blood Square, cursed witches weren't welcome. Yet, bloodsuckers and soul dealers were? The world wasn't fair.

Ziggy stood at his glass counter, polishing small gold spoons. He motioned to the far corner of the store. "Demetrius and the new problem you're staking your life on are in the corner."

"I have a name, you know," a man's voice called from the direction Ziggy had pointed to. He sounded young. I didn't have to see his face to know he would look scared. I could hear it in his shaking voice. "And it's not *the witch's new problem*."

"Yes, yes, as you've reminded me," Ziggy said, shaking his head as if the very idea of showing consideration to the man was an imposition. "I would hurry this up, Ailis. You're a sitting duck in a field of wolves. It is only a matter of time before someone sells the wolf's whereabouts to Pack. Being owed a favor from Pack is worth more than a soul around here. I doubt very much you want to be caught with a werewolf *and* the Master of the City when Pack comes sniffing around."

Demetrius stepped around the first row of shelves, careful not to touch anything. He could probably smell the layers of taint on every tchotchke, relic and marble in the place. Behind him was a man who looked like a younger version of my old professor, Dr. Calvin Bishop. Rome was just over six feet tall and built like he had played rugby or football his entire life, moving with the same fluidity as Pack. His brown, curly hair was pulled into a loose ponytail at the base of his skull, revealing a scared yet warm face and striking jawline. He was every bit like his father with his piercing gray eyes that took in everything and missed nothing. For his age, I was surprised to see he had lost that youthful look. He looked like he had lived more than nineteen years. Every inch of him, from his skin to his movements, looked well lived in. But I suppose running for your life from Pack aged a person. It had certainly added a few years to my life.

There was something almost charming about him, an old soul that gave off a calming feeling, even with his anxiety at a setting that crawled across my skin and gave me secondary nervousness. My necklace had stayed silent, mirroring my thoughts. He was just a kid trying to stay alive. One look in his eyes and the red flags went down, leaving the urge to put myself between him and harm.

I blurred my vision and watched his aura as he stepped toward us. The center of his aura was green and made me smile. Deep down, he was a loving person. Around the edges, it flared with yellow and burnt orange. He was scared, but so would I have been in his position. The closer he got to me, the muddier his aura became. I didn't need to see his soul to know he was terrified. He was scared of me and the pending decision I'd make — whether to leave him to the wolves or give him a fighting chance. His hands trembled along with the rest of his body as he approached.

"Hi, Rome." I extended my hand. "I'm Ailis Kyteler."

He glanced at my hand and swallowed hard. "You're a witch?"

I smiled. "A good one, most days."

"Most days," Ziggy mocked.

I rolled my eyes. "You're one to talk."

"It's okay, Rome. She's the friend I was telling you about," Demetrius said, nudging Rome. Both Ziggy and I snickered at the word *friend*.

"Thank you for meeting with me, Miss Kyteler," Rome said, shaking my hand quickly and pulling back, wiping his hand on his pants. He wasn't the first person to clean their hands after touching me, and he wouldn't be the last. I let it go. My energy felt like static and standing too close to a fire. On a bad day, I felt like lightning before it struck. My mood at the moment was closer to a thunderstorm.

"Demetrius, why don't you keep an eye out while Rome and I talk? Maybe take a short walk?" I asked. Rome's eyes grew wider at my suggestion. "We're only talking, Rome. You're free to walk out whenever you want. No one will keep you here. I have questions, and

I don't want Demetrius to influence how you reply or the emotions I feel from you."

Rome finally nodded. Demetrius went to the door, looking back once. His eyes said it all. If I touched a hair on the boy's head, he'd hunt me down. I knew the look. I had a similar one of my own.

"What would you like to know, Miss Kyteler?" Rome asked.

"Just Ailis," I answered. "How about you tell me what happened to you?"

"I feel like I've told this story hundreds of times," he said. His eyes darted around the store. His nerves were shot.

"We're alone here," Ziggy said.

Rome nodded. "A few years ago, when I was walking home from campus after dinner with my father, I saw what I thought to be a werewolf. I mean, up until that moment, I didn't think they were real, but I figured, like the other species of shifters, they had stayed hidden until someone else outed them. I went in the other direction like I would for any other shifter. Only this one started to follow me. I freaked out and ran back toward the campus, screaming for help. It chased me down and attacked me."

Rome lifted his shirt. Four scars ran down his chest and ended in a twisted knot at his stomach. Ziggy hissed, and I stepped back.

"He clawed me up and dragged me off into the bush, half burying me alive. I watched him shift back into his human form and later came to learn his name was Nathaniel," Rome said, dropping his shirt. My stomach rolled with anger. I had always known Nathaniel was scum, but this was worse than I could have imagined. "I don't remember much of what followed after the attack, but I was told I was found by two of my kind and carried back to a church. I was in and out of consciousness for a week while my body fought against the virus. The first time I shifted, though. Holy hell, I remember that clear as day. It hurt more than the attack did. I was scared to death and was caged in an underground shifter complex. It's where they hold new shifters who haven't mastered their animals."

"When did Pack get involved?" I asked. "Have they always known about you, or did they happen upon you by fluke?"

"Nathaniel was the one creating us. He would hand us over to Julian to be forced to remain in our wolf form. When Nathaniel was killed, the new Pack Leader started hunting us," he replied.

"I had no idea," I answered. My heart cracked at the news. Pack had killed the werewolves held at Julian's house the night I'd killed him.

Rome's smile was weak, almost sad. "A few months ago, some of us started to go missing. At first, we thought the new Pack Leader had picked up where Nathaniel had left off. But those of us who are Alpha could hear them call out for help. They were being hunted by Pack. But we couldn't save them. If we tried, we'd have been next. Those who went after them in the first few months, to try to save them, are dead. Pack doesn't even leave their bodies for us to bury. They burn them."

I winced. They heard the death of their own people. "I'm so sorry this has happened."

"Go to the media," Ziggy said out of the blue. "If you're out, Pack can't randomly kill you all. That would risk them coming to the attention of the public."

"Are you fucking insane?" I turned to face Ziggy, surprised at his suggestion. "And if going to the media doesn't work? It'll be a bloodbath. All he'll end up doing is ensuring the death of them all and tonight. Just knowing about them is a one-way ticket to a dirt nap. Lord knows what would happen if they outed Pack all together."

"Rome is no more cursed than any other shifter out there," Ziggy said. "I'm not saying to out Pack. I'm telling him to out his kind, werewolves. They are their own species of shifter. Pack has no authority over whether a different group must stay hidden or not. And they won't try anything if Rome and his people are in the news. Bringing attention to themselves is against Pack's own laws. Plus, they're already being hunted. They lose nothing if it doesn't work, and gain freedom if it does."

"I don't think that's a good idea. If it backfires, Pack will call in help from outside territories. Do we really want to risk a few dozen outside Pack members helping..." I paused and cursed. Miguel had invited a couple dozen outside Pack members not long after he killed Nathaniel, and told me they were lone wolves. Had he lied to me? Covered up the hunt of werewolves with bullshit? I'd deal with that later, if I lived long enough to confront Miguel. "Rome, do you have a safe place to hunker down for a few days until I can talk to my grandfather? Maybe he knows about some law that'll get you out of this?"

"There are werewolves everywhere, Ailis, in every country. Hundreds of them," Ziggy said. "If any come forward without some sort of a backup plan, someone who can save them from Pack, they're as good as dead. I've watched it happen time and time again. Someone more powerful than Pack needs to step in, or Pack will kill them all. That is simply the way of the world, from mice to monsters."

"I'm not more powerful than Pack," I reminded him, pulling up the sleeves of my shirt and showing off the scars I still had.

"Samuel is," Ziggy replied. "Get him to your grandfather."

Ziggy turned toward the entry as my necklace pulsed. I twisted to face the front of the store, shoving Rome behind me. I could feel the rolling energy pulsing under the door. Demetrius stepped outside and flicked the lock shut behind him. He looked calm, but his eyes said all hell was about to break loose.

"We need to go. Now," Demetrius said. That his voice was calm was uncomfortable.

"Why?" I asked and felt the first wave of Pack energy. "Shit."

"Pack is here," Demetrius replied, confirming what I'd sensed.

"Don't look at me. I didn't call Pack." Ziggy raised his hands. "Ailis, they can track better than any other out there. Whoever you go to next, make sure they can fight, because Pack is going to follow you there."

Rome gripped my arm. I could feel his body tremble under his sweaty palms. "They're going to kill me. They've killed five of my people this week alone. I'm dead. Oh, Jesus, I'm dead."

"Demi... Demetrius," I corrected myself. He didn't get his nickname while I was about to sink for his favor. "Go outside and meet them. Stall them for as long as you can without causing a war." I grabbed Rome's hand. "Ziggy, buzz the backdoor. You know the drill."

"Don't let them take him, Ailis," Demetrius said. "Please. Don't let anything happen to him."

"I'm taking him to Samuel's house. It's the only place Pack won't burn to the ground." I yanked Rome through the shop of cursed objects and left behind one of the reasons Pack would add me to their list of why they're pissed off tonight. I stopped at the rear door and waited for Ziggy to buzz it open. He watched his outdoor security and finally gave me a thumbs up. "When we get out there, stay beside me, Rome. I will shield us until we get to my car. Do not look back, do not speak, do not answer anyone's call. I don't care if Demetrius is the one calling out to you. Do not trust that he hasn't been taken. Whatever you do, don't let go of my hand for any reason. Do you understand?"

He nodded. "Thank you, Ailis."

"Quiet as the wind, let's roll," I said, releasing my aura to cover us both. I shuddered a breath once I felt his fear. His energy turned my stomach sour. He felt wet, like tears, against my aura. "Breathe, Rome. I'll get you to safety, but I won't be able to carry you if you pass out on me."

I pushed open the door and pulled Rome into the alley behind Ziggy's shop. Rome had a death grip on my hand and moved at the same pace I did. He was terrified. Utterly and painfully petrified of dying. The feeling was familiar. I felt it daily, had done since my parents were killed. Demons tend to leave a lasting impression on a child. I squeezed his hand because that was all I could do. Telling him it would be okay was a load of crap, and I wasn't going to try to kid him. This was so far outside of okay. We were both screwed and counting down the minutes until Pack came for us both.

At the end of the alley, I paused and closed my eyes, listening. I waited, looking back toward the shop. Above the awning over the door, the small light flicked on and off. It was safe for us to move. Ziggy had helped me on more than one occasion to escape the bad guys. I'd owe him again. I hated owing a demon, even ones who wore witchy meat suits and took chocolate as a payment. A debt was a debt, and I always ended up screwed when it was time to pay up.

"My car is parked directly out front. It's black, and it has a witch's broom hanging on the rear mirror," I said. "I'll hit the locks as soon as we get there. You jump in the back, hold your door closed, and do not slam it until we're long gone. If someone comes, shut your door and lock it. Stay down and do not get out or open it for anyone or any reason."

We bolted from the alley to my car. The sidewalks were empty, and I winced at what that meant. Pack had cleared them out, knowing they'd be causing a scene. I had experienced it once before, in Mexico. At the end of the sidewalk ahead of us, vampires from every dark corner of Blood Square were blocking the road toward my car. Only murmurs could be heard. It was calm for now. Once Pack realized I'd taken Rome and bolted, things would heat up, and tempers would flare. I wanted to be on the other side of the city when that happened.

Rome climbed into the back seat in one fluid motion, holding his door and ducking down. I got in the front, turned over my car, reversed and turned us around, heading in the other direction. A block away, we slammed our doors and locked them. My heart pounded until I pressed my hand into the center of my ribs. I gripped the steering wheel with one hand while

I tried to keep my heart from breaking through my chest and onto my dashboard.

"Stay down." I dialed Samuel's number as soon as we were out of Blood Square.

He picked up on the second ring. "Miguel just called here again, looking for you. He's called three times, Ailis. You didn't tell him you rescheduled our training? What's going on?"

"It's not good, Samuel," I said, my voice thick with fear. "I need a safe place to stash a werewolf."

"A what?"

"He's a kid, Samuel. He was attacked three years ago by Natt, who was giving his victims over to Julian. There's an entire group of them. They're just like the rest of the shifters. If I didn't help, Pack was going to kill him. They're hunting Rome's people down and killing them for no reason," I replied. "Please, help me? I ran with him, and now we're both pretty much screwed. Sam, I'm in a lot of trouble here, and I don't know what to do."

"Come home. I will always help you."

"Thank you." I sighed a breath of relief. I didn't think he'd deny me, but eventually there would be a day he would say no to me.

"Stay on the line with me. If Pack gets to you before you get to me, I'll redirect you to a safe place," Samuel said. "When you get here, I'll come down for him. Pack won't approach if I'm with you, or at least, none who wish to see the sun rise again."

In the background, I could hear Samuel moving around and the telltale sound of him double-checking that his guns were loaded. Samuel could blow the fur off a Lycan from a mile away, with power alone, but a gun came in handy for making the kind of statement

Samuel liked to make. Bullet or magic, he wasn't picky about how someone died, not when it came to family. I'd prefer it not come down to death, but my wish to stay alive drastically outweighed my squeamishness at the death of others. Contrary to my current decision-making, I didn't want to die.

"We're coming up your block," I said with a shaky voice. My insides flopped like I was driving top speed down a dirt road. "The streets are empty."

"Pack is near. I can feel them," Samuel replied. "I'm heading out front. Stay in your car until you see me."

I hung up and glanced from side to side. I didn't see anyone, but I could feel them and their eyes on me. I pulled up in front of Samuel's building and clicked the locks as soon as Samuel stepped onto the sidewalk. "It's okay, Rome. This is my grandfather, Samuel. You can trust him. He's a retired guardian. Do you know what that is?"

"Yes, Demetrius explained who Samuel was before he left to ask you for help," he replied. "Will I be okay here?"

"I trust him with your life and mine," I answered. "And so did Demetrius."

That was answer enough for him. Rome sat up and opened his door. Samuel grabbed his hand and pulled him into his arms, shielding the young man with his body. They went straight into the building. I locked my car and followed them with the feeling of spiders dancing down my spine. Inside, Samuel got Rome settled with tea and a plate of food while I double-checked every window. I didn't think anyone would be foolish enough to bust into a guardian's house, but people proved how stupid they were on a daily basis. One look at social media proved that point.

"You must be starved, son," Samuel said, his hand on Rome's shoulder. I blurred my eyes and watched Samuel's aura coat him, calming him. As Rome relaxed, Samuel read Rome's soul like a book. "You're safe here. You're now under the protection of the guardians, shifter. No one I do not wish will cross that doorway, and not many are stupid enough to try, including Pack. We will find a way to gather your people into a safe place until we can figure a way out of this."

"Thank you, sir," Rome said, shoveling food into his mouth like he hadn't eaten in weeks. Living with a vampire obviously had some setbacks, like food not found inside veins or blood bags.

Samuel pulled me to the side. "Start explaining, young lady. Why is my block filled with Pack? There are two dozen out there. And why the hell do you have a werewolf in your possession and smell like vampires and demons?"

"You might want to take a seat for this one, Samuel." I told him everything, from the Master of the City approaching me to meeting with Rome in Ziggy's shop. "I know what I did was against Pack law, but I couldn't just leave him there. I'm not Pack, and even if I were, I'd never let an innocent die simply because Pack believes they should be eradicated. I'm not built that way. He's not cursed. I'd feel it if he was."

"That they would have. Pack has hunted and killed them for as long as there have been werewolves to hunt," Samuel said. "But like you, I feel no curses, either. He feels like a shifter. But my word won't stand up to Pack law. And neither will yours."

I groaned. "I just need a moment to think this out. It was spur of the moment. It's not like I had intended to do a dine and dash."

"You've put yourself between Pack and a werewolf, at the request of a vampire, in the house of a demon. This is worse than ducking out without paying your check. You're up shit creek now. This one is going to leave some marks, Ailis, on more than just you. Anyone who helps you will be seen as an enemy of Pack."

"Shit. Should we leave?" I asked. "I'm sorry, Samuel. I wasn't even thinking of that."

His laughter filled the room. "I do not fear Pack. They'd be fools to come here. You are family. Pack will expect you to come home, and I'm sure they're having a hell of a time trying to find a way to get around me to get to you and Rome."

My phone buzzed for the tenth time since walking through the door. "It's probably Miguel again."

"You're going to have to answer it eventually," Samuel replied. "Rip off the bandage now and see just how deep this creek is. You need to know what's waiting for you out there."

"I know what's waiting for me out there. Pack." I groaned at the thought of facing Miguel, but Samuel was right. Miguel had been calling me nonstop since I got to Ziggy's shop. I breathed in and out until my hands stopped shaking and answered my phone. "Hello, Miguel."

"Did I just see you speeding away from Blood Square with a werewolf?"

"I don't think you want to hear my answer."

There was a knock on Samuel's door, and I froze. "It's me, Lish," Miguel said, and it did nothing to calm my nerves. "Open up. I'm not going to do anything to you."

I closed my phone and walked toward his voice. "I'm sorry, Miguel, but I can't. You can't come in. Rome is under Samuel's protection."

"Don't do this."

I swallowed a rock in my throat. "I'll talk to you at home, Miguel, but you're not stepping a foot into this house."

"Please, Lish, you're not going to like our conversation at home if you don't let me in."

"And you won't like what I'll do if I open the door and you try to take him," I answered. "I will see you in an hour. Take your Pack with you, or I don't leave the protection of Samuel."

"One hour," Miguel said. Seconds later, he was gone.

Samuel lifted his finger, tilting his head. It felt like hours before Miguel and his people left. "I'll get Rome to Mairi's house and find the rest of his people. No one steps foot on Mairi's property unless she wills it so. We can hide out there until the end of time."

"Thank you, Sam," I replied. He pulled me into his arms for a hug I could feel down to my soul. "What the hell do I do now?"

"Face the music, Ailis. You broke Pack law, and now you must answer for it. But if I may make a suggestion? Ask Miguel for help, away from Pack. He's not just a Lycan. He is your mate. Ask him to help you."

"Help me?" I huffed a laugh. "I'm pretty sure he's about to throw me to the waiting jaws of wolves."

"If he throws you to the wolves, you will return with your own Pack. You are not alone, and he is smart enough to know that," he replied. "But truthfully, I don't think he will. Be grateful Miguel isn't quick to kill, or you'd already be dead."

"I'll never needle someone for being squeamish about killing again."

"If either of you approach this as Pack, you will pay the same price as Pack. But he will help you if you ask. Swallow your need to be right, or this will end badly for us all."

I nodded. "I'll let you know how it goes. If you don't hear from me in a few hours, I'm dead."

"Miguel will give you time to run, Ailis. He won't kill you outright, and he won't let his Pack do it, either. But if he tells you to run, you get your ass back here," Samuel said, and I smiled. It wasn't often I heard him swear.

"Thanks, Sam." I hugged him again, just in case it was my last one. I breathed him in and blinked away the threat of tears.

I gave Rome my cell number and left him in the hands of the only person on this side of the gate who could keep him alive while I went to face the music. I ignored the rapid-fire texts coming from Cisco and Philip, and the calls from the fang who'd sunk my ship, Demetrius, or Demi to his friends. But I was not his friend, not anymore. Because of him, I was in deep and sinking fast. I'd once told Miguel he was a bleeding heart. I was worse. I dug graves because of my sappy heart, and this grave was exactly my size.

Chapter Five

The drive home was faster than I had wanted. Any other day, it took me forty-five minutes to get home from Samuel's house. Tonight, however, it felt like I hadn't even listened to an entire song on the radio before my street was in view. In between the safety of Samuel and the pending doom awaiting me at home, I hadn't thought of a way to spin this in my favor. I had no solution that didn't end with me hanging or the death of an entire species of people. Neither was a resolution I could live with. Although living wasn't exactly on the table for me or Rome. I either sacrificed myself or handed over souls to save my own. As much as I loved having a pulse, I didn't lead lambs to the slaughter for any reason or for anyone.

I turned down my road and felt the prickly heat of Pack roll across my body like the embers from a fire. I breathed through the initial shock of it. It was stronger than ever before, edged with anger and something that felt close to hate. The energy was coming from every direction, in waves that sped my pulse. My stomach sank, and my anxiety climbed. For a long minute after pulling into my driveway, I debated how well I knew Miguel. I knew the man, but I barely knew the Lycan. I gripped my steering wheel and wondered if he'd kill me or not. It was heartbreaking to not know if the man I loved would kill me before the sun rose. I wondered if I could kill him to protect myself. That I couldn't answer instantly told me how utterly screwed I was.

Miguel, Sofia, Cisco and Philip stood on my front steps. I didn't want to get out of my car. Seeing them waiting for me, having them make me dread the idea of coming home, made me angry. Anger was useful to me. It always had been. But under all the bravado of temper was my fear. I was scared for myself and for those I put myself in front of. Getting between Lycan and anyone, shifter or not, was a death sentence.

I let the memory of Rome's terror fill me. I knew exactly how he felt. I had been in his very position many times, thinking I was about to die because I was a witch and people wanted my kind dead. Hundreds of years of being killed for who we were was woven into the very fabric of my soul. It was something werewolves and witches had in common. We were killed because someone else thought we were undeserving of life. I had been chased down, kidnapped, tortured, hunted, tied to the center of a lit bonfire, had my house broken into and vandalized, and had more death threats than any other person I knew. Knowing how alone Rome was gave me new resolve. If I was the only one to stand with him, so be it. I'd make sure he didn't walk his path alone. No one should face the monsters on their own. If the stronger didn't fight for the weaker, the stronger deserved the same fate.

That I considered Pack to be the monsters in question made me pause a little longer.

"Will you walk into my parlor? Said a spider to a fly," I whispered, to my amusement. The sight of Pack on my front steps, the feel of them circling around my yard, made me feel like the silly little fly. I wondered if I'd ever come out again.

I wasn't sorry for what I had done, whatever the outcome. I knew, in my heart, I'd done what my soul knew was right. Pack law would never trump my soul. They would never decide what I had to do to be able to sleep at night. Turning my back on an innocent was not who I was, not even if I stood over my own hole in the ground. It was not who I had been raised to be. I hadn't come back from hell to waste my second chance. If this was my last deed before death, I'd make it count.

"Into the parlor, I go." I touched my charm necklace. It was cold. If it didn't sense my death coming, I trusted I wouldn't die tonight. I bit the bullet and got out of my car. I grabbed my workbag from the floor of the backseat and walked up the path to my house.

When I met Sofia's eyes, she winced. "I'm sorry, Ailis."

"I'm sorry I put you in this position," I said.

Miguel opened the door for me and motioned to the others. "The rest of you have somewhere better to be."

"I live here," Cisco said, but one look from Miguel had him jumping off the front stoop. The others followed.

"Hell, sweet hell," I said, stepping into my house with Miguel following. I kicked off my shoes and put some distance between us. His energy prickled along my skin to the point it was painful. "So, what's it going to be? Ripping out my nails? Waterboarding? Or a good old-fashioned phonebook beating? If I get to pick, I've been waterboarded twice and have had all my nails torn out already. I'd be down to try something new."

Miguel stood in the middle of the living room with his arms crossed. Each time he opened his mouth, he closed it. Time stood still when he began to pace. I could tell he was trying to calm himself down. When Miguel stepped toward me, I backed up, stumbling over my chair and falling to the floor. I rolled and was on my feet within the blink of an eye, positioning myself for whatever came next. My hands were loose at my sides, and my stance was wide enough for me to lash out if needed.

"I'm not going to hurt you, Lish," he said, frowning as though I had overreacted.

"Great, good. Take a step back then. I've never felt the kind of energy that's pouring off you, Miguel. I need you to give me a few extra feet of space because everything in my body is telling me to run or fight my way out of here."

He stepped back. "Do you understand what you have done?"

"Not really. I mean, I know what I've done. I've broken the laws of your people. But I don't know what that means for me."

"You've bitten off enough to choke on," he replied. "You lied to me."

"No, I didn't."

"When you didn't call me and tell me you had met with Demetrius, or that you were meeting with a werewolf, that is the same as lying to me. Withholding information is no better than lying to my face."

"I'm glad you feel that way," I said. "Tell me something, when you invited Lycan from other territories, was it to hunt down the werewolves?"

He closed his eyes and sighed. "Yes."

"So, you can concoct an elaborate story, blatantly lie to my face and bring your entire Pack into it, but I can't withhold information that will directly result in someone dying?"

"That is not the same."

"I agree. I didn't lie to you. I just didn't call you," I answered. "You don't own me, Miguel. And you certainly do not get to tell me what I can and can't do. I'll take the consequences for what I've done over the prospect of you or your Pack controlling me in any way. You, of all people, should already know I'd burn in hell before handing over my freedom to anyone."

"You'd rather die?" he asked, a hint of surprise in his voice. "Because what you've done could end in your death."

"Yes, but trust me when I tell you, I won't be the only one to die over this."

The tension in the room started to build again, and my stomach flopped. We could fight until the second coming of Christ without needing a bathroom break on a good day. But today was not one of those days. If I didn't stop this from turning into a holy war, things would take an ugly turn, and I'd never dig my way out of the mess I had climbed into. I took another step back and breathed in deeply, calming the roar in my head. I was torn between wanting to fight and wanting to climb into a hole and wait it out.

I thought about what Samuel had said and swallowed my need to be right. I needed to stay alive more than I needed a feather in my cap for winning an argument. "Miguel, I know you have things to say and questions to ask. But before you talk to me as Lycaon, can we talk as people?"

"My feelings will be the same on this matter."

"Please," I asked. "Just listen, then you can say whatever you'd like. If you want me to listen to your side, you need to be willing to hear me out first."

He finally nodded. "Yes. I can do that."

My nose began to tingle, a warning tears were soon to follow. "You've never been hunted. Not like I have. You've never sat in a room thinking you're about to die. I have—many times. Do you know what it's like to be alone in the world? To have people trying to kill you because of who you are, and there's literally no one to help you? To cry yourself to sleep because you may not wake up the next day?"

"No, I don't. I've always had my people."

"It's absolutely terrifying, Miguel. To not know how many days or hours you have left. Every noise sends you into a panic. A knock on your door makes you cry. You look over your shoulder and can't sleep without a gun in your hand. To know that there will be no one coming to save you kills the soul. It's not just terrifying. It's utterly and brutally heartbreaking to face the end on your own. I can't even explain how painful that is."

"I'm not sure how this includes Rome?"

I huffed. "He's there, Miguel. Waiting to die for what he is. I couldn't let you kill him. I'm sorry. I can't. He's not cursed. He's just a scared kid, trying to stay alive."

"If you help him, Lish, you will lose Pack protection. It is the law. No Pack member can aid in the escape of a demon, or harbor one."

"Help me, Miguel. Please. He isn't a demon. I swear it to you." My chin quivered. "I don't want to die for him, but I can't let you kill him. I'm asking you not as Lycaon, but as my partner." My throat tightened, and the first tears began to fall. "Help me. I know you disagree. I know you hate that I've done this. I know you're mad at me. But right this very moment, be Miguel for me. I'm scared, and I don't think I'm going to live through this. Please. I'm asking for you to be another set of eyes watching my back."

"You're putting me in a bad spot. I can't ignore law, not even for you."

"Do you trust me?" I asked.

"Always."

"You know I would have walked away if he was what you think he is. You know I wouldn't harbor a monster. He's not cursed. I felt him with my aura. Samuel did the same and said Rome feels like a shifter."

"That isn't enough for Pack."

"I don't know what to do," I whispered. "I don't know how to help Rome without dying for it."

"Do you trust me?" he asked, and I stared at him for a moment. "It hurts that your answer didn't come as quickly as mine did."

"I trust you, Miguel, but I don't trust your Pack. I don't trust that you'll help me over your Pack. I don't trust that you'll pick me. Give me a reason to trust that you won't let your Pack kill me, and I'll put all my eggs into that basket."

"I want all of the truth, or I can't help you," he said, leaning against the chair, his body finally relaxing. The energy swirling through the living room calmed enough for me to stop fidgeting. "Just start with the truth, and we will work forward from there. I give you my word. If you tell me the truth, I will try to help you."

"Okay, I can do that," I replied. "Remember my friend from university, the exchange student from Russia? The one who you thought was flirting with me until I told you he was gay?"

Miguel blushed. "Yeah, I remember."

"That's the Master of the City," I said and watched Miguel's face as he processed the same surprise I had felt when I found out. "Demitri Belov, Demi, is Demetrius."

"You've got to be fucking kidding me," he said, stumbling. He gripped the back of the chair to keep himself from falling over.

"Yeah, that's the same response I had tonight. I never knew, Miguel. I swear to you, not once did I suspect him to be a vampire. You know I would have told you had I known," I said. "I found out who he is when he came to the school this evening and asked for help, not as Nest, but as an old friend. I agreed to meet Rome at Ziggy's shop."

"Why didn't you call me?"

"And say what? Hey, Miguel, just to let you know, I'm going to meet the Master of the City – your nemesis – and a werewolf at a demon's shop?" I asked.

"Why did you go at all?"

"To see if what Demetrius was saying was true, and it was. I couldn't risk saying something in case he wasn't lying. I'd have killed the boy by telling you. And if Demetrius was lying, me and Ziggy would have stabbed him in the heart and hid the body," I answered. "Miguel, there are hundreds of them – werewolves – all over the world. They're not cursed. After a few weeks, if the person is strong enough, they survive and become shifters. There's an entire underground group of shifters helping each other survive attacks. They have places to keep them when they're first infected. Once they master their wolves, they're no longer a threat."

"That's not possible."

"I said the same thing until I met Rome. Once I felt his soul, I knew I couldn't let you kill him." I put my hand to my heart. "I swear on all I am that Rome is not cursed. He is a shifter. Natt attacked him three years ago and tried to bury him alive. Natt was attacking innocents and handing them over to Julian, who kept them in wolf form, where they lost their human side. But Rome survived. He was found by his people and was caged for the first few full moons. He's in full control of his wolf. Those we killed at Julian's house were Rome's people."

"What?"

I nodded. "Natt would attack innocents, then turn them over to Nest."

"Sweet Jesus. Pack isn't going to take your word any more than they'd take mine on this matter. Maybe we could have done something before this turned into a witch with a death wish," he answered and released a sigh that shifted into a growl. "I can't help you as Pack. It's against all laws."

"I'm not asking the Lycaon of the Noire Lune Pack for help. I'm asking my partner to help me, please."

"If you want my help, no one can ever know. We'll be killed for it," he replied. "And you're not going to like the route we have to take."

"Phonebook beatings?"

"Worse. I'd rather be beaten half to death than do what I'm about to do," he said. "I will cut all ties. We will continue forward as law demands, and I'll do what I can in the background to help you, but it needs to look like you're on your own. And trust that you'll feel alone. If they see me helping you or favoring you, we're both dead, along with Rome and Demetrius. This would turn into a war, and Pack will win—they always do."

I nodded. "When is it ever as easy as a beating?"

He stood. "When I leave, Pack protection leaves with you. You need to call Caser and ask for his protection to remain."

"Okay."

"You need to sever all ties with the Pack. All of them, including me. Stay as far away from my kind as you can. Trust no one," he said, and my heart dropped to my stomach. "We play this for real, Lish. And the hate you'll feel will be just as real. I still must follow our laws and make orders accordingly. If they see me go soft with you, they will take matters into their own hands and hunt you down, after they rise up and kill me for it. Using the law is the only thing that will keep you alive for now. When I leave, Lish, I'm leaving you as your partner and as Lycaon. It can be no other way. I must treat this as I would if you were anyone else, or Pack will kill you outright."

My breath hitched around tears and the urge to scream. "I've had hell chasing me for a decade. I can take it."

"We are what chases hell, Ailis. Nothing escapes our grasp, not even witches," Miguel answered. "If you can't find a way out of this, Pack will kill Rome, his people, and those harboring him, and there is nothing I can do to stop it. With your protection gone, they won't hesitate to kill you if you shield him. Helping a vampire, harboring a werewolf, these are all punishable by death."

"To save an innocent, I'd do worse things than shield him."

"To protect you, I'll do worse things than I'd care to admit out loud. Do not contact me through the usual channels. Reactivate your old burner email we used. That will be the only non-Pack contact you'll receive from me. Any other contact, through other methods, will be as Lycaon, and you won't enjoy what I'll have to say."

"I love you," I whispered, my throat painfully tight.

"I love you, too," he said and stepped back.

"Wait," I whispered and pulled him back into me. "Just give me another minute. I don't want you to go, not yet. The moment you walk out, I'll be alone."

"You won't be alone. I'll be watching you every step of the way. You just won't see me. You can do this," he replied. "You must, or all will be lost. All of this would be for nothing."

I nodded and breathed him in. "I'm scared."

"It's time," he answered and pulled back. "Ailis Petronilla Kyteler, the Noire Lune Pack no longer recognizes their ties to you. You are alone in the world of Lycan."

I watched Miguel walk out my front door, tears in his eyes, matching the ones on my cheeks. I locked the door and texted Mairi, since Samuel still didn't have a cell phone. I let her know I was still alive then called Caser.

"Little witch, you've sunk yourself good this time," Caser said as soon as he answered. "Cisco and Sofia have been texting me nonstop. Sofia just texted again.

What have you done to make Miguel pull his protection?"

"Oh, you know, just the usual aiding and abetting of a werewolf and consorting with vampires and demons," I replied. I gave him the condensed version but left out the part of Miguel helping me in the background. "Apparently, now I'm alone in the world of Lycan."

"Worse, Ailis, you are now seen as an outsider with the secret of Lycan." Caser sighed. It reminded me of whenever I did something foolish and ran to Samuel for help. "Witch, you dug yourself into a mighty big hole. No Pack out there would believe a werewolf isn't cursed. Your word isn't enough."

"Is it enough for you?"

"Yes, but I'm not the one with your name on my list."

"I need a favor," I asked, and he laughed. "Please, Caser. I need you to not remove your protection from me."

"That's a pretty big fucking favor, witch. You just admitted to breaking our laws. Hell, there were witnesses to your crimes."

"Just give me one week before you remove it. Please, Caser. I won't make it an hour without your protection. I don't know a lot about Lycan law, but I know enough to be scared. They will kill me for knowing their secret. I'm as good as dead the moment I hang up."

"Ailis, I can't go around law, not even for you."

"Bullshit, Caser. When Nichole clawed me up in Mexico, you and your Pack were going to trap me and lock me in a cage if I turned into a werewolf. You were going to break the rules for me then. All I'm asking for is a way around you delaying removing protection for a week. Please. Just give me some options here, that's all."

"Your protection stands for one week. I will schedule a meeting to speak with the elders, and once that's done, I'll have to make a formal decision. I'll push for a trial but, heads up, you will lose our protection if you haven't figured this shit out by then. Helping a vampire is a serious offense. Concealing a werewolf is a death sentence. That you're friends with a demon doesn't look good, either."

"I'm not friends with Ziggy, but I get what you mean. Thank you."

"I'll message Miguel and suggest he hold a trial for you and that I will not pull my protection until you are found guilty. That should get them off your back for now. They can't kill you between now and your trial." Caser swore a few times in the background. "Why the hell were you even talking to that bloodsucker?"

"The short version is that I went to school with him. I didn't even know. I was young. I had no idea what vampires felt like."

"You got used to his energy the way you did with Miguel."

"I'm so fucked, Caser. I don't know what to do."

"I'll call Miguel and make sure he knows you still have Mexico's protection. If things go south, get your ass to Samuel's house. I'll have Anna look into law on our end to see if there are any loopholes or ways out."

"Thank you. I owe you."

"If you live through this, you bet your ass you do," he answered and hung up, calling Anna's name.

Chapter Six

My house was locked up as tight as it could get, and now I regretted saying no to Cisco when he had suggested I install metal sliders over my windows, and reinforced steel doors. I was fully armed, a bug-out bag ready for if I had to bolt, and was locked in my bedroom waiting for the inevitable. Caser may have said I had protection, but I didn't trust the Vancouver Pack the same way I did Caser's Pack in Mexico.

My phone and text messages went off the rails for a solid two hours after Miguel left. I read a few, some threats, some concerns, but deleted them rather than respond. Nothing good would come from me sending middle fingers to keyboard warriors. I reactivated my burner email, the account we had used to share information years ago about demons and hunts. It was fitting, given I was the one who was soon to be hunted. I opened it up to find Miguel had sent me an email.

Lish,

Caser has contacted me to enforce his protection of you as his Grimmwolf, until a trial can be held. He has said he's not available to appear for your trial for one week. You have a week to figure this shit out. Seven days and your protection from the Los Luna Pack is up.

You are now an enemy of the Noire Lune Pack until I tell you I am no longer Lycaon. Do whatever you need to do to stay alive. Please do not hesitate. It will come down to you or them. Choose yourself.

Don't waste the time Caser has bought for you. Make every day count. If Pack approaches you, run. Protection only works if we all recognize it, and most of Pack is calling for your life. Do what you must to stay alive. Now is not the time to hesitate. They will come for blood. Make sure they are the only ones to bleed.

Remember, it won't seem like it, but I am fighting for you. I will do everything I can to keep you alive. I love you.
Miguel

It took me twenty minutes to think of something to say. I wrote several paragraphs, only to delete them. I went with what I would say if he were beside me.

Miguel,
I'm sorry.
I miss you.
I love you,
Lish

I curled up and cried until I had nothing left. Although I wasn't alone, my heart felt deserted. When my tears dried up, and I felt empty, I called Samuel and verified Rome was safe. Samuel had gotten him and his people to Mairi's house. Pack hadn't come sniffing around yet. Their focus was entirely on me. Samuel would check on me later. He repeated the same thing as Miguel—if Pack showed up, run for the hills or shoot to kill. What neither Samuel or Miguel understood was that I didn't stand a chance on my own, against Lycan, not unless I was willing to gain the attention of the Coven for dark magic. To stay alive, I was willing to do worse than break a few Coven laws, but I'd only be climbing out of one fire and into another, one built for bad little witches.

My cell phone rang, and the call display showed an unknown name and number. I ignored it. I didn't need to hear the threats. Reading them was enough. My house phone rang right after, another unknown name and number. A text message popped up after I ignored my house phone.

Answer your phone, please.
- Demi

My cell rang again, and I answered it. "How the hell did you get both my cell and home numbers?"

"You're listed," Demetrius replied.

"No, I'm not."

"A friend of a friend," he said, and I huffed an irritated laugh. I wasn't entertained. "I paid the guard at the university to give me your phone numbers."

"What can I do for you, Demetrius? Do you have some other critter you want me to protect? Maybe a demon, or someone off the FBI's most wanted list?" I asked. "I mean, if I'm going to die at the end of this, I might as well make all my enemies fight over who gets to do the job. Maybe you can dig up a few of the vilest witches to have ever walked the earth, and I piss off the Coven while I'm at it?"

"I'm a little busy at the moment, but maybe we can save that for the next time we meet?" he joked, and I wanted to reach through the phone and strangle him.

"I'm glad you're in such a good mood." I swallowed my need to pick a fight. "What do you want? If it's for another favor, you can fuck right off with it."

"Are you watching the news?"

"No." I sat up. I grabbed the remote and flicked on my television. I was about to ask what channel, but they were all playing the same thing. A live feed from social media of a young man shifting into a werewolf. It was Rome, shifting in plain sight while a camera picked it up and broadcasted it live.

"Is that a werewolf?" the person recording was whispering in the background. I knew that voice. *Ziggy.* "The Lycan have come out of hiding…"

"Oh, fuck," I said, gripping my phone. I put it on speaker and swiped my screen to my emails. I pulled up Miguel's last email and wrote him back.

Miguel, that video isn't my doing. Ziggy suggested it, and I said no. I know this is going to make things worse for me. I don't know what to do. The hole I'm in keeps getting deeper and deeper.

I sent the email and watched the news. The camera panned out. A group of werewolves stepped out of the treeline. Howls went up, and the camera stopped filming. The newscasters began speculating. I flipped through the channels, landing on an interview with Humans for Humans.

"…beasts roaming our streets. We are an open door for new creatures, spat from hell. The time to act is now, before they start arriving in droves. Our good city is a breeding ground for demons and the cursed. Mark my words. Our lives are at risk. License them now before they outnumber us, and we lose our..."

I hit mute.

"I thought Rome was with Samuel?" Demetrius asked me.

"Samuel took him to a safe place," I answered, bringing the phone to my ear. "I just talked to him a couple hours ago. He said all was fine. I don't know what's going on."

My house phone started ringing, and my call waiting began beeping. Text messages about Rome's stunt started flying in. I jerked when I heard someone not just knocking on my door, but banging. It echoed up my stairs, and my heart felt like it had stopped. My necklace heated, vibrating under my shirt.

"Someone is here," I whispered.

"Do you need help?"

"I don't know. Probably. I'm on a pretty big shit list right now. Just a minute, let me check my app and see who's here. If it's someone who can't come in unless I open my door, I'm fine. If it's someone my wards won't protect me against, I'm roadkill."

Cisco had installed cameras around my house so I'd be notified of movement in my yard and could check the live feed without having to step outside. I tapped on the app and clicked the icon for my front porch.

"There are two guys dressed in black standing at my porch," I whispered to Demetrius. "I've never seen them before. I don't know if they're Pack."

"Don't open your door. I'm on my way," he replied.

The banging continued. "We can smell you, Ailis."

"Fuck." My heartbeat pulsed in my throat. "They can smell me."

"It's Pack, Ailis. My guess is Sentinels. Miguel removed your protection. Sentinels carry out punishment for the Lycaon."

"But I still have the protection of Mexico," I said, then remembered what Miguel had said. They had to accept the protection, and some still wanted me dead regardless. "I thought Sentinels were just spies? What the hell would they be doing here?"

"They assess and remove risk, Ailis. They're ghosts of Pack."

I hit the microphone for the front door. "Can I help you?"

The one with jet-black hair looked up at my camera. "You're to attend the Chapel."

"No, thank you."

He smiled, but it didn't look friendly. "It wasn't a request."

"Tell Miguel I said no. I will speak with him tomorrow on neutral ground," I answered. "If he has an issue with it, he can speak to Caser about it."

My front door shuddered under a pounding fist. "If you could please come with us, it would show our Lycaon you have nothing to hide. You can deliver your own messages to him."

"Demi, they're going to kick down my door." My voice squeaked out.

"Run," he replied, an edge of panic in his voice. "Get the hell out of your house."

My door splintered. I was up, shoes on, grab-and-go bag strapped on, gun at the small of my back, and crawling out of my window when I heard my cat. Her screams tore through the house like nails scratching across metal. I landed on the roof of my porch to see one of the men grab the edge of the roof and pull himself up. I turned and climbed back into my room, shutting the window behind me as though it would do any good.

"I can't get out." My voice was closer to a shrill than the whisper I had intended. My throat was filled with the panic I was trying to swallow. I was a breath away from screaming. I unlocked my shields, my aura, and pushed it out around me, blocking my scent and energy the best I could. I ducked into my bathroom, shut the door and waited for a better opportunity to arise. "Jesus, I'm going to die in my own home."

"Fight, Ailis," Demetrius said. "Don't try to hide. You will be found. Do whatever you need to do to get to your front door."

"Then what?" I asked. "Die in my front yard?"

"Stay alive for the next few minutes, and I'll be there."

"Great, we'll both die here."

"It'll take more than two Sentinels to kill me. Do you own a gun?" Demetrius asked.

"I don't have silver bullets," I whispered, straining to hear what was happening in my house. A sickening feeling shot through my stomach, and I wrapped my arms tightly around my middle. It was all I could do to not vomit from the surge of fear. "Fuck. I'm going to die because I was too cheap to buy silver bullets."

"Do what you must with what you have," he answered. "Just get out of that damn house."

I palmed my gun and slowed my breathing. I shook out my arms and legs, preparing for what was coming next. My pulse swooshed in my ears as I listened to nearly silent footsteps. I muted my phone and pushed it into my pocket. The man from outside was in my bedroom now, and the one from the front door was up the stairs and in the hallway. I eased open the door in the bathroom that led to the spare room. When my bedroom door opened, I bolted through the spare room and down the stairs. His hands were around my hair before I hit the bottom step.

Although I had trained for every possible scenario and attack, nothing could prepare me for the moment I've actually been caught. I screamed and twisted, tearing hair from my head as I bent forward. I reached between my knees and grabbed his leg, pulling it with all my might. When he went down, I went down with him. Landing, I drove my head into his nose with every ounce of power I could muster. The sound of breaking bones sent a wave of nausea coursing through me. His grip loosened, and that was all I needed. I rolled from his body and pointed my gun at his kneecap. He lifted a hand to ward me off, but I still pulled the trigger. The sound was deafening. His roar was louder. His hands shifted into claws, and I aimed again. I'd put a bullet between his eyes if I had to. I was pretty sure a bullet in his brain would take the bite out of his fight. Either way, I wasn't going to let him get any closer to me in Lycan form.

The second intruder came down the stairs, taking them three at a time, with my cat tearing at his face with her nails. Halfway down, his claws broke through his flesh, and I swallowed the urge to scream. This wasn't a smash-and-dash. Like Miguel had warned, they'd come for blood, but I wasn't going to bleed for them. They kicked down the wrong door, and this witch was tired of monsters thinking they could do as they pleased and no one would stop them. At that moment, I didn't care if they were the protectors of man. They were in my house, uninvited, and I was pissed off.

I pointed my gun and pulled the trigger. I watched his leg buckle as the bullet hit him square in the kneecap. I bolted through the broken front door, leaving behind two wolves, down and bleeding all over my carpet. I jumped off my patio, rolling across the dirt and rocks, skinning my knees and hands. I ran toward my car, veering off when the two Pack members came from inside, limping, covered in their own blood, my cat putting the chase on them. I abandoned the thought of my car. I'd never have time to get in, get it started and drive away. I turned and made a mad dash down my driveway. I wouldn't get far, but maybe I could get to my neighbors in time. Would they even open their door, knowing it was Lycan on my tail? They were shifters, and so far, no shifter has dared stand against Lycan.

A black sedan skidded to a stop at the end of my driveway. The door pushed open, and Demetrius leaned over. "Get in!"

I dove in, and he hit the gas before I had the door closed. "How'd you get here so fast? Your house is almost two hours from me."

"Does everyone know where I live?" he asked, and I nodded. "When I heard Pack pulled your protection for consorting with vampires and werewolves, I hunkered down, close by, just in case."

"How the hell did you hear about my protection going belly up?"

"I have my sources, just like everyone else," he replied. "Information is power."

"Thank you for coming."

"I owe you," he said, and he more than owed me.

"You can pay to fix my front door," I answered, and he smiled.

My phone continued buzzing. I glanced at the call display to see Miguel and found myself glaring at my phone. My house was my only safe space. It was the only place I didn't let hell touch. I had fought tooth and nail to have a home where I could shut the world out, and his Pack had taken that away.

Miguel texted me when I didn't answer.

Did you get in a vehicle with the Master of the City?

I sent him a middle finger with my response. *They shifted their hands, Miguel. They weren't sent to take me. They came for my life. The next time you send your people after me, I won't just shoot them in the knees. I'll fucking kill them. I swear to God, Miguel. I will kill your people to stay alive.*

My burner email buzzed with an email from Miguel. *You should have killed them when you had the chance. It would have been two less Lycan hunting you. Go to Samuel's, it's the safest place for you.*

I wanted to call him and yell at him, but I knew I had been the one who'd called them to my door the moment I'd run with a werewolf.

I'll remember that for next time.
I'm on my way there now.

I called Samuel next. "Where is Rome?"

"When his people came, he and a few others ducked out," Samuel answered. "We didn't even realize he had left until Mairi was told of the video, not but twenty minutes ago. They did it a few blocks from here and came right back. I'm sorry, Ailis. I wouldn't have allowed them to put you at risk like this had I known."

"I know. It's not your fault." I instantly felt tiny. Like the entire world hated me, and I had nothing left that was mine. "Can I stay the night at your house? Miguel's Pack kicked down my front door."

"Where are you right now? Do you need me to come get you?" Samuel asked.

"No, Demetrius is driving me. But my house is wide open. My cat...she attacked them. She's all alone now."

"I'll send some people to fix your door," Samuel replied. "Don't worry about your familiar. She'll be fine."

"They came into my house, Sam. They chased me away from my home." I started to cry, feeling the flood of adrenaline leave my body. My limbs felt like pudding. "They took my safe place away from me. The monsters always fucking win. They take everything good and turn it into shit."

"They won't win. I promise you. We'll figure this out, Ailis. We always do. I'll grab cookies on my way home. It'll be okay," he said. "I'll make some tea, and we'll take this one step at a time."

"Thank you," I whispered and hung up. I wiped my tears and turned the heat up in the car. "Sorry, I'm in my pajamas. I'm cold."

"I'm sorry they kicked down your door, Ailis."

"You didn't do it. Pack did, and the next time, I won't just shoot them in the legs."

We drove the rest of the way in silence. I had nothing to say. I was angry, but more than that, I was hurting. Miguel had warned me that I'd hate the road we'd walk. But a warning and feeling the reality of it were two very different things. If he got to play the big bad monster, I'd be a witch from hell. I wasn't going to do the song and dance for Pack. The next time they came, I was playing for keeps. To do anything different would mean the end of my life.

When we pulled up to Samuel's, he was already waiting out front for me. He gave Demetrius a nod and wrapped his arm around me, leading me inside before I could say thank you to the vamp who'd started the fire that was now my life. I couldn't count the number of times Samuel had picked me up when things went south or waited for me on the sidewalk and walked me inside with tears on my cheeks. He might not be my blood, but he was my family. And now, my only family. It was a hard pill to swallow. To have everything one minute and all of it gone the next. I didn't regret the choice I had made to save Rome, but it still stung.

"My heart hurts," I said, stepping through the doorway into his apartment. The smell of books filled my lungs and made me instantly feel like I was home.

"Just because you did the right thing doesn't mean it won't hurt," he answered. "Let's get you cleaned up, into fresh pajamas, and a bit of tea into you. You shower, I'll make your favorite vanilla tea."

"Thank you, Sam." I hugged him until it felt like the pieces of my broken heart were pushed back into place. "Why do you let me call you Sam when I'm crying but no other time?"

He chuckled. "You only call me Sam when you're reaching out for love. You've done it your entire life. Now, into the shower with you. You smell of road rash, wet dogs and vampires."

The shower burned the scrapes on my knees, but the soap smelled like home, and my fresh pajamas took away the memory of being bloodied and scared. I was never homesick when I was with him. In the living room, Samuel set out tea and cookies. For years, this had been how he got me to calm down, talk through my problems, or just offer comfort when I needed it. I curled into a blanket on the couch, feeling the sting of the day, and nibbled on shortbread cookies.

"Your door is being repaired," Samuel said, pulling my attention from my dark thoughts. "They're installing a metal frame. It won't keep Pack out, but it'll take a few extra kicks to bring it down. Mairi is there. She's going to redo your symbols of protection for you. She's cleaned the blood from your stairs and living room rug."

"I liked my old door." My eyes watered all over again. "Thank you, Samuel."

"I've seen the video Rome and Ziggtmoy created. The demon has outed Pack."

I nodded. "This isn't going to end well for any of us."

"We will cross that bridge when we get to it," he answered, as though the bridge wouldn't be engulfed in flames with me standing on it.

My phone buzzed, and a photo of Cisco making cookies in my apron popped up on the screen. I read it out loud to Samuel. "Heads up, little red. Miguel is coming your way. He's pissed off that you left with the bloodsucker and did not come to the Chapel to discuss your trial. The wolf and demon outing us didn't help, either."

The door knocked a moment later. Samuel shook his head. "That pup is cruising for a bruising."

"Don't open the door, Samuel," I said.

"I do not fear Pack. They are fools to think this is a safe harbor for them. It isn't. I am a retired guardian, but I'm no weaker today than I was a hundred years ago." Samuel stood, an uncomfortable calm radiating off him, and unlocked his door, opening it to Miguel. "You sent your Pack after my granddaughter, to take her against her will with claws?"

"This is Pack business, Samuel," Miguel replied. He glanced at me once. His face was blank of any emotion, but his eyes were filled with pity.

"Your first mistake was going after the granddaughter of a guardian. Your second mistake is showing up at my door, not once, but twice," Samuel said. In the blink of an eye, I saw the real Samuel and the force of nature he truly was. He grabbed Miguel by the scruff of his neck, reached back and punched Miguel in the face, sending him to the ground, surprised. He crouched down and leaned into Miguel's face. Samuel's calm was long forgotten. "You and your people are not welcome here. Go after her again, and you're really going to piss me off. You will get one warning from me, dog. Fall in line, or so help me, God. Not even the gates of hell will protect you and your people from what I will unleash. Now get the fuck off my property before I start calling in favors from beasts not even Pack can survive. If you do not heed this warning, the next time we speak, I will walk away with your head and fur."

Samuel stepped back and slammed the door. He took his seat and lifted his teacup as if nothing had even happened. "As I was saying, Mairi will spell your house and property. All should be right as rain come tomorrow morning."

"I'm sorry. I fucked up really bad this time."

"You did what I would have done," he answered. "I'd have saved the boy and damned the Pack for getting in my way."

"I think I damned myself instead."

"Tomorrow is a new day with new solutions. Rest easy tonight. You are safe here."

I stood. "Thank you. I'm going to grab some sleep."

I gave him a hug and went to my bedroom. It was the only place that never changed. Everything looked as it had ten years ago. When he'd offered to have it redecorated, I'd refused. It was the only space that I could count on that time didn't touch or ruin. I crawled under a patch quilt my grandmother had made me. I kept it at Samuel's, where I knew it would always remain safe. Everything that was important to me—except my cat—I kept at Samuel's.

I didn't care what time it was. I called Caser, who picked up on the third ring. "I've heard about what happened. Cisco texted me," he said when he answered.

"Oh, you heard? That two Pack members kicked down my fucking door and attacked me?" I asked.

"They attacked you?"

"They booted in my door, and when I tried to get away, one of them grabbed me, and I had to fight him off. They grew claws, Caser. I shot them both in the legs rather than being scratched up. Once was enough for me," I explained. "I thought I had your protection? Since when is Pack allowed to claw people up?"

"They're not. Shifting claws during a fight with a human is against all laws. You should have killed them." Caser's growl filled the phone. "I will deal with them myself. They should not have even gone to your house, let alone put their dirty paws on you."

"I'm going to die with or without your protection." My cry hitched in my throat. "Miguel is going to let me die."

"Are you safe right now?" Caser asked. "Do you need me to send someone for you?"

"Had it not been for a vampire, I'd be dead," I said, swallowing the sadness and replacing it with anger. "Demetrius heard about Miguel pulling my protection and was close by. He drove me to Samuel's house."

"I will call Miguel," he said. "I don't know what the hell is going on there. There is no Pack stronger than the Los Luna Pack. My protection should have been enough, Ailis."

"It isn't," I answered. "As Cisco would say, I fucked around and found out, and now I'm royally screwed."

"Until we figure this out, stick to public locations, and don't go anywhere alone. I'm going to make some calls. I'll find out from Cisco and Sofia what is happening."

"Thanks, Caser," I answered. "If they're planning on killing me tomorrow, can you let me know so I can plan accordingly?"

"Hopefully, I'll have more answers later. Until then, do not let them catch you alone."

We hung up, and I checked my messages and burner email. There wasn't a peep from Miguel. Part of me wanted to call him and scream at him. The other part wanted to kick down his door and terrorize him in return. I should have done this my way, not his. I'd have simply shot whoever came after me, not play this cat-and-mouse game. But as I rolled onto my back, I wished he was curled around me.

Demetrius texted as I settled in for sleep. If I could sleep while being held hostage, being hunted by Pack wasn't going to keep me awake.

Is everything okay?

I wanted to laugh at the question.

No, and it won't be for you either.

The little icon on the bottom of the screen popped up and down until Demetrius finally replied.

I've broken no laws. Pack won't knock on my door. If you need help, let me know. It's my fault you're in this. Rome is back at my house. He said he did the video to protect the others, as Ziggy had suggested.

I shook my head. As if what he had done would buy him freedom.

He's painted an even bigger target on his back — and ours. That wasn't the way to do this. Now we'll all pay for it.

I turned off my notifications and set my alarm. If I was lucky, I'd get three hours of sleep before I had to work. The world didn't stop spinning just because an entire species of people wanted me dead. I still had to work and pay my bills. My mortgage insurance didn't cover my inability to work due to death threats. I had to actually die and stay legally dead for my bills to stop rolling in.

Chapter Seven

The first thing I did when I woke up was check my burner email. It was a ghost town. I don't know what I was expecting, but seeing nothing from Miguel hammered it home a little deeper. I was alone again. I dragged myself out of bed and groaned as soon as I stretched my back and arms. Stiff as a board, scabbed and bruised, I dressed for the day, wondering what one wears on a day that may be their last. I went with what I could run for my life in. So, I dressed like I did most days. I stood in front of the mirror for a long minute and didn't like the person looking back at me. My eyes were dark circled, scared, lost, alone. I had looked in these eyes many times. I thought I had left this part of my life behind when I found Miguel again. But here she was, the girl with all the regrets and nothing to show for the pain of it.

The university was buzzing with gossip and speculation about the new shifter population. I wasn't surprised. I had been jumping out of my skin when I'd found out about Lycan and, through them, several other species of magics I hadn't known about. There wasn't a group of people I passed on my way to the demon wing not watching the video of Rome shifting, or sitting in deep conversation about the werewolves. They were all so preoccupied that this was the first time I had strolled down a hallway without a sneer, glare or downright curse. The only ones not talking about the newfound werewolves were the shifters, and more because they had already known and didn't risk Pack finding out they ran their mouths. As I walked by each shifter group, their faces held pity for me. One look told me they had heard I was being hunted by Pack. I hated pity but appreciated they weren't overjoyed by the news like more of my hate club would be.

I stopped by my lecture hall to see a notice from Philip posted on the door. Hall would be closed for the day, and students were to review the articles he had posted online. I unlocked the door to our shared office, cringing at the thought of facing him, but the lights were still off. Philip, it seemed, had taken the day off. I should have done the same. I'd woken up feeling like hell had been clawing at my mind all night. Any sleep I had managed had been restless and twitchy. I'd woken up repeatedly, jerking to any noise I heard and reaching for the gun under my pillow. It had all been Samuel's early morning racket and not monsters coming to snatch me—he'd spent hours making calls, meeting folks in his kitchen, and sending out word that the granddaughter of a guardian was under threat. Before I had left for the day, I'd met two other guardians, Amos and Amelia, each trained by Samuel and both owing him several favors. Even though Samuel was retired, they still looked to him as if he were their sun and moon. They swore they'd find a way to save me or would die trying. Samuel's family was their family. I didn't want anyone to die for me, but I felt a little braver knowing Samuel had my back, and through him, a few dozen others would keep their eyes on me and my beating heart. It made leaving his house easier.

I made a pot of coffee and wandered around my personal office, which was tucked in the back down a short hallway. The common area, where Philip's desk sat, was more of a library than an office. I picked out a few books from my shelves, as well as the latest species catalog. I could have found it all online, but holding the physical book was somehow better, and it gave me something to do that didn't include hiding out in the backroom of Samuel's house. When I'd announced I was leaving for work, Samuel hadn't argued. He knew I'd never let the monsters keep me locked away. He'd simply picked up the phone. I wouldn't know who he would send to keep an eye on me, but from the sound of it, I'd have shadows wherever I went.

With a fresh cup of desperately needed coffee in my hand and a stack of books on the table, I took a seat at the table in the main room. It was more spacious than my office and gave me a way out that didn't include breaking a window and jumping from the second floor. The last time someone had come for me in my office, it had boiled down to my life or theirs. They hadn't made it out alive. I opened my laptop and pulled up my online bookmarks. There were some books you just couldn't own a physical copy of. The more accurate the book, the harder it was to get your hands on. Samuel had a few of those books, but I never touched them. Just being near them made my skin crawl and stomach cramp. Cursed texts always made me feel sick. Holding them was like standing in a haunted graveyard.

My phone buzzed, and I almost let it go to voicemail. I shook out my hands and scolded myself for letting the bad guys control me from afar. One look at the call display, and I was glad I didn't cower. "Good morning, Mannix. Please tell me you don't have another body."

"Funny, I thought I'd be finding yours this morning," he replied, and I cringed. News traveled fast. "Do you want to tell me why my coworker Jax woke me up this morning and told me to check on you? To make sure you were still alive."

"Is Jax a psychic?"

"No, he's a shifter," he replied, and it made perfect sense. "He said he couldn't tell me why I needed to check in with you, only that you were in serious shit and sinking fast. He followed it up by sending me the video of a werewolf. What's going on?"

"I pissed off the wrong group of people."

"Werewolves, I take it?" he asked. "Before you play your usual avoidance games, it's still all over the news."

"They're involved, but they aren't the reason I should be planning my funeral. I'm sorry, Mannix, that's all I can say unless I want to light my own pyre."

"Do you need help? I've got a lot of banked days off. Say the word and I've got your back. We can hunker down with Coven or one of the safehouses. There aren't many groups out there brave enough to knock on their door. I can call my father, and we can be on his plane in the next hour."

"I don't need any help yet, but thank you." I swallowed the rock in the back of my throat. Mannix willingly talking to his father to help me, reminded me that I wasn't completely alone in this world. I had people who cared, and Mannix was one of them. Instead of letting my emotions pull me under, I changed the subject. "Did you solve those murders? Any more bodies?"

"Nope on both accounts, but people will always be dying, Lish. I don't want to wake up tomorrow and hear you were one of them," he answered. "I can come if you need me. Don't worry about my caseload. I take time off when I need to, not when my workload permits it. How deep are you in?"

I groaned. Wishful thinking, that he'd let me change the topic so easily. "I'm up to my ears."

"If things get really bad, call me or get to a Coven safehouse. Not even hell can be summoned within those walls. And unless it's witches after you, which I've heard no rumblings about, no one without witch's blood running through their veins is getting in there."

"Thanks, Mannix. I should be good for a few more days, but I'll call you if I need help."

"You'd come for me if I was in trouble, no matter who I pissed off. If I don't hear from you in the next few days, I'm coming to find you."

I smiled. Although I'd never call him or involve him, it was still nice to know he had my six. "Thank you."

I ended the conversation before I started to cry, and returned to my books. Mannix was a good soul. I don't know what I had done to be gifted a friend like him. I reread the history of Lycan. After learning about Pack, I'd spent countless hours researching Miguel's people. Most of the information I gathered had been from Cisco, who was a walking history book. According to lore, they were a divine intervention, the original hellhounds. After a deal with the man upstairs, hellhounds were allowed out of hell to protect mankind from the cursed and damned. From the lips of Lycan, they were guardians of man. Which, to me, seemed more like a punishment than anything else. They hunted beasts and the like, and after death, their souls went to hell, where they guarded the Gates of Hell in their wolf form, becoming hellhounds once again. Nothing about their life or death sounded like it was a gift.

I leafed through a book I had purchased from an estate sale, *Accidents of the Natural*. It was one of the few books that differentiated between Lycan and werewolves. It said a Lycan was a curse, a gift from hell, and their curse becomes a virus to those infected, creating werewolves. I wondered if this was how it had begun for all shifter groups. With questions on my mind and no one I could call at home, I dialed Caser's number and waited for him to answer.

"I see you're still alive," Caser answered.

"It was touch and go for a moment there."

"Cisco said Miguel was damn near knocked out by Samuel. Cisco had to reset his jaw," he said with a hint of laughter in his voice. "I warned him the first time we spoke, the guardian would not appreciate his grandchild hunted."

"To put it mildly," I muttered. "Do you have a second? I have a few questions about the history of Lycan and werewolf."

"Give me a minute. Anna would probably have the kind of answers you're looking for. She's more of a historian than I am. She's the brains of this operation." In the background, he called for his daughter.

"Hello, Ailis." Anna's voice was as cheerful as I remembered. Everything about her reminded me of the sunshine trying to reach through a storm. "Dad said you had some historical questions?"

"I've been reading up on the differences between a Lycan and a werewolf. There isn't a lot of information out there that keeps the two as separate species. So far, all I've managed to gather is that Lycan is a cursed mythological animal that looks like a wolf and a werewolf is a person infected by lycanthropy who transforms. Cisco had once told me that a Lycan's true form was a wolf, and you use energy to maintain human form. I'm assuming it is the other way around for a werewolf. They use energy to shift into their wolf forms?"

"That's close. Lycan can control their shift. Werewolves do not have the same abilities," Anna answered. "The stronger shifters can harness raw energy around them, sort of like a witch, and shift as needed. During the full moon, when the doorway between hell and earth is at its thinnest, too much energy leaks out, and shifters change whether they want to or not. Lycans, on the other hand, are not governed by the moon once they master their animals. We have the urge, but can stop the shift from happening."

"How did your people come to be? There has to be a cause or a start. I mean, I know the story from Miguel, but how close to the truth is what he believes?" I asked.

"There's a lot of speculation as to how we came into the world and why we are here. Most, as you know, say we are the original Hellhounds who made a deal with God. If he would allow us to live above, we would protect mankind from hell. And when we die, we guard the Gates of Hell to keep out the innocent and drag in the guilty. If we break this agreement, we will be punished."

"And what is the story about werewolves?"

"Lycan can only be born. It is part of the original deal with God. When a rouge Lycan tries to build an army, he can only make werewolves. We cannot spread the Lycan gene, only the lycanthropy virus. It is believed that a werewolf dies within the first few months, their bodies and minds not being strong enough to take the shift. This is obviously baseless, given there are dozens of thriving shifter species out there. But if a werewolf lives beyond the first few days, Lycan hunt them down and kill them. We are tasked with not allowing the virus to spread. We'd be putting all of humanity at risk, or so says the lore."

"Who tasks you with killing them?" I asked.

"God, apparently, and upheld by the Elders. It is written in our books that werewolves are demons out of hell. They are cursed souls. But I've read every book on Lycan, and I cannot find where the word of God is written. It just appeared. The first few mentions of werewolves are vague until a century ago, when a book of the damned was written, outlining those who Pack believed were demons and devils in disguise."

"You don't sound like you believe this any more than I do."

"It's not that I don't believe it, more that this cannot be the entire story, only part of it. Nothing in this world is so neat and tidy. You have to remember, when these stories were written, we did not have sciences and laboratories and individual voices," she replied. "There are others who are afraid to speak out, that have said Lycan are not much different than demons. During the sixties, a group of Lycan concluded twenty years of research on our kind. Their final report was destroyed, but a few pages here and there are still floating around. One of the pages says Lycan and demons share the same curse, and that is why the wounds we inflict have similar results as a demon attack. Another went as far as to say that people attacked by a Lycan will only turn into a werewolf if the curse mutates the genes responsible for lycanthropy. When you look at the outcomes of an attack, their statement holds a lot of merit. There are only three possibilities after a Lycan attack. The person dies from their wounds, wins the war against the curse, or becomes a werewolf. And of those who changed, their genetic makeup was perfectly matched to host the lycanthropy virus. I've spoken to a few shifter groups who confirm the science behind the virus, the activation of junk DNA, and the coin toss on whether infection occurs or not."

"How is it that other shifter attacks result in the spread of lycanthropy, but a werewolf cannot?" I asked. "When Miguel and Cisco were discussing Julian using werewolves to hold his territory, they had said only a Lycan could infect man, not an existing werewolf. How is that possible? It doesn't seem to be the case with other groups."

"That's where we run into plain ego, elitism and a history so long people stopped questioning it," Anna answered. "There are a few variations to the story, but the overall theme is the same. We are told that our calling is from the heavens, and our curse is a last-ditch effort from hell to doom mankind. When we step off the righteous path, harming those we are sworn to protect, hell gets another soul. Basically, when we attack someone, we spread a curse from hell that kills them. Most Lycan think the story ends there. But the truth is, any shifter can infect a human. It's just that we hunt down one specific group of them before they have the chance to infect others."

"Where did the other shifter groups come from, if not for another group like Pack?"

"Exactly, Ailis," she said, her voice hinting on excitement. "History is riddled with stories of therianthropy, skinwalkers, and beings that could transform between human and animal. Just look at the great cats of Egypt or any of the Gods prayed to in many religions and cultures. It is said that Pack is not the first Lycan to have existed, that many of the werecats come from a line of Lycans of their own. The same goes for the rats and water people. All shifters come from their own flavor of Lycan."

"What happened to them, the original Lycan of the other groups?" I asked.

"There are too many stories to say which is true. Some say they're still here and have blended in with the shifters. Others say they were killed off. Since we don't know what smell each would have, I wouldn't even know how to tell them apart."

"Would Rome smell like a shifter?"

"I see where you're going with this, but he would smell like a werewolf to us," she replied. "Even if he were something unlike anything we could name, he'd still smell like a werewolf, and Pack is tuned to hunt and kill them by smell alone."

"Have you found anything on your end that could help me?" I crossed my fingers.

"I haven't found anything that can help the young man," she said, and I groaned. "The law is simple on this matter. Werewolves are seen as an abomination, the doom of mankind, a plague from hell. To allow them to live is to risk humanity."

"How do I make Pack see him as something different?"

"You would need to make him more than what we see and scent," she answered. "You told my father he isn't cursed. Prove it. You said he feels like a shifter. Prove that he is. You need evidence. You need concrete proof that can't be refuted."

"Ailis." Caser's voice surprised me. I'd forgotten he was still there. "You can't change Pack laws, but you can use them to your advantage. Pack cannot kill an innocent. Prove he is innocent. Prove he is within the protections of Pack."

"How the hell do I make them believe me?"

"I believe you," Anna said. "So does my father."

"I wish that was enough to save my skin."

"So do I," she replied. "I will call you if I find anything helpful, but I don't think I'll dig up anything that will save Rome. His video made things even worse for him."

"That was the work of Ziggtmoy, not Rome," I answered.

"Every Pack worldwide is now questioning if Rome should be taken out to guard our secret or killed because he's a werewolf. Either way, they're looking at him as a problem to Pack."

"Would they still question whether to kill him or not if he were a shifter?"

"They may, but they likely wouldn't act on it. He would be considered an innocent and not sworn to protect our secret," she replied. "It would then fall on Pack to maintain our secrecy, and not that of a shifter."

A shadow appeared on the other side of my door, and my heart stopped. A soft knock, and the door opened. Instinct had me standing and reaching for the bat beside my chair. May's head poked in with a smile.

"Ailis?" Anna called. "Is everything okay?"

"Yes." My heart was still in my throat. "It's May. I have to run. I'll call you when I think of something. Thank you for your help."

"You're most welcome, and I will do the same." Anna and Caser both said goodbye, and I hung up.

May closed the door and locked it. "Why was your door unlocked?"

"To let my students come in," I answered.

"And those hunting you," she said. She picked up one of the books from the table. "*Fundamentals of the Abnormal*, you're not going to find what you're looking for in a book." She scanned the page I was on in the *Catalog of the Unnatural, Tenth Edition*. "You're not going to find werewolves in the Catalog, either. It's kind of hard to be listed when your kind is slaughtered before their first steps." She pulled out a chair and took a seat. "What's going on, Ailis? The city is up in arms, groups are moving in and out. Nest has their day walkers out in full force, roaming the streets. Hell, there are four of them on campus as we speak. Our city hasn't sat on the brink of war like this for many years. Something is coming, and it's starting to smell like a burning witch."

"Where do I even start?" It wasn't so much a question. There was just so much that had gone on. I didn't even know what was important anymore. "I know the Master of the City, or I did once, long ago. He asked me to help him save a werewolf, a survivor of an attack. One thing led to another, and here I am, with my ass in boiling water. If I don't figure it out, we're both roadkill."

"They kill werewolves. Why would you put your neck on the line, knowing you'd be harboring someone they have hunted since the dawn of time?" May asked, and I raised my brows. "Oh, come on. I'm not an idiot, Ailis. I've known about Pack since I was three. You can't train to be a hunter without crossing paths with them. I'm dating a Lycan and have dinner with you all two or three times a week. Do I look dumb enough to believe they're all demon hunters? If it walks like a wolf, talks like a wolf, it's a bloody wolf."

"Is that what they told you, that they're demon hunters?" She nodded to my question. "In a way, I suppose that's true. Still, they're not a topic I can freely discuss *and* keep my heart in my chest."

"That isn't going to be a problem for long." She pointed out the obvious. "The entire world is about to find out shortly. Rome's little stunt has dug up old questions. With tech the way it is today, it's only a matter of time before Pack is outed."

"And if that happens, I'll be the one they blame."

"Probably," she answered. "Do you need help?"

I was surprised by her question. May was the type to stick to herself, keep her head down, stay out of the business of others, and didn't meddle. She and I had the same opinion when it came to trouble. Keep your nose out of it, and it won't come knocking. That is until I decided to have a clandestine meeting with trouble and shove it in the backseat of my damn car.

"I don't think Ben would like that all too much," I replied. "But thank you."

Her laughter was tangible. The energy in the room shifted with it. She was amused. More than that, she had a daring look in her eyes that was familiar. Like me, she wouldn't be commanded by someone else. "And he doesn't own me or make my decisions, Ailis. If Ben and his people are hunting you, you need all the allies you can get. I disagree with arbitrarily hunting and killing a species of people simply because that's what you've been doing for generations."

"Don't you hunt and kill an entire species of people?"

"Only bad little vampires," she replied. "I don't hate them as a group. I hate what they do when they go rogue. How can I help?"

"I need to get Rome and his people out of the city. Any ideas?" I asked. "Before I can even begin to figure out how to get myself out of this mess, I need to keep them safe."

"Have you tried asking the other shifters for help?"

"I don't know any, aside from students and the one I'm currently on death row for protecting," I answered. "From what I hear, they're all too scared of Pack to help Rome. I doubt they'd help the witch being marched to her pyre with a Lycan procession."

"But they may have solutions to the problem that we, as non-shifters, wouldn't think of. They live in this world. We're simply visitors." She pulled out her cell phone. "Let me make some calls. I know a few shifters. I'll see who is willing to talk to you."

May stepped out of my office, and I packed up my things. With or without her help, I felt antsy sitting around. She was right. I wasn't going to find my answers in books too old to understand the world we live in today. Twenty minutes later, May came back in with a smile. I staggered at my table with hope, gripping the edge to keep myself from falling over. Her smile was one step further away from my pending death sentence. Even if it was a dead end, it was still a possible outcome that didn't include a hole in the ground. Hope was always the last thing to die, and I still had some spurring me on.

"Let's go," she said. "Cole, the Mane from the werelion pride is willing to meet you right now."

"Mane?" I asked. "Sorry, May, I don't have the same knowledge as you do when it comes to anything outside the gates of hell."

"Cole is an Alpha of the Dawnguard Pride. Most Prides are led by females. His Huntress, their leader, Rashida, hates Pack with a passion and has given permission for Cole to speak to us," she answered. "But we have to go now. He won't do it later, after dark. He says the city is waiting on a knife's edge for Miguel and Demetrius to war. Demetrius told Miguel, at sunrise this morning, you have the protection of his Nest. Any act against someone under their protection, who has broken no laws, will be seen as an act against Nest and the Elders. Demetrius has gone as far as to say Rome's stunt would look like child's play compared to what he would do to save you. Apparently, he mentioned that his human servant is prepared to call a news conference to confirm the existence of Pack and has decades of photos and surveillance video to back it up."

"Oh, great." I groaned. "I'm sure that went over about as good as bomb in an outhouse."

"I'm sure it was much worse than that. But any additional layer of protection that you can get is worth something, even if it's from a vampire. It'll slow down the hunt for you."

"I never thought I'd hear you say those words."

She smiled. "Again, I don't hate vampires. I hate monsters. I have hunted beside vampires who wanted the same goals as I, to live in a world where no one goes to sleep afraid of what's under their beds." She leaned in. "I kill those who step out of line, whether they are Pack, shifter, demon, or human. If they hunt innocents, I want them dead, equally, across the board."

"What an uncomfortable thought," I said.

"No. The uncomfortable thought is that there will come a time when people like me aren't hunting down people like them," she said and held out her hands. "Keys? We'll take your car—I'm driving. I'll get a ride back from Cole."

We stopped at May's office for her to grab her backpack. She opened a massive safe and strapped herself with weapons. "Are you armed?"

I nodded. "One gun, two knives. If Pack comes for me, it's not like anything I have is going to save my life."

She handed me two knives. "Replace yours with these. They're silver. Might as well fuck them up before you die. Every day, when they look in the mirror and see the scars, they'll remember your name."

"Thank you," I said and traded out the knives on my thighs for hers.

"Please tell me you have silver bullets in your gun?"

"Samuel loaded my gun this morning with silver." I followed her out of her office and through the school. The entire time, I felt eyes on me. I didn't know if they were staring at me because I was a dead witch walking or because the two of us were together.

May's driving was more of an art than a science, if that artist was Jackson Pollock and he was drunk. Her behind the wheel reminded me of Cisco. She weaved in and out of traffic as though she owned the road. Horns blared, brakes screeched, and vehicles came a hair away from taking off my bumpers. She drove in circles, up and down side roads and alleyways. I held on and cursed, waiting for her to wreck us. May took the corner without slowing down, and I was nearly sick. I closed my eyes, said a silent prayer and waited to die. Her laughter at my response was unnerving. I'd died once in a car wreck. Twice would be just my luck.

"We were being followed," she said, putting the car in park. "Samuel's people, I assume."

I opened my eyes. "Is that why you were driving like a lunatic?"

"No, this is just how I drive," she answered. "There's never been a day I haven't been hunted for a living, Ailis. You get used to taking precautions everywhere you go. You should be taking the same safety measures."

We were parked beside a dumpster in the back of a diner in West Van, at Hell's Hollow. It was a no man's land in the shifter world. Neutral ground. It sat at the point of eight shifter groups, but within the walls of Hell's Hollow, there were no Alphas. Langdon Bates, or Lang to his friends, was a retired military man and owned the place. His adopted son was a werehyaena, like his mother, Corky. I didn't know them personally. But from what I heard, everyone with fur and fangs knew of him, and knew well enough not to cause problems in his diner. Silver buckshot was not a good way to be asked to leave.

May walked in, said hello to Lang as though she knew him well. May pointed to a booth in the far corner. She kept her eyes on the door and window, and the back door twenty feet from our side, while she walked calmly and casually. She had me slide into the booth first, giving her the ability to stand at a moment's notice. May was trained for kicking ass. I was trained to do my best at staying alive. It was a wise decision to put me on the inside. There was no question in my mind that the man sitting across the table was Cole. I smiled as soon as I saw him. He was exactly what I would have envisioned for a werelion, with long strawberry blond hair that hung in waves to his shoulders, around a solid, stubbly jawline. There was a ruggedness to him that said he didn't sit in an office all day. His eyes weren't just brown—they were amber, edged in almost black. The moment I sat down, I could feel his energy. I don't know what I was expecting, but it was soft, almost calming. It reminded me of my cat in the way she could calm my nerves and make me feel protected at the same time. I knew there was a sea of power under what he held back, but I appreciated the little he showed me was for my benefit. I settled into my seat and breathed a sigh of relief. For the moment, I felt safe.

"Cole, thank you for meeting with us," May said and motioned to me. "This is Ailis Kyteler."

Cole held out his hand, and I was surprised he offered it. Not many did.

"I'm sorry we are meeting this way, but it's a pleasure."

"Thank you, Mr....?" I asked.

"Cole is fine," he replied.

"Thank you for meeting with me, Cole. I really appreciate it," I said, taking my hand back. My palm prickled with energy. He didn't clean his off, which made me smile.

"So, you are the hunted one," he said, looking at me with pity. I hated pity, and I had gotten a lot of those looks as of late. "Not many are brave enough to stand against Pack, and those who do are dead before the rest of us hear of it."

"It's not been a pleasant twenty-four hours," I said, feeling every hour in my weary bones.

"That you're still alive is surprising. You have strong allies, Ailis. A guardian, a Master vampire as of this morning, and a renowned hunter. Collect who you can, because when Pack finally comes for you, and they will, they will kill you for this."

"I have six days," I answered. "My protection from the Mexico Pack will run out then."

"Six days will go by quickly. Let's not waste any time. If you're here for the aid of my Pride, we cannot help you. Pack will slaughter us. There simply aren't enough of us to fight against Lycan," he said. "My Huntress has permitted me to give information but not protection."

"Any help, even information, I am thankful for," I said and paused, my eyes shifting to someone approaching. A tickle of power swirled in the air around him. A shifter. I reached for the weapon on my thigh and stopped short when May grabbed my hand under the table.

"It's a server, calm down. Lang will shoot you if you fuck with his staff," May said. When he pulled out his pad, I eased down. "Three coffees, cream, sugar. That's it for us today."

"No problem, May," he replied and walked away.

We sat frozen, waiting for the coffee to touch down. The server said nothing else and continued about his business. May used four creams and no sugar. Cole drank his black. I held my cup rather than drink it. I was cold to my core and had been since I'd ducked out of Ziggy's shop with a werewolf in tow.

"Do you know how I'd get a werewolf and his people out of the city?" I asked.

"Not with Pack on his trail," Cole answered. "There are four dozen Pack in town and more on the way, from what I hear. Word is, Demetrius has called all of his children home in case there is a war. They're set to arrive tonight."

"That should please Pack," I grumbled.

"Pack can't stop a Master from calling his children," Cole explained. "It is expected. When a new Master takes over a city, their children follow. Until now, Demetrius hasn't called anyone home. All this over a werewolf. I hope he is worth it."

"Every innocent is worth it. I won't let Rome die because I'm scared of what will happen to me." I tapped on the table. "Which leads me to my next question, how do I prove Rome is an innocent?"

Cole smiled. "You'd have to prove he's a shifter."

"And how do I do that? Pack isn't going to take my word for it."

"Try having him tested for the lycanthropy virus. If he has been a shifter for as long as May told me, he's overcome the curse. It will show up in his blood. It takes a few weeks to show up clear as day, depending on their shift cycle, but it should be there now," he explained. "When any of us are exposed to the virus — or as Pack calls it, the curse — we all must fight it or succumb to it. If our bodies win, it goes one of two ways. We become a shifter, or we do not. Some beat the virus before it has a chance to get a foothold. And for some, their bodies and minds cannot tolerate the virus, and they die or need to be killed."

"It is the same with vampires," May said. "Some do not become, and some do. It's the luck of the draw on any given day. No test can say who will be lucky and who will not. A dozen years ago, they tried to map if a person could be at higher risk of contracting the vampire virus and came up empty, though there's been speculation on what makes the perfect host for the virus."

"The same was done for shifters," Cole added. "Every human being is at risk for it. Lycanthropy is a virus, and viruses don't care who they infect. We all carry the junk DNA the virus mutates. Some victims are bitten multiple times and don't catch it. Others receive the smallest of scratches and shift. If you can catch a cold, you can catch this virus. But like a cold, it varies in severity."

"Will the bloodwork show a werewolf, though? They've never been tested before. I checked."

"If he's a shifter, it'll pop up as lycanthropy. Deeper genetic testing will show his strain is lupine in nature, which will be a new one to add to the list. If he's not a shifter, you're back at the start, and Pack will slaughter you for housing a hunted wolf."

"If he has it, Pack cannot kill him," May said. "He would be an innocent."

"Cole, I don't know if this is a personal or protected question, but where did your people come from? Who created the werelions?"

"We come from the same place as werewolves," he replied. "Our original line can be traced all the way back to ancient Egypt. My people were protectors of man. The pure lions, Lycan, were seen during great times of suffering. When the wall between man and hell opened, my people came out of hiding. Unlike Pack, we gave our gift to the strongest warriors of man in hopes we could drive the devils back to hell. In turn, the devils created demons, who killed all Lycan of my line, leaving only werelions behind. The werelions stepped forward and continued the fight their ancestors died for." There was something more than pride on his face. "It is a death sentence to our people to spread this virus. For some, it is seen as a curse. For us, it is a gift and not one given lightly. Only the strongest are selected, and only those who are close to our Pride. To change someone against their will is heinous and is met with the full force of Pride. No one should ever be forced to live a life they didn't choose."

"Is it the same for all shifters?"

"Their backgrounds vary, but we all come from the same place, Lycan."

"Does Pack know this?"

"They know but do not believe. They see shifters as inferior. We are nothing more than a virus. Whereas they see themselves as chosen by God." Cole huffed a laugh. "We are all chosen by God, or we wouldn't be here."

I fought the urge to roll my eyes. The whole 'we are all God's children' rhetoric was tiring for those of us who had been dragged through the fire one too many times. "Thank you, Cole, for answering my questions."

May drank down the last of her coffee and took my still full cup from my hands, since I wasn't drinking it. "I can help you, Ailis. We can use the labs at work. Let's bring Rome to the school, or we can go wherever he's hiding out and do a blood draw."

I half laughed. "I'd suggest we probably not go to him. The vampires are protecting him."

"Yeah, I'm not walking in their front door," she said and I agreed.

"How about I do a blood draw and meet you in the bio labs?" I asked, and she nodded.

Cole reached across the table and squeezed my hand. "I do not envy your position. To go against Pack, for any reason, takes a lot of courage. If it's any consolation, the rest of us haven't answered the call of Pack, to hunt the traitor. None of us are answering."

"They're asking for outside help?" My voice cracked at the news, and he nodded. "Just because I won't hand a kid over to Pack to be killed doesn't make me a traitor."

"Unfortunately, it does. And if you're caught with the Master of the City, you forfeit your life on the spot. Pack has made it clear to all, if you're caught with either the wolf or Nest, you're to be killed."

"I'm damned no matter what I do."

He shrugged. "If you want some sage advice, I'd relinquish your ties to Pack. All of Pack, including your ties to Mexico. It's the only way you won't be held to Pack law. The protection you're receiving from Caser, which hasn't done much for you, is keeping you tied to the laws that will end your life. Do not give them another rope to hang you with."

"Without the little protection I do have from Mexico, they'll kill me for the knowledge I have." My response was thick with fear. Caser was the only one standing in the way. Right now, I was being hunted. Without him, I'd be outright killed.

"They're going to kill you anyway. Take a few reasons off the table. You'll die sooner for breaking their laws than knowing who they are. Right now, in their eyes, you are Pack, whether you shift or not. Holding onto Caser is keeping one foot in their door." Cole pointed to a way out for me. It was a slim chance, but more than I had at the moment. "I hear you're getting a trial. Lessen the charges against you. If you go to Pack as a human without ties, they can't punish you according to their laws. You're still on the hook for knowing about them, but at least it's only one law you're fighting against."

"I'm so fucked." I groaned and set my forehead on the table. "How the hell do I fight knowing about them while I'm standing in front of them?"

"You can't," Cole said, and I nodded, pressing my hot face into the cool table. "This is deadly information to have, and they've killed to guard the secret of Lycan since the dawn of time."

"Cole, could I grab a ride back to campus? I need to talk to the lab." May stood, and I turned toward her. Whatever look of dread I had on my face made her chuckle. I was glad someone was enjoying my misery. "Meet me at the bio labs in three hours. I'll get Dr. Vincent to come in and run the tests. I trust him implicitly, and he owes me a few favors."

"Thank you, Cole, for everything," I said as he got up.

"I wish you the best, Ailis." He walked out the door with May.

I called Demetrius. "Nest protection? Press conference? Calling your children home? Have you been drinking tainted blood? They're going to kill me for this."

"Not as fast as if you didn't have it. Right now, Pack is figuring out if my protection means anything to them and, if it does, how to get around it. With Nest and Mexico offering you protection, it limits what Miguel and his people can do," he replied. "I tried calling you a dozen times before I issued my protection. I didn't know if they had you or were holding you. I did what I could to buy you more time."

"We'll talk about this later if I'm still alive to yell at you." I calmed the anger inside. I could see why he'd done it, but I knew I'd pay for it. "I need a blood draw from Rome. I'm going to try to prove he bested the curse and is now a shifter."

"No problem, I'll do it myself."

"Not with your teeth."

"You've always been such a funny witch. Where do you want me to drop it off?"

"Can you meet me at the university in three hours, at the bio labs?" I asked.

"Yes. I'll go beforehand, make sure the coast is clear. If something's up, I'll call you."

"See you then." I groaned as a familiar wave of energy rolled through the diner. "I have to go."

I felt Sofia before I saw her. Through the front doors, she came. She had always been a presence, but today, her energy was hot. Her eyes zeroed in on me the moment she was inside. No one turned to look at her, even though the energy in the room skyrocketed. Everyone was used to it, I suppose, given this was a neutral ground. Behind her, Cisco strolled in. His usual smile was fixed on his face. He ordered two coffees and a few slices of pie before following Sofia to the booth. Sofia took the seat across from me while Cisco sat beside me, pushing me deeper into the booth. I couldn't help it, but I started to shake as though I had been dropped into a pool of ice water. The tears began to fall before I could control them.

"Please don't kill me," I whispered, my words getting caught in my throat. "Please, I don't want to die."

Sofia flinched. "Jesus, Ailis, we're not here to hurt you."

"I can't give you Rome."

"We're not here for him either," she answered. The server set down two coffees and three pieces of pie.

"What? I'm hungry. I'm a stress eater," Cisco said and offered me banana cream pie. I shook my head. "More for me."

"Why are you here?" I asked. "How did you find me?"

"The app on your phone tells me where you are," Cisco said. "And the fob on your keys is GPS equipped."

"If you know where I am, Miguel does," I said and pulled my keys from my pocket, cursing myself for not realizing it sooner.

"I changed the passwords as soon as I heard you had gone to the dark side," Cisco said. "He doesn't know where you are, but I've been keeping an eye on your movements in case things went south."

"If you're not here to kill me, why are you here?" I asked.

"Because we threw in our hat with you," Sofia said. "Caser called us and filled us in on what's been going down. He said you're trying to find a way to save the kid. And now that Miguel and Pack know you've received the protection of Nest, shit's about to get real, real fast. Pack is livid and calling for your head. You're in deep, sinking fast, and could probably use your friends right about now."

I glanced at Cisco. "You couldn't give me a heads up the other night when Sentinels came kicking down my door?"

"By the time I found out, you were jumping in a vehicle with a bloodsucker. Both Sofia and I came as soon as we found out. We got there in time to see you make your getaway," he talked around a mouthful of pie. "What the hell, little red? Werewolves and vampires? Meeting them with a demon at your back? How many laws were you trying to break at once?"

"First, I didn't know he was a vampire when we went to school together," I said and finally grabbed the slice of pie. My stomach was growling. "Second, Nathaniel attacked the kid a few years ago, and he survived. His reward? Being hunted by you all. What the hell did you expect me to do? Step aside and let you kill a kid who doesn't deserve to die?"

"We've been on the trail of a few rogue werewolves for months," he answered.

"He's not rogue. He's scared and hiding."

"Call him what you wish. We've been tracking werewolves for months."

"He was attacked three years ago, though," I said, my point getting lost. "Obviously, he isn't the rampaging lunatic you all think werewolves are, since he's been one for three years. There's an entire population of people just like him all over the world. The local group is over a decade old. They found Rome after he was attacked. It seems that if they can live through the first few weeks, they survive. If they can gain control over their wolf, their own people let them live. They are shifters, innocents, not beasts to be dropped into a hole. That Rome and his people are still alive and our city isn't filled with bodies suggests they can control themselves just like any other shifter."

"Fuck," Cisco growled. "Miguel isn't going to like this."

"Miguel can kiss my ass." I swallowed a rock in my throat. "He sent two Pack members to kick down my door. They came into my home, and my cat attacked them. They shifted their hands into claws. They weren't there for a friendly invitation to the Chapel. They came for my life."

"Miguel didn't order it. Pack demanded it and took matters into their own hands." Sofia said. "When Cisco received a notification from your home security app, we booked it. We got there just in time to see you jump in the corpse's car."

"If it wasn't for my cat..." My voice hitched in my throat. "My poor cat."

"Cat is okay," Cisco added. "We left when Samuel's people showed up with a new door. But I went back once they were gone. No one else has been in your house besides me and Sofia. I warned Pack, if they touched our cat, I'd kill them. No one touches a familiar and lives to talk about it."

"*Our.*" I smiled. "Thank you."

"So, what's the plan?" Sofia asked. "Please tell me you have one, because we don't. We left Pack and are now rogues in a territory that doesn't allow them. We still have Caser's protection, but that's going to wear out pretty damn fast once we're seen with you."

"I'm testing Rome's blood to see if he has the lycanthropy virus. If it pops up positive, you all can't kill him. If not, I don't know what to do next."

"That's your plan?" Sofia shook her head. "We need to get the hell out of dodge. We're Packless, and you, Ailis, are a human with knowledge she shouldn't have."

I took a few bites of my pie then pushed it away. It tasted like cardboard. I sat for a moment, thinking about what Cole had suggested. "How do I relinquish all ties to Pack?"

Cisco grinned. "Making it harder to kill you?"

"Yes. It's all I have."

"Call Caser and relinquish your protection," he replied. "Agree to keep your oaths but request to sever all ties. Shit will hit the fan once you do. The fact that Caser has enforced his protection after this Pack removed theirs is the only reason you're not dead. After the Sentinels kicked down your door, Caser threatened to kill Miguel and his entire Pack if he went after you again. No challenge, just death."

"Shit has already hit the fan. I'm splattered in it." I dialed Caser. Pack was gunning for me. Cole had been right. Sooner or later, they'd pull the trigger, regardless of Caser.

"Ailis, you're still alive," Caser answered his phone. "Miguel told me Nest has given you protection? Do you have a death wish, witch?"

"No more than usual. I didn't ask for the protection. I found out through May."

"Get on a plane," Caser said. "I can hide you here until we figure it out. No one, not even Miguel, would be foolish enough to come here for you."

"You know I can't do that, Caser. But I love you for offering." I paused. Sofia pushed a piece of paper across the table and mouthed for me to read it. "Caser, Lycaon of the Los Luna Pack, I relinquish the ties that bind me to you and the Los Luna Pack. I swear, on my blood oaths, I will uphold your secret with my own blood, protection and love, unto my death."

Caser chuckled. "Sofia, I heard you went rogue. I was wondering how long it would take for you to find our little lost witch."

Sofia smiled. "Hello, Caser."

"And Cisco," Caser added. "You two do nothing without the other."

"My wolf would not allow the hunt of an innocent, Pack law or not," Cisco replied. "Ailis is my sister. I could not have her stand on her own."

"Miguel is your brother," Caser reminded him.

"What has happened is wrong. I can't sit by and do nothing. I warned Miguel I would leave if he did not protect Ailis. He chose Pack. I choose family."

"Law is law," Caser said but sighed in the background. He didn't like it any more than the rest of us.

"Then the law needs to change, if what Miguel is doing is right," Cisco replied. "Pack is demanding Ailis is executed and the kid alongside her. No trial."

"They are not demanding her head for protecting the wolf," Sofia said, leaning into the phone. "This stopped being about Rome the moment Pack saw her in the demon shop with Demetrius. They want her dead for consorting with a vampire."

"Come again?" Caser asked, surprised.

"Pack wants her dead for having an existing friendship with a bloodsucker," she said. "They see her helping him with the kid as a slight against them all. What they went through with Julian, they say this is a slap in the face."

"This is absurd," Caser said.

"Ain't it?" Cisco asked. "Pack is using the laws that state no Pack member can consort with a vampire. Ailis has the protection of Pack and is a Grimmwolf. She was aware of the laws before she broke them," Cisco explained, and I was as interested as Caser, given I didn't even know what my charges were yet. "Once she became aware of her previous connection to Demetrius, she should have reported it, but she didn't. She then met with a werewolf, knowing they were outlawed. They're saying she went against Pack to hide a demon—what they're calling Rome—and lied to Pack to protect said demon and a vampire."

"The kid isn't a demon," I interrupted. "Trust me, I'd know. Demons are kind of my thing. He feels like my neighbors down the street, like a shifter."

"Great. Now, how will you prove it?" Caser asked.

"Blood work," I said. "I'm going to see if he has the lycanthropy virus."

"If you want a good sample, you need him in full shift," Caser added. "Get one sample in his wolf form and one in human."

Sofia nodded. "Concrete proof. Pack won't be able to deny it if you have both samples, showing it is the same person."

"How the hell do I do that?"

"If he was strong enough, he'd be able to control his shift. With the amount of stress he is under, I don't know if he'll have the control needed for it." Sofia raised her brows. "If all else fails, do you think you can pull it up the same way you did with me?"

I groaned. "He's being hidden by the Nest. I'm not going there to yank a wolf out."

Caser's laughter filled the speaker on my phone. "Did your bravery run out? You're being hunted by someone much bigger and badder than a shifter. You've just relinquished your rights under Lycan law. Pull the fucking wolf to the surface, Ailis, or you're going to find yourself up close and personal with wolves more terrifying than Rome. Pick which wolf you want to be in the same room with. It's up to you."

"Goddamn it." My shoulders slumped. I didn't want to be near any wolf in full shift for any reason. Once was enough for me. "I'll see if he can be brought to Samuel's house. I'm not going to the house of blood and pain. That feels too much like climbing out of a boiling pot of water into a sizzling frying pan."

Cisco finally spoke up, having polished off two and a half pieces of pie. "Any advice for us lone dogs on the run, Caser?"

"You two are the bane of my existence. You still have my protection, and neither of you is an easy mark. That'll slow them down. Anna has been busy for the last day, scouring our history books, trying to find a way out for you all. So far, her exact words are 'they're all fucked.' But if anyone can find a way out of this, it's Anna. She has spent her entire life nosing through our history and law."

"Hopefully, I'll be alive tomorrow to thank you," I replied.

"Tick-tock," Caser said. "You're running out of time, and I have my own shit to deal with. The moment I let Miguel know you no longer have ties to Pack, you're running for your life. Nothing is stopping them except a vampire, and Pack doesn't recognize their bids of protection. Come sunrise, if that, your head is on the chopping block. I hope you know what you're doing."

"Not even a little," I answered. "Thanks, Caser."

We ended our call, and I contacted Samuel next. Samuel was an easy sell. Anything to help me dig my way out. He was happier, knowing Cisco and Sofia were at my side. Less happy that it wasn't Miguel, but beggars can't be choosers. He agreed to help me pull the wolf, if I had to, but only if we were at Mairi's, in case everything went to shit and we needed to trap a werewolf. Demetrius was a harder sell. He had only heard of Mairi, and from what he had heard, he didn't trust her. But I did, with all my heart and soul. It was enough to get him to agree, but he wouldn't leave Rome alone with me. Once his blood was drawn, Rome would go back into hiding. I can't say I blamed the man. If I could hide until this was over, I would, too. But dead or alive, there wasn't anywhere I could hide from Pack.

Chapter Eight

Demetrius stood on the other side of the gate to Mairi's house. There was no way in hell she was going to invite a vampire onto her property for any reason. He didn't take insult to it. In fact, he agreed. A cautious witch was a long living witch. He gave her a few pointers on where the wards were weak enough for someone to walk through without much trouble and where the spells used for protection didn't affect him as they should have. Mairi thanked him, but still looked him over with suspicious eyes. He ignored the glance as though he was used to it. I wondered how many decades it had taken for him to have grown accustomed to being hated for what he was, but I wasn't brave enough to ask the question. Instead, I did what he did. I ignored the hate and paid attention to the energy around us, feeling for pending doom. Demetrius took up his position and stood with his eyes on the road. His people were spread out through the neighborhood, watching for Pack and those doing their bidding. So far, we had felt nothing coming, but the night was young, and Pack hungered for my blood. I rechecked my phone but saw nothing from Miguel. That it was quiet made my stomach turn. Silence didn't mean they'd given up. Just the opposite. They were in regrouping and planning mode.

"You look like you've done this before, keeping under the radar of Pack," I said to Demetrius. "You had a plan before we were even off the phone earlier."

"I've done it once or twice, just like every other group in town. Pack isn't known for compromise or negotiations. After one hundred and fifty years, I have a plan for everything. But Pack or not, you can't be careful enough."

"I was thinking the same thing," Sofia said, taking up a position beside him. Her eyes zeroed in on him until he took a few steps away from her.

"Do not let your hate for my kind blind you to the true dangers of tonight," he replied and put a few extra feet between them.

"And do not let your friendship with Ailis give you a false sense of safety. If you step out of line, I'll kill you."

His laughter filled the air and made my skin crawl. It wasn't joy I felt, but sorrow. "She was once a friend, but a friend no longer. She would kill me to protect you in the blink of an eye, without question, without thought, but she wouldn't kill you to protect me for any reason."

"You're already dead, Demetrius," Sofia said, her voice thick with contempt. "You're just not smart enough to crawl into a hole where you belong."

"You forget, young wolf, not all of us have had the privilege of choice. Not every vampire you meet has decided their fate," he answered. "Most of us were forced into the life of darkness. Pulled into this world of blood and death against our will. Trust me when I tell you this everlasting life is not one many of us would have chosen. I certainly would not, had I been given a choice in the matter. Alas, I was not."

"You claim this, yet you have made countless children. Did you give them all the choice? Did they honestly know what they were signing up for, a life of death and darkness? Surviving off of blood and misery?" she asked.

"Four is not a countless number. Each was terminally ill, and all made the choice to become," he replied. "It has been decades since I've made a child."

"Four, my ass," she said, echoing the thoughts I didn't say out loud.

"Your hate for me blinds you from the truth." His remark curled Sofia's lips, but not even her snarl made him pause. "Those I have called home are not of my making, but of my adoption and trade from Masters who delight in torture. If trading favors and gold to save someone from a life of horror at the hands of their maker makes me a monster, I will gladly take that title. I've been called much worse."

Before they could continue, I stepped between them. "Can we focus on keeping my ass out of the dirt? You both can go back to this bullshit later when I'm not digging my own grave. If not, you both can leave. We don't have time for this nitpicking."

"Later works," Sofia said, making Demetrius grin.

"You and everyone else in this city know where I live," he said, shaking his head.

I left them standing at the gate and walked up Mairi's driveway. The vines on either side moved as if they had a soul of their own and they were fighting an eternal war for freedom that they'd never get. Each time I came to her house, everything looked the same until you stopped and paid attention. Archways and pergolas were tucked into the thick garden of shrubs and trees and were overgrown with flowers and vines that changed with Mairi's mood. They were scattered throughout the yard, guiding the very few visitors Mairi had around the garden. But it was always the lively vines that caught my attention. They took on a life of their own as they hungrily searched for more pieces of land to expand into, seeking threats to attend to and unfortunate souls who came with harm on their minds. But it was the backyard that took my breath away. Around back was where it was not just magical in the way it was warded, but it was breathtaking. The thick moss-covered mounds contoured around a twisted path that led to a massive outdoor dining room. Tucked in the farther edge of the yard was why I liked visiting. Her stained-glass greenhouse stood tall and offered every type of herb and flower a witch could ever want. The greenhouse had claimed the land first— the yard and garden had been designed around it. Some of my fondest memories were of the hours I'd spent there as a child, learning from Mairi.

At the end of the drive was Mairi's small but proud home. The layout inside changed as often as her garden, but somehow, I always knew what direction to go. In the front of the house, standing on moss and stones, Rome shook like a leaf with Cisco at his side. Samuel and Mairi kept their distance but were close enough to help if it was needed. I was nervous, not werewolf-being-yanked-to-the-surface anxious like Rome, but just the same, my palms were sweaty, and my mouth was dry. With each step I took forward, Rome took a step back. He couldn't calm down enough for me to get close to him. I took another step, and he tucked himself behind Samuel. I glanced at Cisco, who shrugged. I gave him a pleading look to help me, and he scowled. One firm look from Samuel, though, and Cisco nodded. Guardians had all the clout. Unless I was willing to kill, I had none.

Cisco sniffed the air, and his face fell. Whatever he smelled gave him a pained look. "You have nothing to fear from me, little wolf. I'm here to help keep your fur where it belongs — on your back."

"I don't believe you," Rome said. He looked at me next. "I'm sorry, Ailis, but neither of you are coming near me. You are scary enough on your own. Being near those who are actually hunting and killing my people is too big of an ask."

Cisco backed up a few feet, and before I could answer Rome, Cisco began to talk. His energy mellowed into something that felt like a warm breeze on a cold day. Many things could be said of Cisco, but above all else known, it was that he was loving and kind. He was led by his conscience and soul over duty. Of course, he was cocky, witty, idealistic and a pain in my ass, but those were characteristics that made him one of those people you wanted to be around. What I loved most about him was that he never lied to me, even when things were looking bleak. Sure, he tried to soften the blow, but he did that out of love and not cowardice.

"It's okay to be scared. I would be, too," Cisco said with the voice I knew he used when trying to calm someone down. Whenever my head went to dark places, Cisco was the first to jump in with stories, both of defeat and victory. They always worked to bring me away from the edge of a breakdown. "You know, I still remember the first time I shifted. I remember the night, clear as day. The fear I felt stains me to this day. There I was, a beat cop, fighting an unstoppable drug war. The cartels were and still are literally everywhere. They've bought their way into every position of power and politician that made the laws we had to uphold. You couldn't do a drug bust without them knowing we were coming and what door we were kicking down. And here I come along, thinking, I'm going to make a difference. I'm going to save my community. I'm going to matter."

Cisco shook his head and laughed. "The first bullet didn't even hurt. I didn't know I had been shot until I started to get dizzy from blood loss. The second bullet, though, Christ on a bicycle, that one felt like a sledgehammer against my ribs. The funny thing is, it wasn't even the drug lords that took me down in the end. It was a bloodsucker. I was cornered down some dank alley, shot, bleeding out, and scared to death that my last moments were going to be in some shithole smelling like trash and my own blood. I kept thinking, what would my mother do without me? Who is going to take care of her? Before I could make peace with my God, a vampire jumped me and sunk his teeth in, shaking me like a bag of garbage. And that's when it happened. My wolf broke free. Jesus, it hurt. Every inch of my body screamed out in pain. But it was over in an instant. The shift gets easier over time, and faster, but the pain is still there. Still, to this day, when I shift, and I'm not fully prepared for it, it hurts so bad that I fight between lashing out and passing out. If I have to shift during a fight or my fear is riding me, the moment my paws touch the ground, I'm ready to shred whoever is near. I've come pretty close to clawing up those close to me. Those first few seconds, my human side is lost to the shift, and my wolf defends me to the death."

"And?" Rome asked.

"And that's why I'm here. It isn't to hurt you. You're already hurting. It's to make sure, when Ailis pulls your wolf to the surface, you don't lash out and attack a witch hell-bent on dying to protect you," Cisco said. "Pulling it up isn't going to hurt nearly as much as pushing it back down. Your wolf is not going to want to go home. You're too scared. He's going to want to hang around for a bit to make sure you're all right. But Ailis is going to shove it all back inside, and it's going to feel like drowning in boiling water and breaking all your bones as you struggle."

"And if I do try to hurt her?" Rome asked.

"I'll kill you," Cisco answered honestly. "To protect her, I'll do what I must. I'm sorry, Rome, but protecting an innocent is my first duty. I'll try not to kill you, if that helps?"

Rome stepped around Samuel. "Keep them safe. I'm scared and do not have good control when I'm scared."

Cisco nodded. "It's the same for all shifters."

"You believe me that I'm a shifter?"

Cisco nodded. "You're the first werewolf I've met that has been alive for as long as you have. But you no longer hold the scent of hell. You smell and feel like a shifter to me. But my word means nothing. I'm rogue."

I finally approached Rome. "I'm sorry, but this is going to hurt."

Rome nodded. "Cisco, what happened to the vampire that attacked you?"

Cisco laughed. "I tried to eat him. I was sick for days with food poisoning. I wouldn't recommend trying to eat a walking corpse. We can't eat rotten meat any more than a natural wolf can. It makes us sick."

"You all wound me," Demetrius shouted from the gate.

"You're lucky we need you, leech," Sofia said and jogged up the driveway.

"Always a pleasure to work with Pack. Remind me never to do this again," he replied and received her middle finger in return.

Sofia would be taking Rome's blood. I wasn't going anywhere near those claws while he was in wolf form. Samuel and Mairi stepped to the side, preparing to contain Rome if needed. Mairi's hair floated above her shoulders as she gathered energy. Samuel held her shoulder and nodded. They were ready.

Sofia approached Rome slowly, her hands up to show she wasn't armed. Even though her greatest weapon was deep inside her soul, ready to tear out of her flesh at a moment's notice. "I'm going to take your blood in human form first. This will give us a baseline. Once you've shifted, I will take your blood in wolf form. Hopefully, we'll be able to find the Lycanthropy virus in both human and wolf form, proving you are a shifter."

"And if you do, this will help?" Rome asked.

"It'll do more than help, little wolf. It'll keep you and your people alive," Cisco answered. "Pack cannot indiscriminately kill shifters. Our Elders would sentence them to death for the murder of an innocent."

Rome nodded and held out his arm. Sofia tied a band around his forearm and had him flex his fist a few times. In quick and practiced movements, she cleaned the crook of his arm and inserted a butterfly needle into his skin. Blood flashed into a tube. She took three vials then removed the needle from his arm. She stepped back and began securing the blood in the small cooler Demetrius had brought. The life of a vampire was too strange for me to even begin to ask questions.

"I don't think I can do this." Rome ran his hands through his hair. "I can't calm down enough to concentrate."

"Let me help you," I said, stepping forward. "I can bring your wolf to the surface."

"Will it hurt?"

"I don't know any way to do this that doesn't hurt," I said.

"Okay," he finally said and stripped out of his clothes, covering his groin with his hands. "It's so that I have something clean to wear after."

"Don't worry, we brought warm blankets," Sofia said. "I'm always cold after."

"I could eat a horse after I shift," Cisco added.

"You have," Sofia teased him, gaining a grin from Rome.

"Touché," Cisco said and turned back to Rome. "Are you ready?"

The smile on Rome's face faded, replaced with fear. His eyes watered, and he started to shake until his teeth chattered. "I'm scared."

"It's okay to be scared." Sofia reached forward, and this time, Rome didn't pull away. "I know that fear. Trust your wolf. Trust that we will keep you and the others safe. I give you my word. We won't let you hurt anyone."

He nodded. "Thank you."

I closed my eyes and focused my aura on Rome. I could feel his energy as if it were my own. Fear mixed with gratefulness. I pushed beyond the energy and breathed in the scent of his wolf. His wolf wasn't as scared as Rome. He wasn't as angry as I thought he'd be, to have me poking around. Sofia's wolf had been terrifying, all angst and anger. But Rome's wolf felt like meeting a natural one in the wild. Curious, careful and ready to walk away if given the chance. In the back of my mind, I could see him. His hair was brown like Rome's, and his gray eyes were more piercing than those of his human counterpart.

"Please don't attack me." I reached forward with my aura, nervous. "I'm sorry, Rome."

As soon as my hand touched his wolf, I grabbed on. It wasn't like when I had pulled Sofia's wolf to the surface. I had a little more time to be gentle with Rome. I pulled but didn't haul him up, clawing and biting. He protested, but I begged. I didn't want to hurt him. I didn't want to force him. This time, I coaxed the wolf to the surface. He followed me up until the last moment when I pulled. I kept my eyes closed as Rome shifted. The sound of skin falling off and hitting the ground made my empty stomach roll. Rome's groans turned into a low and painful growl.

Cisco's energy pulsed over me as he stepped up to my side. I could smell Cisco's wolf. He smelled like the coming rain on a hot day. "Easy, Rome. It's okay."

I opened my eyes and stepped back. My brain told me to run, to get away. Monsters were on the loose. But I stayed planted. I grabbed onto Cisco's hand and stared at Rome, who stood a few feet in front of us. He was roughly the same height as he had been in human form, much smaller than a Lycan. He was close to what

I thought he'd look like and every bit as scary as what I had imagined. His larger but still human eyes glanced down at my hands gripping Cisco, and he took a step back.

"Not...hurt," Rome said. His jaw was massive and dripped spital as he spoke. His teeth turn my legs to jelly.

Sofia smiled but didn't back up. "I'm going to take your blood now. Is that all right?"

Rome nodded awkwardly. "Not...hurt...you."

"I know, and I'm not going to hurt you, either," Sofia replied.

"Allow your wolf fully to the surface, Rome," Cisco said. "If you stop fighting him, you'll learn to become one. It'll make speaking and moving much easier."

"Um, how about you do that when I'm not here," I countered. "I'm not really interested in seeing how becoming one with a wolf goes."

Cisco laughed. "His wolf feels exactly how Rome does. He's calming. I feel no threat from him."

I blurred my vision and looked at Rome through my aura. Green, with only a hint of fear. Sofia stood in front of him, whispering nonsense, keeping him calm, while she drew three more vials of blood. Her aura coated Rome, sending small waves of energy to keep him still. Under the blues of her aura, I could see her wolf sitting at her side, wisps of white energy flowing from the wolf to Rome. This must be what Pack had been talking about when they said they used the energy of their wolves to keep new pups calm. I refocused my eyes and waited until Sofia stepped back. She marked the vials and put them away. With another nod, it was time for Rome's wolf to go home.

"Are you ready?" I asked Rome, and he shook his head and held out his hand as if to ask for a moment. I couldn't help but stare at his claws. My stomach flopped again. It felt like I had drunk butterflies staggering around in my stomach and slamming into my ribcage.

Rome breathed in, expanding his chest and shuddering. He nodded once, and I closed my eyes. I didn't need to see it. I had enough nightmares. Watching a wolf shift back into human form was not something I wanted to haunt my dreams. When I reached forward, Rome had already begun the shift on his own. Instead of pushing, I touched his wolf and led him back down. He pressed his head into my hand and trotted home. In the background, however, it was all bones sliding, wet skin falling, and Rome half-screaming and half-groaning. The smell was awful, like hot meat cooking. I finally tuned around and vomited in Mairi's flower bed. Before I could apologize, the ground opened, and my mess was gone. I stepped back from the flowers, shivering. Every time I went to her house, there was a new reason I got creeped out.

"Hurts," Rome said from the ground through chattering teeth. "Hungry."

"They don't build wolves like they used to," Cisco said and moved forward quickly, picking Rome off the ground. "It's okay, Rome. You did good. Let's get you into the car before you freeze. The old blood bag has food and warm blankets in the car for you."

"Demi...blood...bag..." Rome tried to laugh, but it came out as pitiful groans. Rome touched my shoulder on his way by but passed out before he could say anything. Sofia picked up his clothes and followed.

I hugged Mairi and Samuel. "Thank you for helping me."

"We will always help," Mairi answered.

"Keep an eye out for a witch's pyre," I joked, although part of me meant it.

"You will not fail," Samuel replied. "But it certainly is going to hurt."

"A little pain is worth the lives of an entire species," Mairi added, and I agreed.

"Just another day in the glamorous life of a witch." I dashed down the drive behind the others. I had thirty minutes until I was due in the bio labs with the samples.

Chapter Nine

I paced back and forth in the hall outside the bio lab at the university. I felt like an easy mark standing out in the open, waiting for a computer to ding. The lab in question belonged to Professor Vincent. Dr. Vincent was a very particular man and didn't like the idea of people in his personal laboratory. "*You people,*" he'd said, making Sofia clench her fists, "*have to wait in the hall.*"

I was used to being unwelcome. She wasn't. Dr. Vincent was as close to the word *snooty* as anyone I had ever met. But, he was a true genius among his fellow man, or as he would say and had, many times, he was a prodigy among goblins. He had more acronyms beside his name than any other professor on campus. However, he still taught Biology 101, ran a science camp in the summer for middle school kids, and led a free adult study group for those trying to earn their high school diplomas. I could see why his students looked up to him and wanted to follow in his footsteps, but also why he rubbed people the wrong way. Putting aside his lack of social skills and verbal filter, I hadn't ever minded the guy. We had a lot in common. Pissing off everyone around us was one of those things, and we both came by it naturally.

My phone buzzed non-stop while I walked from one end of the hall to the other. Calls and texts from Miguel came in like rapid fire. I answered none of them. It wasn't until my email went off that I reached for my phone. My burner email had one unread email from Miguel.

Lish,

Caser has informed me that you've severed your ties to Pack. Smart move. It'll change your coming charges, but now you're out of time. Pack no longer has to hold to the rules of trial. There are no laws standing between Pack and a witch. You can trust that I'm doing all I can to keep you alive, not as Lycaon, but as your partner. I love you.

"Can I trust Miguel?" I asked Sofia, putting my phone back in my pocket.

"Not as Lycaon, his duty is his Pack. But as someone who will die for you, yes," she replied. "If he wanted you dead, he wouldn't be dragging this shit out. When me and Cisco hit the road, he didn't fight us. He let us go, knowing we'd be coming to help you. And he hasn't allowed anyone to come after us, which would be his right as Lycaon."

"Don't you both have Caser's protection?"

Cisco laughed. "As if that would stop Miguel. Miguel could clean the floor with Caser. If he wanted us dead, we'd be dead. He didn't move on us because he knows we're with you, keeping you alive."

My phone rang again. It was Miguel. Instead of ignoring it, I picked up. "Hello?"

"Pack is coming. Let them take you," he said in a hushed voice. "Don't fight them."

"Are you insane?"

"Please, trust me. I won't let Pack kill you," he replied. "I'm sorry, but Cisco and Sofia aren't coming with you. I need them elsewhere tonight."

"How the hell did Pack get onto campus?" I asked and knew before Miguel said the words.

"Philip gave Pack his keys and passcodes. They're coming, and you need to let them take you."

"I need more time," I said, biting back my panic. "I don't have the answers yet."

"I do," he answered. "Please, trust me. I would never tell you to come unless I knew you'd be walking away with your life. You asked for my help. Let me help you. You will face trial tonight."

I hung up as both Sofia and Cisco were putting their phones away. Both looked torn. They obviously received the same message from Miguel. I took a deep breath and settled into my fate. Unless I wanted a bloodbath and have Cisco and Sofia kill their own people for me, I was leaving the campus with Pack. I had asked Miguel for help, and now I had to trust that he would.

"Stay here with May and the lab results," I said to them both. "Do not let those fuckers get their hands on the results. I'll get Pack to follow me away from here."

"Miguel won't let Pack kill you," Cisco said.

"He won't be able to fight the entire Pack if they turn against him," I pointed out the obvious.

"But he'll buy you the time you need to get away," Sofia said. "If Miguel tells you to run, head west. It'll take you into Nest territory. Your bloodsucker will know where you are. You're under his protection. Find Nest if this goes south."

"If this goes south, I'll open up the gates of hell to save my ass," I said, knowing I'd do worse than calling up a few demons to stay alive.

"When you get there, ask for your guardian, a lawyer," Cisco added. "They are the caretakers of those who are weaker, and you, Ailis, are weaker in the eyes of Pack. It is law to grant you council for a trial."

I nodded and left them in the hall. I didn't jinx myself by saying goodbye. I didn't want this to be our last conversation, but I refused to end it with something so concrete. I jogged from the lab across the campus toward my office. I circled the building and felt Pack before I saw them. Before I could react, I was falling forward as my head burst in pain. My nose filled with the smell of Pack as I fell. The world faded to black before I could scream, curse, or call for help. If they killed me, at least I'd sleep through it. It was better than the alternative, fighting to my bitter end.

But I wasn't so lucky. A blink in the dark was all I would receive. Just as I was stretching out in my oblivion, I woke up face down on a cold rock. I knew where I was without opening my eyes—Stanley Park, the original meeting place of Pack, long before they began meeting in the Chapel. I could feel Pack's energy rolling over me. It felt like sitting on an air mattress in the middle of the ocean during a storm. Such hate, the kind most people reserved for actual monsters and demons, not witches who were trying to do what was right, nipping at me from every angle. I felt pushed and pulled by the emotions around me. I firmed up my shields, protecting me from the onslaught of negative energy.

I groaned, rolling over and wincing once the back of my head touched the stone. My head swam, and my vision tracked and sparkled. The back of my head felt like it had been hit with a bat. I rolled my head from side to side, feeling it thump over a freshly formed goose egg. I breathed in the night air and assessed the rest of my body. Aside from the head wound, I was in pretty good condition for a run-in with a group of wolves who wanted me dead. I had a few cuts and bruises, likely from falling, and a mushy brain.

I blinked away the blur until I could see clearly. I rolled to my side and slowly stood on shaking legs. Days of living on coffee, cookies, adrenaline and fear hadn't done me any favors. I was weak and trembling. I stood in the middle of Stanley Park, in the center of the thick forest, with Pack surrounding me as I stood on a massive stone. My eyes zeroed in on Philip first. He stood closest to the rock with his arms crossed. I had never seen the look he was giving me on his face before. He was disgusted with me. My eyes watered. How could someone so close to me hold so much contempt for me? Philip finally looked away as if it were too painful to see me. I took my time to make eye contact with every Pack member. I wanted to remember their faces. If I died tonight, I'd want to know who did nothing to help me. I'd be going to hell for eternity, and when Pack died, they'd be coming downstairs after me. I'd beg, borrow and steal to make their afterlife as hellish as mine would be.

"You've got to be fucking kidding me," I said as soon as my eyes landed on a witch's pyre erected on the far side of the stone I stood on. A massive wooden version of a witch's broom, there was a wooden stake in the center, and logs and branches built up around the base. My heart hammered in my chest as the reality of my night's end hit me like a punch in the chest. They planned on burning me alive tonight. I didn't know what was worse, being ripped apart by wolves or being burned at the stake.

"Ailis Petronilla Kyteler." Miguel's voice made me flinch.

I turned to face him. He stood at the rear of the gray stone in torn jeans and a faded white shirt, no socks or shoes. His hair was free and twisting around in the breeze. He was dressed in his shifting uniform — easy to remove and battered enough to toss out if he wasn't quick enough. His face was unreadable, and from this distance, I couldn't see his eyes. I swallowed the urge to scream. My legs shuffled with the impulse to run away. It's nearly impossible to silence the will to survive. My legs twitched as blood ran into them, preparing me for a run I'd never make. I'd never outrun a Lycan. *Hell, I can't even outrun a housecat.*

When Miguel stood a few feet from my front, I balled my fists. "Where are the two men who kicked down my door?"

Miguel frowned. "They're not here."

"That's not what I asked you, Miguel. I want to know where they are. When we are finished here, I'm going to kick down their doors and terrorize them."

"Caser has recalled them to Mexico. *When* and *if* you leave here, you're free to discuss that with Caser."

"There will be nothing left for me once Caser is done with them." I crossed my arms. "Who hit me?"

"One of my people."

"Before I leave, and I *will* leave here alive, I want his name," I said. "I owe him a bat to the back of the head."

"If you leave, you're welcome to dig another hole for yourself."

I rolled my eyes. "Why have I been brought here against my will?"

"You stand accused of consorting with the enemy of Pack, vampires," he answered. "And you are accused of aiding the cursed and the damned."

"I want my guardian, my lawyer," I said. "Don't I get one?"

"You may select one from Pack."

"Oh, hell no. I'm not taking a lawyer from the same group of people that want me dead."

Miguel stepped forward and gave me a look that asked for a world of trust while I stood on the precipice of death. I slapped his face instead. "Get the fuck away from me."

"Trust me," he whispered when he grabbed me. I shoved him again but nodded.

My tears were real. My fear was real. It didn't matter what Miguel pulled out of his hat. I was inching toward death. I turned when I heard a voice tell someone to move before she moved them for herself. The edge of my mouth raised.

"I am here to represent Ailis Petronilla Kyteler," Anna's voice cut through the night. She moved through Pack to the front of the stone. "As per law, she is free to choose her guardian from her *original* Pack. She informed me three days ago that she wishes for me to represent her. I have been in your territory since early evening, with your permission, Miguel, collecting the evidence which will clear her of these said crimes against Pack."

"Step forward." Miguel motioned to Anna. "Ailis, do you confirm you wish for Anna to be your guardian through this trial?"

"Yes," I said and stepped toward her. "Thank you, Anna."

"Very well," Miguel answered.

Anna set her briefcase on the stone and clicked it open. The sound echoed. It felt like the world was holding its breath, waiting to hear what Anna had to say. It's not like I had any kind of defense that wouldn't end in witch-burning.

"Thank you, Miguel, Lycaon of the Noire Lune Pack," Anna said, standing up with a small stack of files. "As you are aware, Ailis relinquished her ties to Pack prior to aiding the individual, Rome. As such, the accusation of aiding a cursed, against Pack law, is baseless."

I kept my face blank as Anna lied. I prayed she could back it up.

Miguel raised his eyebrows. "The Los Luna Pack continued to provide protection to Ailis. That is not severing ties. One of you is lying."

"Is my Pack on trial here? Am I being called a liar?" Anna asked. Miguel said nothing. "I didn't think so. Ailis relinquished her ties to Pack, and my Lycaon offered to maintain his protection of her, as is his right to do. She is a human witch who is often in need of help, which…" Anna was cut off by murmurs in the group. "*Which*," she raised her voice, "was approved by a panel of five Elders as a token of their appreciation for saving the lives of countless Lycan in Mexico. It was a debt paid for her services. As you are aware, my Lycaon did not remove her protection. She is still considered under his protection. He merely informed you of the severed ties. That you accosted a protected person of the Noire Lune Pack and the Elders of Mexico on several occasions is troublesome but is a matter for you and my Lycaon to discuss."

"I would like to see the approval of this, in writing," Miguel said.

She stepped forward. "Here is a signed affidavit from the Lycaon of the Los Luna Pack. It formally states Ailis' request to remove herself from Pack was approved. And here are the statements from five ruling Elders, prior to said charges, granting permission for Ailis to sever her ties and the Los Luna Pack to maintain their protection of her."

"Your Lycaon has only just informed me of Ailis' request to sever ties," Miguel said.

"What my Lycaon chooses to do and when he decides to do it, is not my place to question," Anna replied. "There are no blood ties between this Pack and his. The speed at which he delivers information to you is at his discretion. I imagine, if I may be so bold, it is likely because you and your Pack would have hunted the human for her knowledge, as you've clearly disregarded the protection my Pack has granted her."

"The witch," Miguel corrected Anna. The words knocked the air from my lungs.

A growl escaped Anna's lips. "She is a human. A being. A person. As said by our Gods and by law. Witches are deemed innocents until *their* governing body changes their status without our intervention. I have spoken to a Coven member, Mannix Ashford, who has written a statement confirming Ailis' status as an active member of their Coven. His father, Coven High Priest Torin Ashford, has confirmed Ailis' membership is in good standing. Thus, Ailis is an innocent."

"Very well," Miguel said after reading the letter, which was a surprise to me, given most of what had been said so far was a lie. Miguel folded the pages and looked out at his people. I squirmed as the pressure in my ears rose to the point of popping. "As you just mentioned, Ailis holds the secrets of Lycan. Law demands her life to maintain our secrets."

Anna nodded and pulled out an even larger bundle of papers. "Here is a signed and notarized letter from guardian Samuel Carmine. As you can see, listed on page two is the date. It is dated almost eight years ago. When Ailis' grandmother passed away, her guardianship and parental rights transferred over to Samuel. This is a legally binding agreement, as stated in two legal wills, between the Kyteler family and Mr. Carmine."

"And what does that have to do with this trial?" Miguel asked, handing back the papers. Anna pushed them back.

"Keep reading," she said. "The last seven pages outline Ailis as the granddaughter of a guardian, along with his affidavit that Ailis is his apprentice. It is signed, stamped, and sealed by ten ruling bodies and ten religious officials and supported by two active guardians, as is the custom of the Legion of Guardians. The secrets you claim are the grounds for her death are rendered void by this document alone. Our protections extend to the guardians. This is, in fact, written into our laws. Guardians are not to be harmed, and, under law, it is our sworn duty to die in their place. As an apprentice, this protection extends to Ailis."

The crowd around us began to whisper. One stepped forward, and he spat on the ground. "She helped a cursed. I don't care what your goddamn paperwork says, she helped a cursed escape."

"She did no such thing, wolf. And you will not address me with such distaste lest you want to regrow a tongue. I am your guest. Do not make me remind you of Pack law. I'd hate for this night to end with your death at my hands, but if that is how you choose to die, so be it." Anna turned back to Miguel and pulled out her cell phone. "I did not have time to print this last document, as the results have just been verified by two separate specialists. Rome is not cursed. He holds the lycanthropy virus."

"That's not possible." Whispers of disbelief rose around us. Rumblings of lies and misdirection flowed up from each corner of the group.

"After he was attacked and found, he was brought to holy ground to battle the curse. Those who survive a Lycan or werewolf attack are not cursed. They hold the virus," Anna explained and pulled open her file again. "Here are signed affidavits from over a dozen shifter groups. As you will see, there is a brief overview of their history on each affidavit. They state the originals of their lines were once Lycan, like us. For example, werelions were once a type of lion Lycan, as far back as Egyptian days. They came out of hiding when the gates of hell opened for the first time. They, like many others, did not believe they held a curse, rather, a gift, and shared it with warriors to fight the devils back. The Huntress, Rashida, of the Dawnguard Pride, has stated she will allow Cole, her Mane, to provide you with an oral and written history of her people. He is on standby, fifteen minutes away, should you wish to speak to him."

"And we are to simply take their word on this?" Miguel asked.

"Of course not. I understand the history of animosity between Pack and shifters. This is why I also have two active guardians, Mr. Goelet and Miss Astor, who are with Mr. Carmine. Both are willing to provide you with the oral history of Lycans, which is in line with what every other shifter group is claiming. They are willing to attend, should you need verification," Anna said, and I did my best to hide my smile. I had just met Amos and Amelia when they had tea with Samuel. He had been a busy man. "I trust you would not question three guardians, Miguel. It is not our place to do so. Under law, they carry the word of God. Would you question the word of God?"

"I would not, but the history of Lycan is not up for question," Miguel answered. "The matter we are discussing is if Ailis aided a werewolf, which you've proven she has."

"I have proven Rome and his people are shifters, innocents," she replied.

"So far, all you have given me is information that can't be verified. How could we possibly say they are not cursed without concrete proof?"

"Which is why we've had the blood of my Lycaon, Caser, compared to the blood of Rome. There are commonalities we cannot deny unless you are suggesting Lycan are also cursed demons, along with every shifter group in existence? The very church you've served for most of your life houses the holy Pride, a group of werelions in service to the church. Are you questioning the church's stance on shifters?" she asked, and Miguel didn't answer. "I didn't think so, and neither do the Pack Elders. If they believe Rome is not cursed, neither can you. As we speak, the Elders of Mexico have initiated an order to stop the hunt of werewolves. They are reaching out to the Elders of other territories, requesting the kill order be abolished. Come sunrise, any death of a werewolf will be considered an attack on an innocent. If you do not bend to this law, your Pack will be eradicated to protect the unhuntable. Under the new laws, if you move against the werewolves, you forfeit your life. I am required, by law, to kill you to protect them."

Miguel's eyes widened. "Dear God. We've been killing them."

"Shifters carry out death sentences for those who cannot fight the curse. They govern themselves as any other society. The werewolves are no different than any other group," Anna said. "As you can see, Ailis broke no laws. Just the opposite, she followed them to the letter. She protected an innocent at the expense of her own safety and life. As part of her original oaths, she protected them with her blood and soul. As did the two rogues who left your Pack to stand at her side. The law demands the hunt of Ailis Kyteler ends now."

"Consorting with vampires, the very demons who tortured us," from the crowd.

"No. Ailis killed those who tortured you and almost died for your vengeance," Anna replied. "No laws have been broken here. Ailis has removed all ties to Lycan. She cannot be held to these laws. She is an apprentice guardian. Any act against her is an act against our God. Our laws state she is under the protection of all Lycan, including our Elders. Please, Miguel, do not force me to fight for her life. I will send out a call to arms, and many will answer the call of an apprentice and a wolf. You and your Pack will die before the sun rises tomorrow. I love you and respect you. Please do not let me leave this stone with your blood on my hands."

"You are free to go," Miguel said to me. "You have broken no law, apprentice."

Anna grabbed my hand and pulled me off the rock while the others argued. "I suggest we haul ass right about now before that pyre is lit and we've both tossed on the flames."

Anna dragged me through the trees as Pack began arguing and howling behind us. I tripped enough times for Anna to slow down. I couldn't see in the dark like she could. I put my hands in front of me until I could smell Cisco. My lungs filled with the scent of pumpkin pie, whipped cream and home. Cisco grabbed my hand and lifted me into his arms. He didn't bother leading the way with me in tow. He picked me up and ran. Sofia jogged at our backs. Anna ran to a black Suburban and unlocked the doors. She tossed Cisco the keys, and we jumped in. By the time I'd buckled up, we were long gone, spitting rock behind us. My heart was pounding hard enough for me to lean forward. I wanted to be sick.

"They were going to burn a witch," I said, my throat convulsing around my words. "Sweet Jesus, they wanted to burn me alive."

"Don't worry, little red, we wouldn't have let them light a match," Cisco said from the driver's seat.

I nodded slowly. I was still in shock. This wasn't the first pyre I had seen with my name on it, but it was the first one built by those who claimed they loved me. "How the hell did you get all of those documents?"

Anna laughed. "Miguel and my father have been working around the clock, along with Samuel. Enough favors can buy just about anything."

"Did you know?" I turned to Sofia, and she nodded.

"It was the only way," Cisco answered. "We were all tangled in one big lie."

"What happens to you two now?" I asked. They both shrugged. "Where is Rome?"

"With the corpse," Sofia said. "Now that they have the blood results, Rome can apply to be recognized in the catalog and request a species license. Without it, they can still be hunted by every other group."

I sent a text to Mairi's phone.

I'm alive. Tell Samuel that being his apprentice had better come with perks.

She texted back as though she had been holding her phone and waiting for me.

Thank the Goddess. We love you. Samuel says the perks are being alive.

I sent one more. It was for the vampire that had started all this.

Not dead.

He replied with a series of happy faces.

I know. I was in the trees watching, just in case you needed help.

I made Cisco pull over twice so I could be sick. I knelt in a ditch and brought up all my fear and anger, followed by screams and tears.

"It'll be okay, Lish." Cisco rubbed my back as I cried.

I shook my head. "I'm tired. I'm so bloody tired of this. It's always going to be like this."

"It only feels that way right now," he answered. "Grieve, Ailis. You've gone to hell for an innocent. That has to count for something. Don't let them take that from you."

"Call Caser. I want to make sure he deals with those two assholes for breaking down my door, coming into my home, and making my cat attack them."

"They didn't make it to Mexico," Cisco replied. "They didn't make it out of this territory."

I glanced up. Up until ten seconds ago, I'd wanted them dead. But now, it didn't sit right. "Why? Because they kicked down my door?"

"You're not going to like the answer," he said and took a healthy step back. "Pack law demanded punishment for attacking the Grimmwolf of Mexico. But they didn't just attack the Grimmwolf of the Los Luna Pack. You had the protection of eighteen Pack Lycaons, the Mexico Pack as a whole. Worse, they went after the mate of Miguel. And they touched our fucking cat. Their lives were the cost of reaching too far and touching that which was untouchable."

"I'm so sick of this shit." I got to my feet.

"That makes two of us, witchy woman."

I got back into the suburban, the weight of the last week pressing down on my shoulders. Aches and pains I didn't even know I had began to throb. Sofia drove the rest of the way while Cisco sat beside me. I cried until I hiccupped. Cisco told me about the pies he had waiting at home for us, and all the junk food we'd eat tonight. He was going to break his rule on not eating packaged food for one night only, spurring Sofia on to stopping at a drive-thru to grab us each a banana split. She pulled into a stall and toasted with her spoon.

"The monsters don't get to win, not when you have people who have your back." She echoed the same thing she had written on a card that I had stuck on my fridge.

"Thank you. All of you. I wouldn't have made it without you." I breathed out long and hard, willing the tension in my body to leave. "It means a lot to me that you all showed up."

"Next time, let's piss off a group that doesn't have the power to kill us all," Cisco said. "Like maybe demons, or dragons, something minor and manageable."

"Dragons are real?" I asked. "I thought they were a myth. Though, I also thought werewolves and Lycan were myths."

"They're real. They live in some of the most desolate places on earth, including hell," he replied. "They don't pop up all that often, maybe every hundred years or so. But when they do, they're a sight to see."

"Until they start eating villages by the whole," Sofia added.

"There's that," Cisco said with a shrug. "But I'd still rather deal with a dragon over Pack."

"I bet they're easier to hide from," I added and started laughing. It was the kind of laughter that rid the body of anxiety.

The last fifteen minutes of the drive home made me smile. Cisco gave us plenty of reasons to laugh, even though most of what he said bordered on morbid and uncomfortable. But that was Cisco's way of healing. He laughed when things were too hard to carry. He filled the moment with the reasons he fought so hard to make it home and why he put his life on the line for others to make it home. Love. Family. Laughter. That was gold to him. It was to us all. At the end of our days, when our last breath left us, there wasn't much we could take with us. Love and memories, that's all. As someone who had died once already, I knew love and those memories could keep you going for eternity.

"Pack is here," Cisco said as we turned down my road.

"Who? All of them?" I asked.

"Do you think I'd still be driving toward your house if they were *all* here?" Sofia said with a grin. "It's only Philip."

"Do you want me to beat him up?" Anna turned in her seat. A look filled her face like she wanted me to agree.

I laughed. "I might. Let's see what he has to say first."

"We should do it anyway. He's a deserter and deserves it," she replied. "Pitiful excuse for a Lycan, if you ask me. The whole lot of them should be tarred, feathered and run out of town."

Sofia pulled into the driveway, and we all got out. Cisco jogged up the stairs and brushed by Philip, giving him his shoulder along the way. Sofia shook her head, and Anna paused in front of him. He towered over her, but she didn't step back. If anything, I watched Philip force himself to stay in place.

"Touch her, and I'll kill you, you useless mutt," Anna said and pushed by him.

I stood at the foot of my stairs and stared at my front door. It looked like my last one, but it wasn't mine. It was a replacement because of Pack and people like Philip calling for my head. I didn't care what he had come to say. Nothing would ever be good enough. No reasons would make me feel better. He had once been my friend. I would have given anything for him and his safety. I would have put myself between him and Pack, or any other monster, without question. Worse than that, I'd have killed monsters for him. And when push came to shove, he'd left me hanging to fend for myself.

"A pyre? Are you fucking serious? You were going to burn me alive?" I asked, walking past him. "You're fired."

"I'll clean out my desk tomorrow."

"No. I'll have it shipped to you." I turned to face him. "Hand over your keys, your ID, and the spare key to my house. I'm sure Pack gave them back to you when you sold me out."

"I'm sorry, Ailis."

"Go to hell," I said. I held out my hands, and he handed over the ties he had to my life. "Any university property in your possession is to be mailed to the school." I reached for the door and paused. "Philip, you are not welcome here. If I see you on my property, I will press charges for harassment."

"Ailis," he started, but I walked away, closing the door behind me.

I took off my shoes and set down Philip's keys and ID. I'd deal with his termination in the morning. Cat came from the basement, looking like she had just woken up from her tenth nap today. She stretched once and twisted around my ankles. I picked her up and breathed her in. She smelled like home. Despite the new door, everything smelled the way I remembered it. I thanked my lucky stars for the family I had. They came when I needed them.

"Miguel is in the driveway," Cisco said from the kitchen.

"He can go to hell, too," I said. "Do not open that fucking door for him."

"Do you want me to see what he wants?" Sofia asked.

"I don't care. Not tonight," I answered. "I can't deal with any more emotional crap tonight. I know he did all he could, but that doesn't mean I'm not still pissed off about it all."

I carried my cat upstairs and got undressed. She followed me to the bathroom, where I showered and cried one final cry. My cat curled up on the floor by my shower door and waited for me to let the night roll down the drain where it belonged. Once I was empty of dread, I dried off, pulled on my pajamas and called Mannix. I had a dozen missed calls and texts from him, all asking if I needed help.

"Jax already told me that you've survived a run-in with those he couldn't mention. He was there, waiting with his Mane, in case you needed help," Mannix said as soon as he picked up. "I only had to worm my magic through him twice before he gave up your location. I was getting a group of witches together when he called me to let me know you walked away unscathed."

I couldn't help but laugh. Mannix never used his magic for nefarious acts. He wasn't exactly by the book, but he never used magic for personal gain. "Thank you, Mannix, for being willing to come for me, and for speaking to Anna on my behalf."

"Jax brought her to me and told me not to ask any questions," he answered. "Lish, I've got your back. Come heaven or hell, I'm there. You're my ride or die, witch."

"Same here. Thank you. I'll never forget this. I'll call you tomorrow," I said and hung up. I carried my cat downstairs and called Caser as soon as I had made myself a cup of tea.

"I can't believe you made it out of this one in one piece," Caser said, laughing. "I thought for sure you were a goner."

"So did I. Thank you for helping me."

"You owe me a favor, and you better believe I'm going to call it in. Getting legal documents backdated are a bitch. Do you remember the last time you owed Pack? You damn near became one of us."

I sighed. "I look forward to working with you again."

"No, you don't, and neither do I. If I need someone with your skillset, I'm fucked," he answered. "Anna will be flying home tomorrow. Make sure she gets on that plane. She's talking about how much she loves your city."

"I'll drive her there myself," I replied. "I don't know how you pulled this off, but thank you."

"It wasn't me, Ailis. This was all Miguel. He called in a lot of favors for this one. He and Samuel have been meeting in secret and keeping me updated."

"Miguel can go to hell. For tonight, that's where he can sit."

"I'm sure he's already there," Caser said. "Good night."

My body tensed when my front door knocked.

Cisco smiled. "It's May."

"Your door is unlocked? You learn nothing." May opened the door and came in with a large duffle bag. "Pack is around. I don't trust them."

"What's in the bag?" I asked.

"A rifle and a few more guns. Miguel had me in the trees in case things got out of hand and you needed a clear path out of there. Demetrius and his human servant were with me. A few of his people were scattered about, waiting to see if you needed to be bailed out."

"Demetrius is a block away." Cisco sniffed the air. "And Miguel is on the front porch."

"They can both sit in the cold," I replied. "One of them dragged me into this, the other let Pack drag me to a pyre. I'm not dealing with that baggage tonight."

I dimmed the lights and turned on a movie. The others soon found their way to the living room and settled in with me. I was too tired to care about anyone other than myself. I ate my pumpkin pie and shut out the world. I had earned one night of peace. Saving lives was exhausting, especially when one of those lives was mine.

Chapter Ten

I filed Philip's termination papers as soon as I sat down at my desk. I had thought it would bring me some sort of satisfaction, but all it did was remind me of how at risk I was in my everyday life. The safe spaces I'd thought I had created were as deadly as any hunt I had ever been on. Not even my home was safe for me anymore. It was a hard pill to swallow, knowing I had done it to myself. I sent Philip a copy of his termination package and let the feeling of loss sink in. This would be the last time I initiated contact with him. I couldn't risk having him on campus, not when my life had so little value to him. More than that, I now questioned if he would protect a student if his Pack wanted them dead. There was no room in this world, or in my life, for those who would let innocent people die. The mere questioning of his morals had been the final nail in his coffin. Terminating him was easy for that reason alone.

I made a list of those who had helped me survive my ordeal with Pack and sent it to Demetrius, along with gift ideas he would pay for and sign my name to. I wouldn't need to say 'thank you for saving my life' had it not been for him sitting down at my table and asking for a favor. It took less than five minutes for him to respond to my text, telling me to consider it done. The gift for Samuel, I would take care of myself. I grabbed one of the books from my locked cabinet and stuffed it in my bag. It was an original Hans Christian Andersen, one of my most favored books to be given to one of my most favored people. It wouldn't replace what I knew Samuel had given away to gain my life back, but it would make him smile, and that was all that mattered to me. I wrote a note, slipped it inside the book, and signed it as every guardian before did, taking on the last name of their teacher.

Samuel,
You have all of my love.
Thank you for the home you've built for me.
Your apprentice,
Ailis Petronilla Kyteler Carmine.

Sipping on my morning coffee, I answered a few emails, most of which were from Mannix, who had questions about Rome and his people. Mannix was like a dog with a bone. One detail out of place, and he followed his suspicions to the ends of the earth. I gave him a summary of whatever someone could find in the books on my shelves and kept the rest to myself. I may have gotten away from Pack, but their secrets still held me in a death grip. Running my mouth would only bring them back, and next time, I didn't think they'd knock. After lying through my teeth to Mannix, I collected Philip's things. Thankfully, he didn't have many personal possessions in the office. It was enough to fill two banker's boxes with room to spare. Putting the lids on the boxes felt final. A chapter in my life I had once valued the most was closed, and I had no desire to ever reopen it.

I felt Miguel at the door before he knocked. His smell filled my chest, and I caught my sigh before it escaped. This morning, I had locked the office down. I wasn't taking any chances. The moment I'd pulled into my parking spot, I'd felt Pack. Cisco had warned me before leaving for work they'd be keeping a close eye on me to see if I'd retaliate or if I'd take my licks and walk away. The thought of burning their church to the ground had crossed my mind once or twice, but I'd side with keeping my head down and heart beating. A witch didn't get lucky twice in a row.

I unlocked the door and stepped back. "Good timing, you can bring Philip his things."

He came inside and closed the door. "Can we talk?"

"Are you still Lycaon?" I asked, and he nodded.

"The game isn't over."

"Very well then, I only want to know one thing."

"What's that?"

I smiled with forced pleasantry. It was the same smile I used when I had to attend university functions and rub elbows with those who had more money than brains. "Where do you want me to send your belongings? The Chapel? A ditch? A dumpster? I'm fine with any location. Just let me know."

He sat down at the table, shoulders slumped. "I tried to help you. There wasn't a time I wasn't working my tail off to keep you alive."

"You tried to kill a fucking person. He didn't do anything wrong. And in the process, I was hunted down." Whether we were still playing the game or not, my anger was real. "They hunted me, Miguel. Fucking hunted me. They came into my home. They grew fucking claws, and I had to shoot them."

"Pack law…"

"I don't fucking care about Pack law!" I shouted. Fury coursed through my body, begging for release. "I almost died because of your people again. I understand that I was the one who started this all, but I was damn near burned alive for helping a kid. That's fucking insane. You all are fucking crazy. That's three near misses in under a year. I'm done. Get the fuck out, and this time I mean it."

"I warned you, Lish, this was going to hurt."

I couldn't help but laugh. "I'm not going to be the only one who has to suffer this time. I am not a dog for your Pack to kick. I'm a witch, and a pissed-off one." I lifted the receiver on Philip's desk. "Hello, this is Dr. Kyteler from the demon department. Please send security immediately."

Miguel stood. "You didn't need to do that. I would have left."

"And you didn't need to have me dragged into Stanley Park with a head injury to decide if your people would kill me. But you did. For fuck's sake, they built a witch's pyre to burn me alive."

"If I didn't do it, you'd be dead," he answered.

I let my face drain of anything remotely human. I was a cursed witch, and that's exactly what I showed him. "No, Miguel. Your people would be dead. I'd have made awful deals with awful people to stay alive. And I'd have done worse with my bare hands. You are all alive because I gifted you your lives, but I will not offer it twice. If one of your people comes for me again, I will kill them. I will strangle the wolf inside their souls and fucking kill them. Do you understand?" I asked, and when he didn't answer, I pressed him. "Do you understand me, Miguel? Tell your people to back off and stop following me, or they will know what it's like to have their wolves cursed, never to surface again, never to be able to answer the call. In the end, they will take their lives for me, and all it will cost me is a cup of taint. If I must, to stay alive, my city will never have another Lycan on its soil. I will damn you all."

"I understand," he replied.

"Good. Don't ever say I didn't warn you," I said as the sound of rubber-bottomed sneakers and heavy feet running full speed filled the halls.

Security rushed in seconds later. The first one through the door looked at Miguel, then me. "Dr. K., Is everything okay?"

"Hi, Carl. No, everything is not okay." I motioned toward Miguel. "Please see him off the property. He has a few others with him. Please be sure to ask them to leave as well."

Miguel shook his head, grabbed Philip's boxes and left with security. There was no satisfaction in seeing him leave this way. But until he stepped down, he was my enemy. I locked my door with tears in my eyes and kept it closed until lunch when May came by. She filled me in on what she had heard from her sources, which I'm pretty sure was her boyfriend, Ben. Pack, from what she heard, was falling apart. Ben left, Philip left, and all those who had come from Mexico had been called back by Caser and surrounding territories. Ben mentioned those who had played a part in hunting me, didn't live through their meetings with Caser. Law is law, and Caser didn't take kindly to those who questioned his reach. I wanted to feel bad for them but felt nothing at all. I was numb and cared nothing for Pack.

"How is Rome?" she asked once she saw I wasn't interested in Pack business.

"Samuel got an interim species classification pushed through. Werewolves are now a protected species and are grouped in with the rest of the shifters until the official documents are processed. Rome has to formally apply, along with the rest of his people, but the interim order will keep their necks off the chopping block for now," I replied. "The nutjobs, Humans for Humans, have gone off the deep end, talking about corruption and the cursed high up in our political system. Mannix is having a field day with all the new threats coming out of this."

"The cycle never ends, Ailis. People who hate will always find something to be angry about and someone new to target over it," she replied. "Did I see Miguel being escorted from the building by security earlier?" she asked, and I nodded. "Ben said Miguel was working behind the scenes, though."

"If Ben trusted Miguel so much, why did he leave?"

"Good point. Have you heard from the Nest?"

I shook my head. "I sent Demetrius a text this morning with a list of gifts I am making him pay for, for everyone's help. You?"

She nodded. "When I went home this morning to get changed for work, I got a basket of chocolates for my troubles. Do you want them? I don't accept gifts from those I usually end up hunting down in the end. It just opens the door to problems I don't want."

"Since I didn't send you a gift basket, it's probably a wise choice," I replied. "But when you get a box of handcrafted Ashwood stakes, don't give them away. They're from me."

"Fancy, and a pretty penny. I'll make sure to save them for special occasions." She leaned in as if she had a secret. I debated on whether I wanted to hear it. "Ailis, I heard the board held an emergency meeting last night. Rumor is, they're going to ask you to resign."

My heart plummeted, but I nodded slowly. "To be honest, I've been waiting for it."

"I'm sorry."

I posted a note on the lecture hall door, saying that class was canceled until further notice, and I went back to my office. I didn't bother waiting and began packing my things. While I was removing books in the front room, Dean Michaels came into my office. He had this way of getting under my skin, no matter what we were discussing. Perhaps it was his presence, or maybe it was simply a feeling of irritation he caused in me. Whatever the case, I never really liked the man. He dressed as stuffy as his nasal voice. He was the type of man who should always be holding a cup of tea in one hand and his trust account in the other. He was less approachable than I was, and no one wanted to approach me.

"What can I do for you, Dean Michaels?" I asked, not skipping a beat on my packing.

He cleared his throat. He was nervous, but everyone was when they were around me. I had gotten used to leading conversations and prying information out of people because of it. "The board has been reviewing your position at the university. You have caused a great upset, Dr. Kyteler. Over this last year, you've needed security well over fifty times. A woman died just months ago. And you were kidnapped from campus just last night. Your personal life has risked the safety of students and staff, along with our reputation."

My only surprise was that it had taken this long. I wanted to be shocked. I wanted the disbelief. I wanted to have the kind of life where conversations like this weren't expected. But I had been waiting for this since shoving a human servant out of the window to her death. The kidnapping was just the icing on the already burnt cake.

"Am I being fired or forced out?"

"You will be asked to resign," he replied.

"I'll have my desk cleaned out by the end of the week."

"Thank you," he said and breathed a sigh of relief. I half wondered how he thought I'd react for him to seem so relieved at my calm response. "Of course, we will provide you with excellent references and a severance. This is not a matter of performance. You are an excellent teacher, and your students speak highly of you."

"Of course." I grabbed the box I had already packed, dropped my ID and keys on the table, and opened the door. I took one more look around and shook my head. I was ending a chapter in my life I had worked my fingers to the bone for. It was expected, but stung just the same. "Please lock up once you are done in here. I'll have movers schedule the removal of my belongings with your assistant. My files are up-to-date, and all grades and assignments have been uploaded. You should have no issues with the transition."

I walked straight to my car. My nose prickled, and my eyes blurred. I was on the verge of tears. I had never been politely fired before, but it felt like every other time I had been given the boot. It was just one more badge earned for a cursed witch, to lose job after job for who we are and who we attracted. I put my box and bag in the back seat and got in. It took me a few minutes to calm down, but I finally pulled out of the parking lot. When I'd woken up this morning, I hadn't thought the day would end with me unemployed. But it was still better than yesterday, when I'd thought I wouldn't make it to sunrise.

Alchemy Co. popped up on the call display the moment my vehicle was out of the parking lot. "Ziggy? Is everything all right?"

"Ziggtmoy," he corrected. "I heard you're no longer employed. I have a job for a witch with your skill set. Money is no issue. It has no value to demons, only humans. Name your price."

"How the hell did you find out?" I asked. "I'm not even off campus proper."

"Eyes and ears everywhere, Ailis. I'd be a sorry witch if I didn't keep a finger on the pulse of my city," he replied, and I huffed a laugh at his comment about being a witch. "As I was saying, I'm offering you a job. Think about it. You'd have complete access to every spell you could dream up, and the tools and permission to use them. Imagine what you could learn."

I groaned. "Thanks, Ziggy. If I get desperate, I'll give you a call."

"Desperation is how most find their way through my doors," he replied. "It's how you have always ended up in my shop."

"I'm not desperate yet. Thanks, though." I hung up.

I ignored his call back, and the three other attempts at luring me into his little shop of horrors. I'd be lying if I didn't say I was curious as hell to know what he held in his storage and the second level of the shop. But curiosity kills, and I was fresh off the pyre. I turned off my Bluetooth and turned up my music. My drive home was filled with thoughts about taking a vacation, a real one, with my newfound freedom. I might not have a steady job anymore, but I still consulted with various organizations and could probably take on a few more cases here and there. They paid well enough for me not to worry. I wasn't destitute, I was just pissed off.

The hour in traffic helped cool me down until I pulled into my driveway. Miguel was sitting on my porch. I grabbed my things from the backseat, walked around him and into my house without saying a word, locking the door behind me. Cisco and Sofia were in the kitchen making dinner. I took off my jacket and shoes and jogged up to my room. I opened my window and began throwing Miguel's things onto the lawn.

"What about my duffle bags?" Miguel stood on the grass, looking up at my window. "I have two."

I tossed his two bags out last and shut my window. I changed into comfortable yoga pants and a sweater and met Sofia and Cisco in the kitchen. Cat was sitting in the spelling pot on the table, watching us all walk back and forth. Every now and again, Cisco would sneak a treat into the pot as though I wouldn't notice my cat had gained a few pounds since Cisco showed up. All the two of them did was lie around and snack, with my cat sitting on Cisco's lap. Out of the dining window, we watched Miguel walk back and forth, picking up his things. Random socks and shoes, books, and clothes scattered my entire front lawn. I ignored him. Cisco and Sofia didn't.

"How long are you going to punish him?" Cisco asked, sitting down for dinner.

I pushed my food around with my fork. "Until I decide not to. Because of my personal life, I got canned today. So, when I'm gainfully employed again and hell freezes over, I'll consider it."

"It's mighty cold out here." Miguel popped up in front of the kitchen window. "I think hell is starting to freeze."

I closed the curtains.

"Can I have some dinner? I haven't eaten all day," Miguel asked.

"Get off my flowerbed," I scolded. I turned and motioned for Cisco to make a plate for him. I passed it through the window. "You can eat outside like the dog you are."

"I didn't want to come in, anyway," he replied and carried his plate to my patio.

"He slept on the bench out there last night," Sofia said. "To make sure Pack didn't come any closer."

"May would have shot them," I replied. "She brought a few boxes of silver bullets."

"This one time..." Cisco started, and I took a seat with my eyes on the window. "Actually, every time your life has been at risk, from the moment Miguel met you, he has found a way to save you. You might not like how he did it this time, but he did it in the only way he could without risking all of our lives."

"And if it didn't work?" I asked. "I'd be dead."

"He did the best he could in a situation he didn't create," Cisco said, pointing out the fault was mine. It was. But I didn't have to agree with being hunted for it.

"As if he'd let you die." Sofia laughed. "Miguel would have had them all killed before they could touch you. He had us close by, several members of the Pack ready, and Samuel with his crew a few blocks away.

May was in the trees with Demetrius and a few dozen of his people. Miguel wasn't going to let you die, but he wasn't going to kill everyone unless he had to. You know him. He's squeamish about premeditated murder."

"I'm not," I muttered.

"We know, and that's why we love you," Cisco replied.

"I'm sorry, but I can't deal with any more Pack shit right now." I pushed my dinner away. "It's been one giant nightmare from the start."

Cisco nodded. "Give yourself time, little red, but don't leave him in the cold forever. It's a lonely place to be. You know firsthand what it feels like to have everything taken from you in the blink of an eye, to be alone, to be without many options."

"Am I supposed to feel sorry for him?" I asked. "I lost everything. I lost my job, Cisco," I said, eyes watering. "I loved my job, and I got fired because my personal life risked the lives of those who attended that campus. And you know what? I can't even be angry at the board for their decision. I would have done the same thing. I'm a walking timebomb. People die around me. And it feels like I've lost important parts of myself. I feel like I'm being punished for doing what was right, and you know what? It's not fair. I'm allowed to be angry."

"People are alive because of you," Miguel said, tapping on the kitchen window. He passed his empty plate through to Cisco. "It's not fair. It's never fair. And I'm sorry you're being punished for it."

"Fuck off, Miguel. You don't get an opinion on my life, not tonight. That one goddamn favor in Mexico has cost me everything."

"Not everything," he replied.

"Everything worth having," I said, feeling the sting of those words like a punch to the gut. I'd lost my job, my family, my partner, my friends, and the safety of my home. I'd gained nothing more than a long-winded nightmare. Sure, I had saved a life, but it cost me my own. I was allowed to be angry about it. I walked out of the kitchen before anyone could see the tears rolling down my cheeks.

Chapter Eleven

It had been two weeks since I'd lost my job, and my entire professional life had been reduced to nothing more than a moving van full of boxes. Years of whispers behind my back, backhanded comments, ignorance and downright hate mail, shoveling shit and thinking it was worth it, and all I had to show for it were boxes and severance pay that wouldn't get me very far. It was a stark reminder of how little I had meant, how replaceable I was to those I had held in high esteem. It was enough to send me on an ice cream diet while I binge-watched every movie I hadn't gone out to see because I'd had to work early the following day. The world still rotated without me, and I was fine not being out there to watch it turn.

After ignoring the maze of boxes in my living room, me and Cisco moved a few hundred books worth of boxes into my basement. Cisco sat on the floor, thumbing through each one before putting them in the order I asked, while I sat on the couch, testing the limits of my pancreas with another tub of ice cream. It was the closest to a vacation I took. I wouldn't risk the song and dance it would take for me to enter a new territory, not when the powers controlling them knew I had escaped the grasp of Pack and still had the protection of Nest. The werewolves had lit a fire with his video, and I still didn't know where I'd land in that mess once the smoke cleared. Until Miguel left his place with Pack, I had nothing but enemies following my every move.

I had worked two more cases for Mannix, a dead vampire, leaving behind ashes, and a dead shifter. This time, the vampire's killing had been caught on someone's yard security camera. It wasn't clear enough to make any identifications, but it did give us a good enough picture of his final moments, hunted down by five unknown assailants and stabbed in the heart with a wooden stake.

The body count now totaled ten, five of which I had seen firsthand. Five had happened while Pack was trying to burn a witch. Each murder mirrored the last. All were stabbed, beheaded, or burned, in the case of the vampires. After a bit of digging and consulting with those who were still willing to talk to the blacklisted witch, I found out they were all lower level, weaker compared to their brethren, and easy to pick off. All from influential backgrounds with families who had political pull. After a little more brainstorming with Cisco and Sofia, we found our link. Those with the strongest voices, opposing the laws that protect non-humans, were being targeted, their loved ones slaughtered. Perhaps it was a scare tactic, or a message to silence those who were fighting for the rights and freedoms of all magics. Either way, Mannix was taking that lead and running with it. It was the closest we had come to a solid chance in hell since bodies had started turning up around the city.

After declining several invitations over the years, I finally agreed to meet with Mannix at his office. It's not like I had any other pressing matters outside of looking over my shoulder and flinching at every sound outside. I stepped into the Vancouver Special Forces Police Department and let reception know I had a meeting with Mannix Ashford. VSPD was the first of its kind in North America, a pilot program designed to assist the local authorities in crimes touched by hell. If a metaphysical being was involved, VSPD was called. Mannix's team had been called everything from Monster Hunters to Freak Feds to their current name, the Spook Specialists. They were all nicknames that were nicer than what people usually called me and much more creative than my usual tags.

Mannix showed me around the building, giving me a grand tour that included a massive library, a free coffee shop and a cafeteria, making sure to point out all the vegetarian options, before finally ending in his office. Each stop along the way was to pique my interest, and one look told me he had already practiced his speech before I had arrived. The little notepad on his desk held bullet points detailing why VSPD was a good place to work. The final point simply said, 'Please.'

"Just think about it, Ailis." Mannix glanced at his notes. "The pay and benefits are better than what you made at the university. VSPD Arcane Division covers the cost of our insurance, malpractice, licensing, and even our Coven dues. And if a demon pops up, we get hazard pay. Who doesn't like getting a few extra hundred bucks for doing their job? We get paid time off for Coven duties, or if you were a shifter, for full moon shifts. They even installed a wet sauna and small pool for the water people, but they're always down for some company. I'm taking diving lessons from a water nymph during my lunch breaks. I'm having a spelling lab installed just down the hall, in case you were interested in trying out a few flammable spells."

"The Arcane Division, is that what you're called now? A few weeks ago, there were more words in your department than in the most complicated spell I know."

He shrugged. "They didn't like my suggestion of the *Sin Squad*."

"I can't imagine why not."

"The demon department would kill to have you. Try it out on a probationary period. If you don't like it, you don't like it. Earn a few bucks until you have something better."

"Ziggy offered me a job two minutes after I was canned."

Mannix cringed. "Okay, if you're thinking he's a better option than the Sin Squad, you're crazy."

"Sin squad? Yeah, it's not going to catch on, Mannix, no matter how many times you say it." I laughed. "Who would be my supervisor?"

"Me." He grinned. "Captain Troy Holland is above me."

I nodded. "What training would I need?"

"For you, with the experience you already have, boot camp, then you'd have to be paired with me for a few months until your probation period was up."

"Hourly or salary?"

"Hourly, with as much O.T. as your little witchy heart desires. And if you move to a level-two witch, your pay goes up."

"Not a chance in hell. There's not enough money in the world to make me involve myself with Coven anymore than I absolutely must," I replied. "What about out-of-town work? You're always in and out of town."

"Ever notice it's when my father is in town?" he asked and chuckled. "It's not mandatory, but smaller regions reach out to us when they have a problem. It's double bubble pay when you're away. It's a full-expense paid trip to bum-fuck nowhere, but it's still better than being in town when my father visits. I could cut you in on a trip out of town when Coven is around, if that sweetens the deal?"

"What are the benefits like?"

"Full benefits across the board, except psych. That's in-house only, and mandatory once a month. Most of us make appointments for every two weeks, but you don't have to go that often if you're not comfortable with it."

"And now, what are the reasons I should say no?" I asked. "I'm done drinking the juice. Tell me why I *shouldn't* do it."

"It's life and limb out there, Ailis. You know that. We deal with the cursed, cases the rest of the world can't handle. We're not only dealing with hell. We're eyeballs deep in everyone's business. If they can pull on hell, smell like hell, think like hell, or have a return address to hell, it's our problem. But you have a badge and can shoot them, so there's that," he answered. "That's not even the worst part. Humans are what cause us the most stress. That we can come and go in and out of any scene we deem fit rubs a lot of people the wrong way. We're now a federal branch and no longer have to be invited in. We get a lot of attitude for it. But if it even hints of hell, the scene is ours, and it should be. I have no idea why humans would want to work a case involving demons and magics, but just the same, we tend to piss a lot of people off. The crimes we work on could help a cop up the ladder, and we snag it out from under them."

I leaned against his door jam and scrunched my nose, thinking. "What about the team? How do they treat you?"

He frowned. "Good, why?"

"I wasn't Miss Popular at the school."

"There's normal office crap, over office supplies and holiday rotations, but we're a pretty tight group. When you're looking into the eyes of hell on a daily basis, it tends to bring you together, not push you apart," he said, his face softened. "I'm sorry you faced that kind of treatment at your last job, Ailis. That shit doesn't fly around here. It's not just because of policy. It's because none of us would stand around and watch a team member be abused. We're all really close and have each other's backs inside and outside the office. How could you possibly trust the man at your back if you're scared he's holding a knife?"

"I get to continue teaching. I want a guarantee that I can host classes here for those who want to learn, and the classes will be free and on topics I select. Not just for the department, but for anyone I approve."

"Done," he replied. "We have a massive education budget. It won't be an issue."

"Three months," I finally said. "I'll see how I feel about it at the end of the probation period."

"Seriously?" he asked, first surprised, then grinning ear-to-ear. "Holy shit. I'm going to get such a sweet bonus for this. You're for real, right? You're not screwing with me?"

I nodded. "I expect you to take me out to dinner with that bonus."

He jumped up and hugged me, lifting me off the floor. "Hot damn! I've been waiting years for you to say yes."

"Specialist Ailis Kyteler does have a nice ring to it," I replied. I couldn't help but laugh at his excitement. "Three months to start. That's all I can promise. We can renegotiate when my probation is up."

"Once you meet everyone, you won't want to leave. Trust me." He leaned in and hushed his voice. "If you stay, I'll negotiate a nice signing bonus for you. Maybe you can buy yourself a better car."

"What's wrong with my car?" I asked.

"It smells like you bought it off a lot in hell, and it's a piece of shit. How it stays on the road during the winter is beyond me," he answered. "I'll start your paperwork. Meet in a week to go over the details and sign your waivers?"

I nodded. "Thanks, Mannix. I appreciate this. I was getting nervous I wouldn't get hired anywhere and would have to take Ziggy up on his offer."

"I've been asking you to come on board for years. I wasn't missing this opportunity. You're one of the most coveted witches in the city. I can't believe you weren't snagged by someone else."

"I'm blacklisted right now for the werewolf mess. I got a few calls, but no one I'd like to work for."

"Who tried to nab you before me?"

"Oh, you mean aside from a demon?" I laughed. "The government, some research facility, a few hunter agencies, and Coven."

"You'll fit in here much better than those places. I promise." He grinned again. He was more excited about this than I was. "I'll email you with your contract to review and the entire welcome to the Sin Squad package."

I rolled my eyes. "Sin Squad."

"Oh, it's going to catch on. Just give it time."

"I have to run. I'm meeting friends for dinner," I said, glancing at the clock. "Thanks, Mannix. I'll catch you later."

"Call me if you have any questions about the information I email over. Captain Holland will push your paperwork through and get you into boot camp in the next couple of weeks. I hope you can do push-ups."

I cringed. "You owe me more than dinner for boot camp."

"I'll get you a shiny new gun and add your name to the gun range program," he replied. "Free access for VSPD."

"A gun? Now you're just flirting with me."

"Do you want me to walk you out?" he asked.

"No, I'll find my way." I left him beaming in his office. Before I left, I heard him make a call.

"She said yes... If she said yes, she won't back out... I will. I'll start working on the paperwork now... We're going to be the most requested team out there."

I walked out smiling and feeling a lot better than when I had walked in. I was no longer unemployed, and no one would freak out when I showed up to work with a gun or a giant knife. Being wanted was the part I thought I would enjoy the most. It's a hard life when no one wants you to have a pulse. After a few wrong turns and some friendly directions, I cleared the building. I looked back once and grinned before I jogged through the rain to my car with a bounce in my step and headed to East Van for dinner. I called Samuel as soon as my Bluetooth connected.

"I accepted the job," I said as soon as I heard the line connect. I didn't realize I was excited until Samuel answered his phone.

"Good for you, Ailis," he replied. "Mairi," he called out. "Ailis took the job at VSPD."

"Well, hot damn, I'll have to keep my fire setting and crimes on the down low," she replied.

I laughed. "I just wanted to let you know. I thought... I don't know. I wanted to share it with you. I thought you'd be proud."

"I'm glad you called. Your good news is my good news," he answered. "I'm very proud of you. I've heard a lot of good things about Mannix and his team. I think you'll like it there a lot more than the University."

"Thanks, Sam, for everything," I said and pulled into the parking lot. "I have to run. I love you both."

"We love you too. Are you still coming for dinner over the weekend?"

"Unless hell swallows me between now and then, I'll be there with or without a demon on my back," I answered and hung up to his laughter.

I pulled my hood over my head and ran from my car into Demented Dave's. It was a little dive that was popular with those of us who touched hell. Like every other establishment run by non-humans, plays for power were frowned upon and handled with a shotgun full of silver and salt. I slid into the booth beside Rome. Across from me was Cole, the werelion, and the vampire that had started all this, Demetrius — or Demi, to his friends, as he always added after introductions. All three looked odd together, but in this place, they fit right in. Demetrius was dressed as casually as I had seen him since his return to Vancity, in dress pants and a turtleneck. Cole was exactly as he had been before. A beaten-up jacket, jeans and strawberry hair that I was dying to touch. Rome was the only one who looked better than the last time I had seen him. His haunted eyes were replaced with a look his father always had when discussing something exciting. His hollowed cheeks had filled back out, and the frantic energy had soothed into something calmer, like waves on a sunny beach. I ordered a soda and fries as soon as I sat down. My stomach had been grumbling for the last hour.

"How did your meeting with Mannix go?" Demetrius asked, leaning in. He looked like he wanted to be excited but was saving it in case the day had been a bust. "Are you a new member of the VSPD?"

"I accepted the job offer," I said as soon as my drink was set in front of me. I couldn't help but smile. "I agreed to three months, for now. I can't sit around unemployed. And plus, it's better than working for Ziggy."

"Congratulations, Ailis." Demetrius lifted his untouched drink. "I feel safer already."

Cole clinked his glass against mine. "A friend of mine works with Mannix. He speaks highly of the team and of Captain Holland. I think you'll fit in well with them, given your desire to save everyone no matter the cost."

I shrugged. "If those of us with power do nothing to protect those without it, I don't deserve the life I have."

"Which is why me and my people stood in the trees the night Pack finally called your number," he answered, to my surprise. "Your path will be rocky, Ailis, but you now have a lion in the trees."

"Thank you," I replied, my throat feeling tight.

"Working with Ziggy would have been interesting. He was a nice fellow," Rome said, clinking his water glass against mine.

"He's a demon wearing a witch's meat suit," I replied, and Rome blanched. "Nice enough for a demon, but I wouldn't trust him, Rome. Bad things happen to good people when they start depending on demons."

"Don't you depend on him?" Rome asked.

"I'm a prime example of that rule. Did you not notice the shitshow of my life over the last month?"

"Good point." Rome laughed.

Rome passed over a copy of his species status application from The Commission of Natural and Unnatural Statics and Civil Registration, coined The Commission. I went over it while I waited for my fries. I hadn't seen one before, since every species I had ever dealt with—Lycan aside—was already listed in the catalog. It was as convoluted as any other government document I had seen. Aside from name, birthdate and address, the rest might as well be written in a dead language. I had no idea how to answer most of the questions.

"Holy crap, they want a lot of information," I said. "Jesus, the small print on the back makes my brain hurt."

My fries came while I Googled most of what the document said. The terms were obnoxious, the directions were vague at best, and the spaces to print were too small to fit all the information. Anyone filling it in would have one hell of a time trying to complete it. I bet most applications were denied simply because the damn thing was impossible to complete, and they had given up. I lifted my head with everyone else at the table and watched Miguel walk in. He sat in a booth next to us, leaving three feet of space between me and him.

"Miguel," Demetrius said, nodding his head once.

Demented Dave's wasn't exactly a neutral space, but it was close enough. Dave, the owner — a shifter — would start tearing off limbs if people tracked their problems into his dive. Most places run by the metaphysical were run the same way. Keep your shit at the door, or don't open it.

Miguel looked over casually. "Oh, hello. I didn't realize you'd all be here."

"Hello," I replied. I glanced at Sofia and Cisco on the other side of the room. They both looked away guilty, lifting menus to cover their faces.

"Ahh, the species status. Those are a pain," Miguel said as if it wasn't a big deal that he was sitting beside us. "If you want to speed it along, you will need a reference letter from a physician indicating you are not a risk to the general population due to your species type, and one from clergy, saying you're not cursed." He pulled a stack of papers from his jacket. "Here, these should help. The specialist is the grandson of the original doctor who helped the shifters gain civil status. He's now a specialist in London and is willing to come over to help if need be. There's a letter from the clergy, as well. The two extra letters are from two Commission officials, stating they are in support of your status application. They owed me a favor, and since I'm not likely going to need the help of The Commission, this seemed like a good place to use them up."

Rome stared at Miguel, frozen in place. He was scared. I didn't blame him. He'd been hunted to near death by Miguel and his people less than a month ago. He blinked and looked back down at the table. I reached underneath and squeezed his hand. I wanted him to know it was okay to be scared, but he wasn't here alone. He had friends. He had people who had his back.

Demetrius took the papers and finally smiled. "Thank you, Miguel. The process is pretty complex, and there is not much for instruction online. Are you familiar with the document?"

"I am. I've helped those of half-blood lines complete them," he replied. "The Commission makes it difficult in hopes fewer groups apply, I think. Humans for Humans have their fingers in it, mucking up a once simple application. But if you have the blessing of the church, they seem to push the documents right through."

"Do you mind taking a quick look for Rome?" Demetrius asked. "See if we've filled it out correctly?"

"Not at all," he said, and Demetrius handed the pages over. Miguel read the first page and asked for Rome's pencil. "Do you mind me making a recommendation that would speed this along?"

"Ahh, not at all," Rome said. His voice was quiet. "Thank you."

"You're a new subspecies of an already existing group. You would fall under the already cataloged Lycanthropy species and would be listed as a sub-group, an addition. If you go that route, it would be nearly impossible to deny you," he said. "Do you have your testing results from the lab?"

Rome nodded. "I had them verified by two more labs, as well."

Miguel passed the paperwork back. "I've underlined the areas you need to check off and sign at the bottom of each page. On the last page, it asks you what supporting documents you are including. Add what I've given you and your laboratory results. Do not miss any documents, and do not add documents you've not listed on that page. They'll toss it based on completing the documents incorrectly. It's best not to give them a reason to reject you."

"Thank you," Rome said, looking over his paperwork and smiling. "So close, I can almost taste it."

"Thanks, Miguel," I finally said.

"Well, we should be on our way." Demetrius stood, clearly uncomfortable. I groaned internally at their leaving. "Come on, Rome. I'll give you a ride home."

I climbed out of the booth and gave Rome a hug. "Soon, Rome, and you're home free."

"Thank you," he replied. "I can't tell you how much I appreciate your help."

I smiled. "The basket of goodies was enough. We ate all the chocolates in one sitting."

Demetrius laughed. "It's the basket May sent back to me."

"I know. The card was still tucked inside." I shrugged. "I still ate them after giving half to Ziggy for his help. They're from the witches' market. That stuff is expensive as hell."

"See you at the party this weekend," Cole said, standing. He waved to Cisco and Sofia, who waved back. He glanced at Miguel once and nodded. "Miguel."

Demetrius leaned in and kissed my cheek. "You can meet Webb. He's crawling out of his skin to meet you, especially after he heard you tossed Elizabet out of a window. Every time we've met, he's asked to come."

"As a human servant, you think he'd feel bad for her," I answered.

"He's more than that, Ailis. He has been with me for nearly a century. He is my life partner," he replied. "And no, not many feel bad for the fate of that woman. Elizabet earned her fate."

I nodded. "Tell Webb I'm looking forward to meeting him."

"Thank you, Ailis." He waved to Sofia and Cisco and stopped at Miguel's side. He offered his hand, and to my surprise, Miguel took it. "Thank you for helping Rome."

Miguel stood. He was usually a dominating presence, but tonight, he was toned down. "Thank you for doing what you could to keep Ailis alive. I won't forget it."

"Be well," Demetrius said, and walked out with Rome following.

The moment the booth emptied, Sofia and Cisco jumped up and shuffled right in, packing Miguel into the booth with them. I rolled my eyes and took my seat.

"Can you believe it? They actually invited me and Sofia to celebrate with Rome and his people?" Cisco asked. "The invites were on the doorstep this morning."

I smiled. "Rome really likes you, Cisco."

"He's a good pup," he replied and turned his attention to Miguel. "So, how are things with you?"

"I convinced Philip to return, and I've stepped down," Miguel said.

I raised my eyebrows but said nothing. I hadn't received an email to my burner account from him since the one asking me to trust him. My heart sank into my stomach. He hadn't told me. The realization that we had found what could break us strangled my heart. This was happening again. And for the same reason—Pack.

"I'm a wolf without a Pack or a home, really. The market here is cutthroat."

"Try Blood Square," Sofia said to Miguel, reaching under the table to squeeze my hand.

The blood roared in my ears. All the anger that had been burning inside me was instantly pulled away with the current of my sadness. Up until that point, having someone to be angry at had made waiting for the dust to settle easier. I had known that, eventually, I'd have to face the reality of my actions and what that would mean for Miguel and me. I just hadn't expected to be sitting in public when my world crashed down. Hope was the last thing to die, and I sat in Demented Dave's while the last of my hopes that Miguel would come home to me fizzled out. Staring across at Miguel, I smiled. By the grace of God, I didn't cry. I swallowed it.

"Where have you been staying?" I asked. "You haven't been on my front porch in weeks."

"Your garden shed," Cisco answered, and Miguel blushed.

"It's no five-star resort, but it's not the worst place I've slept," Miguel said with a playful smile.

I nodded slowly. I pulled a twenty from my bag and stood. I opened my mouth but closed it without saying another word. I pushed Sofia out of the booth and walked away. I made it to my car and out of the parking lot before the tears started. I wouldn't regret what I had done for Rome and his people, but that didn't mean it didn't hurt to pay the cost. I lost part of my family to keep someone alive. It didn't seem fair. But not much was fair in the world, which was especially true when you put your nose in matters of monsters.

Chapter Twelve

I tossed and turned in bed until my restlessness had me going downstairs. Sofia and Cisco were playing cards at the kitchen table, a game called War. It usually resulted in slapping each other's hands until they were swollen and red and the table being cleared off. I put on my slippers and went outside, the instant chill of the night making me feel bad for the squatter in my shed. I opened the door to find Miguel sitting up on a cot with a book in his hands. It was cramped, cold, dingy, and smelled like my gas lawn mower.

"It looks like my first apartment in here, only roomier." I pulled the door tightly behind me to keep the night wind out. "It smells better, too."

"I've slept in much worse conditions — like your first apartment." He smiled. "The rats in the parking garage of that building were the size of wererats. It was life and limb every time I needed my car. Thank God I can't catch rabies, or I'd have died within a month."

"You can stay with Cisco until you find a place," I said and rolled my eyes at his sudden grin. "And you can pay rent, since I'm unemployed."

"I thought you just accepted a position with the Arcane Division?" he asked.

"I won't start for another few weeks, and I'm not feeling very charitable," I answered.

"Do I pay what Cisco pays?" he asked, and I shook my head.

"This is Vancity. You can pay the top dollar for a basement suite. I hope you find a job soon. I want to be paid on the first of the month."

"Mannix offered me a job." Miguel quickly held up his hands when he saw the 'I don't think so' look on my face. "I said no. I already accepted a job with a private company used by the church. It's how I got the letters for Rome. I included them in my signing bonus."

"Thank you for that. I know he appreciates it," I replied. "Let's go inside, it's freezing out here."

"It's not bad, but I much prefer *not* sleeping in a shed." He followed me in.

"Anyone want cake?" Cisco asked as though he knew I'd finally go out and bring Miguel inside. "I bought one from the Italian bakery in East Van today. It's red velvet with little chunks of dark chocolate inside the layers. It's to die for."

He didn't wait for any of us to answer. He pulled out the cake and cut us each a piece. I ate mine in the corner of the kitchen while the three of them chatted. They didn't talk about anything important, but I didn't feel like I was part of the group anymore. I washed my plate, left them all sitting in the kitchen, and went into the living room. I wrapped myself in a knitted blanket and stared at the wall. I felt like I was out of place. I was still numb, almost empty, and raw in a way that could only be felt in the soul. Sitting on the brink of life and death had this way of draining a soul. One would think I'd have gotten used to it by now, but I wasn't.

"Are you good here, Ailis?" Sofia asked from the front door. "Do you need me to stay the night?"

"No, I'm good, but thank you," I replied.

"Okay. I'm going to head out then," she said, giving Miguel a look that carried more meaning than words. A warning not to start trouble. "I have an interview tomorrow with a hunter firm."

"You're not returning to Mexico?" Miguel asked.

"No. I think I'll hang out here for a bit," Sofia answered. "At least until the city calms down."

"Good night, Sofia." I mustered my best smile that didn't say I was uncomfortable. "Dinner tomorrow, on me. You can tell me how your interview went."

Cisco gave her a hug and locked the door behind her. "I should be going to bed as well. I have so much to do tomorrow. I have a nap at eleven I can't miss again and a late lunch with myself that is flagged as a must."

I rolled my eyes and watched him open the basement door and shut it behind him. My cat trotted across the room and pushed into the basement at the foot of the door. "Cisco!"

He opened the door. "Yes?"

"Did you cut a hole in my basement door?"

"Yep," he replied. "I was getting tired of going up and down the stairs. My damage deposit should cover the replacement."

"What damage deposit? You don't even pay rent," I countered.

He shrugged. "Tenant harassment is against the law, you know."

"Good night," I said, and he closed the door.

I shifted from being uncomfortable to instant nervousness. My pulse picked up, and all I could hear was the swooshing of blood in my ears. Miguel took a seat at the other end of the couch, raising my blood pressure until my temples throbbed.

"It's okay, Lish," Miguel said.

I nodded but couldn't shake the nervous energy. "I feel awkward."

"Can we talk?"

"What's there to say?"

"I love you," he said, his voice tiny. It was unusual to hear his vulnerability. He was always so sure in everything he did.

"I love you, too, Miguel," I replied, and his shoulders shook.

He looked up at the ceiling, blinking away tears. "I didn't think I'd ever hear you say that again."

"I'll always love you." I pursed my lips to keep back the millions of other words I had inside. I folded my blanket and felt the first tear fall. "Good night, Miguel."

Miguel reached for my hand before I could step away. "Wait."

"You didn't message me," I whispered and pulled my hand back. Feeling his touch hurt my heart. "After you stepped down, why didn't you message me? You said you would. I waited for you. I checked my messages dozens of times every day, waiting for that email, but it didn't come. I waited for you to come home, and you didn't. I've been playing the game, doing this song and dance, and waited for the moment you'd come home, but you never did. You stepped down and never came back to me. I know I fucked up, but like a fool, I thought you'd still come home."

"As soon as I stepped down, I came straight to you. It's taken a couple of weeks of negotiating with Philip to ensure Sofia, Cisco and myself could remain in this territory. But I wasn't walking away until I knew for sure you'd be safe," he said and tilted his head, a look of puzzlement filling his face. "Is that why you were suddenly so sad at the diner this evening? You thought I had stepped down and didn't tell you?"

I nodded and took a seat. "The thought crossed my mind."

"I'm done with the Noire Lune Pack," he answered. "As soon as it was official, I came here looking for you. When I couldn't find you, I called Sofia and Cisco to find out where you were."

"Oh." I released a heated breath. "I thought you left me."

"It would take more than you bringing us to the brink of war for me to leave."

"I love you, Miguel, but I'm not just done with the Noire Lune Pack. I'm done with all of your world. I'm done with Pack, completely." I felt awful for saying the words, but I meant it. "I won't survive them. I can't do it. I damn near died again."

"I know you don't want to hear this, but at the time, I did what I could. I'm sorry it wasn't enough." He glanced over, cheeks wet with tears. "I'm so sorry, Lish. I can't begin to tell you how sorry I am. It killed me inside to know what you were going through."

"I know. I have no doubt that I'd be dead without your help. I know you did everything you could, and I can't thank you enough," I replied. "I'm so sorry, Miguel, for all of this. I understand the position you were in. I put you between an impossible choice and a hard spot that could have killed us all. I am grateful for what you did for me. I am so thankful you did all you could to help me. I recognize all of it. I know you did your absolute best and got me out of a situation I put myself in. I'm not angry with you. I wanted to be. I wanted to blame you. I wanted to point a finger at someone else, but you're not the one who did this. I am. I am so sorry for putting you between me and Pack."

"I feel like there is a *but* coming."

I nodded. "*But* it'll always be this way, you standing between me and them. I can't live with Pack hanging over me. I'm not one of you. And when I stood up to your people, I found myself at the very end, without many options. It was a terrifying place to be, and I never want to be back there again."

"You were never alone. I made sure of it." He smiled. "I'd say you did pretty good for a lone witch."

"I stayed alive, Miguel. That's what I did. But one day, I'm not going to be so lucky, and I'm going to be forced to take lives. I don't want to kill just to stay alive, but I will. But I don't want to live a life where every day boils down to my death or someone else's."

"I don't want that for either of us," he replied.

"I love you with everything I have to give. There is no part of my soul that doesn't love you." My voice hitched in my throat. "But I can't be in a relationship where there is a question of where your loyalty lies. I don't want to be in a relationship where we're pushed to opposite sides of a decision. I'm under no illusion that we will disagree, we will have different opinions, that one of us will do something that angers the other, but I never want to worry that I'll die because of it. I don't want to ever be afraid of being in a room alone with you or your friends. I can't be with you when I know you would put Pack before me. The result will cost me my life. I thought I could, but I can't. I thought I could walk in this world of mythical beasts and suffer no consequences, but I can't. I wish we could go back to the way it was before I knew about your people."

"You've severed your ties to Pack," he said. "I have done the same. I'm out. I will have nothing to do with this Pack. I am rogue. I am a wolf without a Pack anywhere."

"What about Caser?" I asked.

"Caser is family, but I am not a part of his Pack either," he answered. "I have the Pack I need and want with you."

"I'll always be in danger."

"You'll always be in danger regardless. But together..." Miguel's chin shook. "Please don't leave. We're stronger together. It's hell on earth out there. I don't want to walk it without you. I won't make it, Lish. My wolf won't settle unless I'm near you. It's why I've been in the shed."

"What the hell do we do?" I didn't want to wake up tomorrow and have him gone. I couldn't do it twice. I'd barely made it the first time I left him. But I also didn't want to wake up tomorrow and have it be the last day I had a pulse. "Find us a way out, Miguel. Find us a way that won't end in one of us dead."

"We stick together. We have always been stronger as a team."

"Swear it, Miguel," I replied. "Swear that it is me and you against them all. No matter what, we stand shoulder to shoulder against any and all who come. We won't leave the other to face the monsters alone. We face them together."

"I oath myself to you, Ailis, to us. Whatever comes, we're in it together. Whoever comes, I'm at your side."

I slinked across the couch. "You must know that we're going to die together if we stay together. That will be our ending. We're not going to grow old together on the front porch, sipping iced tea. We'll go down in a bloody battle. We'll be running for our lives until the bitter end."

"There's no one else I'd die for and no one else I'd rather have at my side," he answered. "Please."

"I won't let you kill the people in my life because you are Lycan," I replied. "I can't be held to the rules you grew up with."

He smiled. "I'll keep my claws to myself."

"We don't talk about work or Pack or Nest or any other monster unless they're on the front steps."

"Deal."

I inched closer. "And you don't let Pack steal me away in the night for any reason."

"I am a rogue with no ties to this Pack. My loyalty is to you and no one else. You are my Pack, Lish. I'll die defending you."

"If they come for me again…"

"I'll kill them," Miguel finished my sentence. "But if you could please stop putting yourself in positions where I have to keep you alive?"

"I'll do my best," I replied, and he laughed. "Kiss me."

He pulled me onto his lap and hugged me. He breathed me in, and his entire body shuddered. Once he'd rubbed his cheeks over my body, covering himself in my smell, he finally pulled back and kissed me. Cupping my jaw, he kissed me like it was the first and last time, all mixed together. His warm lips felt sad and loving at once and filled up the parts of my heart that felt empty and numb.

"I don't want to go another day without touching you," Miguel said, sweeping the hair from my neck and nuzzling his nose into my skin. "Without feeling you against my soul."

"Let's go to bed," I said, my body reacting to his touch. I stood and gripped his hand. "You can bring your things inside in the morning."

"This wouldn't be the first time you've thrown my things out a window." He followed me to the stairs. "Remember when you tried to throw out my television and dropped it on your foot? You broke your toe, and we spent nine hours in the emergency room arguing."

"How we keep finding our way back to each other is beyond me," I answered, remembering one of our first arguments. Miguel had shoved me out of the way during a demon hunt, thinking he was being the hero. I'd landed on the lap of a ghoul, who'd pulled out a handful of hair before I could get away.

"And me," Cisco's voice came from the other side of the basement door as we passed it. "It's us against them all. You are my family. You are my Pack."

"Us," I replied. "I love you, Cisco."

"I love you both." Cisco shuffled back down into the basement, the pitter-patter of little furry feet following him.

"He stole my cat," I said, walking up the stairs.

"The night the Sentinels came here, Cisco and Sofia beat the shit out of them in the driveway. Cisco broke bones because he smelled your cat on them. He's protective of you in ways that only a brother could be," Miguel answered. "And Sofia had to be pulled off of them because they stepped foot in your house."

"Never mess with a witch's familiar or her home."

"I wasn't nearly as calm as Cisco or Sofia."

"What did you do?"

"As you well know, they didn't make it out of the city," he replied.

"Are they dead?"

"Yes. They died for touching my mate."

Inside the bedroom, I shut the door behind me. Miguel took a seat on the foot of the bed and wiped his palms on his jeans. His nervous energy filled the room and brought a smile to my face. Miguel had the confidence of a warrior from hell and could command the attention of a whole room, but away from the rest of the world and the problems that rode our souls into shards of glass, with me, he had always been soft. Tonight, he was uncertain. It was a very human emotion for a man who was very much not a human.

I walked to the bed and positioned my knees between his thighs, lifting his chin and eyes to meet mine. When he raised his hands to the waistband of my pajama bottoms, I pushed his hands away and grinned. "You're not in control tonight," I said, leaning into his mouth. "I am."

"Sweet Jesus," he groaned.

His entire body shivered. I stepped back and pulled off my top. He licked his lips as I ran my hands down my breasts to my hips. I turned my back to him, pulling my bottoms to my ankles, bending over and giving him a full view. A moan escaped his lips and whispered curses soon followed. I watched him from between my ankles, fighting his urges. He gripped the bed as his hips jerked, the blanket seams ripping as he held himself in place. I grazed my fingers up the inside of my legs, stopping at the apex of my thighs.

"Oh, fuck, not that," he moaned. I lightly danced down my lips and back up. "Fuck me."

"Not yet."

I let out a small moan as soon as my fingers found my sweet spot. In the background, Miguel echoed my delight. I snaked my hand farther through my legs, sliding a finger into the wetness, sending small darts of excitement through my body with each movement I made. Between my legs, I could see Miguel and his bright orange eyes. The torment on his face made every thrust of my finger all the more enjoyable. He had always loved seeing me touch myself, but he'd never been able to contain himself for longer than a few minutes. Giving up control wasn't a skill he possessed. Being teased would only last so long. He inched his hips forward.

"If you get off that bed, you do not get an orgasm," I said to motivate him.

"I don't need one."

"And you do not get to make me come, either," I answered.

"Fuck."

I brought my hand back up to the tip of my cleft, rubbing small circles around my clit, pleasure jolting through my middle. Miguel's growl filled the room and rumbled through my chest. The smell of his wolf filled my lungs, and I moaned.

"Come for me, Lish," Miguel said from the bed. "Show me how you make yourself come."

I felt the tension building in every inch of my body. My breath came out in ragged pants, sharp and filled with need. I alternated between slipping my fingers inside and rubbing firm circles around the bundle of nerves that weakened my knees. Hearing Miguel groan from the bed as he forced himself to remain seated sent me over the edge. The heat spread from my hips to my legs and breasts, tingling my nipples and electrifying my flesh. I jerked against my hand, and finally, my orgasm hit me, and I went to my knees, groaning as I cupped myself. Wave after wave rolled over me, arching my back and setting the world on fire around me. My vision blurred, and for a moment, my body filled with the sensation of falling.

I turned around and crawled toward Miguel, my body still pulsing with pleasure. He leaned forward on the bed, his rear barely touching the bedding beneath him. I knelt between his thighs and leaned up into his mouth, licking his lips.

"Take your shirt off." I kissed him once and pulled back. His shirt was over his head and on the floor in an instant. He reached for the button on his pants, and I pushed his hands away. "Let me."

Miguel leaned back. I ran my hands over the contour of his cock beneath the fabric. His hips bounced to meet my touch. I pulled the button on his jeans, popping the top of his jeans open. Slowly, I unzipped him. With newfound freedom, his cock sprung through his pants. I cupped my hand around his head and squeezed, bringing a hiss from Miguel's lips. With a tug at the waist of his pants, he lifted his hips, and I pulled them down to the floor. One by one, I freed his legs. I gently traced my fingernails up his thighs to his stomach. Every movement made his cock twitch. I grazed him from top to bottom, running my nails over his sensitive skin. Pre-cum rolled down his shaft. I rolled my thumb over his pleasure then pulled my hand away.

"Please," he whispered, his hips lurched to find the touch he wanted.

I smiled. "Please, what, Miguel? I want to hear you say the words."

"Stroke my cock," he answered.

"Like this?" I grasped him firmly and ran my hand from base to tip, gently squeezing at the base.

"Harder."

I leaned in and licked him, holding him with both my hands, working him harder. Miguel enjoyed a hint of pain, just enough to add another layer of sensation. I ran my hands up and down forcefully until his body tensed and his cock hardened to its fullest potential. His breathing turned from soft moans to something frantic. I placed my lips around his tip and sucked him into my mouth. Miguel sat straight up and gripped my hair.

"Oh fuck, I won't last like this," he said, trying to pull my mouth off him.

"You are not in control," I repeated and slapped his hands away.

I darted my tongue around the head of his cock and continued working my hands in tandem. I stretched my mouth open and swallowed as much of him as I could. Miguel fisted the blankets and jerked below me. He knew I wasn't stopping. I dropped one hand below and cupped him, gently squeezing. Miguel growled the moment my mouth roamed his shaft freely, sucking and flicking him with my tongue. I alternated between stroking him and plunging my mouth down as far as I could go.

I pulled away just enough to settle my lips around the head of his cock and glanced up to meet his eyes. With my hand pumping him, my eyes on his, he drove his hips up and down. Miguel's brow furrowed. His breath turned to pants. He grabbed my hair and pressed my head down, holding me in place as his orgasm pulsed through him. In a voice I could barely hear through the groans, he called out my name. Miguel's cock erupted inside my mouth. I swallowed as he pulsed and jerked uncontrollably under me. I pulled every drop from him, teasing out his pleasure. Miguel pulled my head back, leaned down and kissed me. His tongue pushed between my teeth as he lifted me to my feet and turned me to sit on the bed.

"My turn," he said.

My stomach lurched at the promise. Miguel knelt between my legs and lifted my thighs into his arms, gripping my ass in his hands. I looked down the line of my body to see him on his knees. He opened my legs and breathed me in, licking his lips and moaning. He leaned forward and licked me from bottom to top, pressing his tongue flat against me. My elbows gave out, and I fell onto my back. He let my body rest on the bed and reached each hand to my breasts, rolling my nipples while he pushed his face into my thighs. His tongue danced across my bundle of nerves. I arched my back and wiggled my hips against his mouth. As soon as my breathing shifted into pleasure, Miguel pinched my nipples.

"Don't stop," I groaned, working my body to get that perfect rhythm.

I squirmed between the pleasure of his tongue and the firm grip on my breasts. I panted, so close to release. Miguel released my breast, and within an instant, my body was full. He worked his fingers in and out while his tongue darted across my clit. I gripped my bed as the world fell out from under me. As my orgasm neared, Miguel pulled my hips to the edge of the bed to meet his hips. In one fluid motion, not skipping a single beat, Miguel pushed himself inside me.

"I want to feel you come," he whispered into my ear. "Come for me."

Miguel's cock reached the end of me and pulled back out, over and over, hitting the spot deep within that sent fireworks through every nerve and fiber. I closed my eyes, arched my back, and screamed his name as my orgasm smashed down. The build-up was fast and dirty and hit me hard. I dragged my nails down his back and gripped his ass, pulling him harder and faster against me. I threw my head back in pleasure and moaned his name as the last pulses roared throughout. Every corner of my body had felt the touch of that explosion.

Miguel picked me off the bed, wrapping my legs and arms around him. I held his face to mine as he pushed me against the wall, driving his hips in and out. My lips bruised against his with the force of our bodies moving. Holding me tight, Miguel's pace shifted. He buried his head into my shoulder and rushed toward his final climax.

"Fuck, fuck..." Miguel moaned. He drove himself upward as he pulled me down onto his hips.

"Come for me," I said, and that was all it took to send him over the edge, finishing in a fierce growl that filled the room and shook the art on the wall.

He pinned me, his body jerking and pulsing against me. We both heard Cisco running up the stairs and pausing once he realized neither of us was in danger. I laughed until Miguel's legs gave out with his own laughter. When my arms and legs worked again, I got up and stood over Miguel, nudging him with my foot.

"Get up, you lazy hound."

He rolled onto his knees and crawled to the bed. "The floor is still more comfortable than the shed."

"I'm sure the shed isn't as bad as that time you locked me in a trunk and forgot about me," I said, helping him to the bed.

"For the hundredth time, I didn't forget about you. I was unconscious."

"Why were you sleeping in my shed, Miguel?" I asked. "It can't be because there's no rentals in town."

"I was scared Pack would come back for you. After they kicked down your door, I haven't been far from you, just in case."

I kissed his cheek. "Thank you. I love you and our ridiculous life together."

"We have had quite the run, hey? Every memory I have, the ones that carry me through my darkest moments, are with you. Even the times we fight, or things go south. You are the reason I keep fighting and keep getting back up."

"You keep me from becoming the witch I should not be. You keep me from shaving off my soul for the wrong reasons." I climbed into bed beside him. I rolled my back to him, and he pulled me tight against him. "I do enjoy our making up."

"I love you." Miguel kissed my shoulder.

"I love you, too," I replied and told the app on my phone to turn off the bedroom lights.

"Well, aren't you a fancy witch?" Miguel laughed.

"Cisco's laziness has rubbed off on me." I closed my eyes, but this time, I wasn't so naïve to think tomorrow wasn't going to bring doom and gloom. This time, I went to sleep knowing it would come, but I wouldn't try to do it alone. Some people were worth suffering for and with. Miguel was that person.

Chapter Thirteen

"The mariachi band was a little much, no?" I asked Cisco while we stood at the edge of the crowd. In the center of the hall, a ten-person band and six dancers weaved in and out of partygoers. Their bright red and yellow clothes drew the eye, but it was the music that gained our full attention. Mexican music was made to move you. It pushed your feet to dance. It was designed to instill emotion, and I felt the range of them all with each song. Between the suave harmonies, the rhythms, and the gregarious singers, I couldn't help but smile.

"You're just jealous that Rome liked my gift more than your charm necklace." Cisco clapped his hands, grinning, and bumped his hips side to side in rhythm with the music. "It's not every day you become a legal werewolf citizen. The celebration called for a mariachi."

It had taken mere days for Rome's application to go through, gaining full status for himself and a new section in the catalog. The party to welcome Rome and his pack into society was a massive celebration. They were officially a species of shifter, protected under the law, with the same rights as everyone else. Every power in the city had turned up to the event, presenting them with a gift. They were small tokens but meant the world to the werewolves. It said they were welcome and no longer had to hide or fear who they were. I had given Rome a charm for his necklace and given his pack my phone number. I'd come if they needed help. Hopefully, the next time wouldn't require me to run for my life or owe a demon several slabs of chocolate.

When we'd arrived, Rome had introduced me to his people and his Alpha, Boyd Grayson. I received hugs, tears, smiles, handshakes, and invites to dinner. Not one of them cleaned their hands after touching me. It was small things like those that really made my day. Miguel had stayed with Samuel while I'd been introduced to the rest of Rome's pack, knowing how the others felt about him. He was willing to befriend them, but not push for it too soon. Rome had been the bigger wolf and welcomed Miguel with a hug. Miguel was tense at first but warmed up quickly and relaxed into the celebrations, dancing and socializing with others. Unlike him, I didn't feel at ease. I kept my eyes on the room and the energy flaring here and there. Species at war with each other were mingling, leaving their issues at the door. It left me confused. Generally, when I hated someone enough to try to kill them, I didn't dance with them at the next party. But the world of fur and claws wasn't mine, and I prayed this world would never become my own.

"Yours is flashy for a night. Mine is useful," I answered Cisco.

"He's a wolf, little red. Why does he need a charm that'll alert him to demons?" he asked. "He can literally smell them coming."

"First, when he met Ziggy, Rome couldn't tell that he was a demon. Second, the charm doesn't warn against only demons. It will alert him to all danger," I corrected. "In the world we live in, why wouldn't someone want something like that?"

"I'm sorry your world needs charms, Lish," Cisco replied. "I hope one day you won't need them."

"Pretty to think, but I'm going to hell when this song and dance is over. It's too bad I can't take the charms with me."

"That sucker would blow up if you brought it down there." He said, and I finally smiled. Cisco always tried to smooth things over with humor. It was one of the reasons I liked being near him when it felt like fate was inching too close to me. "Don't worry, I've got your back in the pits. From this life onto the next. Plus, your cat will be there. Not even demons like fucking with familiars."

Cisco tucked me under his arm and swayed back and forth, bumping his hip into mine. We watched as the others danced to the music as though the hall wasn't filled to the rafters with monsters. Miguel spun Sofia around in circles until her laughter filled the room. They had hit the dancefloor as soon as the music started. Seeing them both smiling in the center of every other shifter group in the city was unnerving, but they didn't seem to mind. They were the only Pack at the party. The others weren't invited. But every other flavor of shifter had attended, and there were way more than I had ever suspected.

Until I heard the music, I hadn't thought of how badly either of them would miss home. "Are you homesick, Cisco?"

"I *am* home," he said. "I miss certain parts of Mexico, and certain people, but I don't see Mexico as my home anymore. Why do you ask?"

I motioned to Miguel and Sofia. "Do you think they are?"

"No. You are Miguel's home and have been since he met you," he answered. "As for Sofia, home is wherever we are."

"We should take a trip back when things settle down."

He chuckled as if I had told a joke. "None of us lead lives where things are settled. This problem will go away and will be replaced with a new one. But I get what you're saying."

"Do I need to ask Caser's permission to enter his territory? What if he says no?"

"It is customary to ask, yes. But it's more like we'd be giving Caser a heads-up to prepare for the return of four holy terrors," he replied. "Don't worry, he wouldn't say no. You're family. Because of you, he still has his daughter."

"Well then, we should get a trip in before we're all too busy to take one," I said, smiling at the thought of returning to Mexico and not being there to hunt witches and demons. "I think it would do us all some good to laze around on a beach for a week."

"I'll give Caser a call later on. I'm sure he and Anna would be happy to have us."

Throughout the night, dozens of people came and went like a revolving door. There were faces I recognized and had never known they had been a shifter, and some were new to me. Each person I pointed to or had come for a handshake, Cisco would tell me what brand of fur they were. Rats, lions, tigers, two bears, panthers, and apparently, one of the rarer of the species, a boar.

"Do you think there are werefish?" I turned Cisco, who stared at me like my ears had just fallen off. "What? All I have are folklores and the catalog, which isn't exactly brimming with information. If a species doesn't want to be found, they keep off the map."

"Werefish? Like mermaids?"

"There hasn't been a mermaid seen in decades, and even then, it was speculation and not fact."

"And they like it that way. They tend to stay in the more tropical waters. There's a small tribe of them living between Mexico and the Cayman Islands," he answered to my surprise. "You doubt me? You're talking to a future marine biologist here. Their numbers are pretty low compared to other magic groups, but that has more to do with their reproduction rates than anything else."

"Why aren't they in the catalog?"

"If you could have remained a secret, wouldn't you have?" he asked, and I nodded wholeheartedly. "There are a few species of water people not in the catalog. Some have a species name of their own, and some are classified as shifters. Most, if they can, stay off dry land until they have no other choice."

"I have cataloged eighty-seven species of water-dwelling magics," someone said from behind me. I turned to face a man standing with Demetrius, their hands locked together.

"Ailis, allow me to introduce Webb Bentley," Demetrius said.

Webb extended his hand with a smile. "Dr. Kyteler, it is a pleasure to finally meet you. I have heard so much about you."

"Please, call me Ailis. The pleasure is mine." I smiled and shook his hand. "You were saying?"

"Throughout my years, I've managed to catalog eighty-seven species of water-dwelling magics. Some are long gone, but for those still thriving, they live in regions inhospitable to man. I can't really blame them for that. We're not exactly known for having a live and let live mentality," he explained. He turned to Cisco and held out his hand. "I have drawings and photographs, if you're interested in seeing them?"

Cisco stiffened for a moment. Vampires and Pack had a long history of hunting each other into shallow graves, and an even longer history of simply hating each other. Pack law put Cisco in an odd position. Fraternization with the enemies was a death sentence, but would it count if Webb was still human? Webb noticed the discomfort and tried a different route, dropping his hand without making a big deal of it.

"How about I send them to Ailis, and she can share them with you," Webb said and leaned in. "I understand your position. No one needs to know they're from me."

"Thank you," Cisco finally answered. "That is kind of you to offer. I've only cataloged three dozen."

"That won't do. I have charted their migration routes and nesting grounds if ever you're brave enough to dive into some deadly locations," Webb replied. "A few months back, I chartered a boat off the Northern Isles of Scotland and was lucky enough to watch the migration of a clan of selkies. On my way back, I caught sight of a sea dragon."

Cisco leaned into the conversation. If he were sitting, he'd be on the edge of his seat. It was as if their history had vanished with one conversation. The awkwardness between Cisco and Webb had disappeared. Once the initial discomfort had passed, I stood with Demetrius, my eyes scanning the room for trouble. He did the same, while always keeping Webb in his line of sight. Webb was charming, cheerful, and everything Demetrius wasn't. He laughed loudly, cursed, dressed colorfully, and seemed like he was more the life of the party than Demetrius would ever be. However, not sitting on a throne gave everyone the freedom to live authentically, and everything about Webb was genuine. Although Webb didn't say nasty things about Elizabet, he didn't hide his joy that she was dead. She was a monster in her heyday and broken near the end. Death was a mercy.

Demetrius and Cisco made polite conversation, which was a pretty big step. Some wars would never end. The one between Lycan and vampire had been raging since the dawn of time and wasn't about to stop any time soon, no matter the topic at hand. Sofia, from across the room, kept her eyes on Demetrius the entire evening, watching his every movement. The vampire didn't care. I think he was used to it. Part of me felt sorry for him. I knew exactly how it felt to be hated. The other part understood why vampires were feared. I might have known Demi, but I didn't know Demetrius. He may have been peaches and cream today, but tomorrow was a different story. I wasn't inclined to count my chickens before they hatched. There would be no benefit of the doubt when it came to monsters.

"You're both standing around as though a war is about to break out," Webb said, nudging Demetrius. "It is next to impossible to get Demi to take a day off."

"Days off are for people who don't touch hell daily," I said and paused. "Can no one else feel the tension building in here?"

"We've filled this hall with the greatest powers in the city. It's bound to feel uncomfortable," Cisco answered.

"All of us under one roof. Isn't this a brilliant idea?" I glanced around the room again. I rubbed away the feeling of spiders on my arms. "I'm going to mingle a bit and call it a night. I don't like that we're all here. I feel uneasy, like my skin is crawling."

"I do hope we can spend more time together. I'd love to get to know you away from the glamour of deadly high society," Webb said, pulling me into a hug before I could shake his hand. "We can leave the bullies at home and do a lunch date at Gotham. They have an amazing selection of vegetarian dishes I think you'd love, and a cheesecake that'll make you sob."

"That would be nice," I replied.

Demetrius and Webb wandered back to Rome, and Cisco followed me to the buffet. He filled two plates, and we took a seat beside Miguel and Sofia. I had four bites of my pie before Rome tapped on the table.

He held out his hand to me. "Demetrius mentioned you would be calling it a night shortly. I wanted to introduce you to someone before you left, if that's okay?"

"Of course, lead the way." I stood. We made our way through his people, who had made a wall between the three Pack members and the far tables behind them. I grinned as soon as I saw Rome's father.

"Dr. Bishop," I said when Rome introduced us. Demetrius and Webb were already with him, saying good night as well.

Calvin stood right away and pulled me into his arms, hugging me until I couldn't breathe. His body shook from silent tears. "Thank you, Ailis. For putting your neck on the line for my son. From the moment I met you, I knew you'd do great things with your life."

I pulled back with a laugh. "You sure didn't grade me that way."

"I graded you hard because I knew you could do better, and you did," he answered. "If you ever need anything, anything at all, my door is always open. I am a safe space for you, any time of day. I owe you my life."

"I didn't do it to be owed favors, Dr. Bishop. I did it because it was the right thing to do."

"And that is why I will always come to your call," he replied. "Because you are deserving of it."

I didn't spend long chatting before I began to yawn. I was not a night owl, at least not a social one. Whenever I was awake during the witching hour, it was because someone was dead or trying to kill me. I politely excused myself, giving Rome another hug before leaving him to celebrate with his family and people. Miguel found me wandering back, smiling. He tugged me into his arms and kissed my temple.

"Marry me," Miguel said, leaning back to see my face.

I raised an eyebrow. "And the next time I'm pissed off at you, I'd have to get a divorce. Those will be expensive fights."

"I'll pay for your lawyer every time you file for one." He pulled a ring from his pocket. "I was going to ask weeks ago, but death threats got in the way."

"As they do."

He knelt and held out a black ring box holding a raw diamond ring. It had flecks of black, just like my soul. "Marry me?"

I smiled. "Yes."

Over the cheers and questionable glances, Cisco's laughter rose above it. "This last fight is not the worst one they've had. Ailis lit a house on fire, once, with Miguel still inside."

"He was crawling out of the window," I said, rolling my eyes.

"A match made in hell," Samuel said, handing each of us a glass of champagne. "Welcome to the family, Miguel."

"I'm sorry, Samuel, for the troubles you went through," Miguel said.

"I'm not sorry for punching you. Next time, I'll break your legs," he said and walked away.

"I think you got his temper, Lish," Miguel whispered into my ear.

"I *am* his apprentice, after all."

"You're much more than that to him."

"And he's much more than that to me," I replied. "Take me home?"

"To bed." He winked.

* * * *

Miguel and I had just crawled into bed, our hands roaming each other's bodies, when my bedroom door flew open. Cisco ran in, in a panic, and I scrambled and screamed. "What the hell, Cisco. I'm not in danger."

"The times I came upstairs was not to save you, witch. It was for that lovestruck pup of yours. He'd let you carve the heart from his chest," he said, snickering. "I hate to break up your sexy time, but Mannix is here and needs you downstairs."

I pulled up the covers. "Why?"

"Humans for Humans bombed Rome's party," he answered. "A half-hour after we left."

I shot out of bed, pulled on a T-shirt and underwear, and ran down the stairs. Mannix was standing at my front door, looking like he had just crawled out of bed and into my living room.

"What happened? I was just at his party. Everything was fine when I left."

"It's not fine anymore." He tossed me a badge. "Get dressed. It's all hands on deck for tonight. Everyone has been called in. There's too many dead and injured, and they're all metaphysicals."

I ran back upstairs. I dialed Samuel's phone number while I dressed. My heart hammered. "Please pick up, please pick up." When no one picked up, I called Mairi's cell phone, cursing out loud that Samuel still hadn't gotten his own.

"Ailis?" Mairi answered. Her throat sounded raw.

"Where is Samuel?" I asked. "Is he okay? Are you okay?"

"I'm okay. Samuel has been rushed to Van General," she said over the noise in the background. "I'm on my way there. Humans for Humans bombed the hall. They screamed their rhetoric before blowing the hall to bits. They're everywhere. I don't trust them not to attack the hospital, where the victims are going, so I'm headed to Samuel now. Where are you?"

"I'm at home right now, but I'll be on my way to the scene with Mannix," I replied.

"Be careful."

"I love you both. Keep me posted," I said and hung up.

Miguel was already dressed. "I'll go to the hospital to make sure no one goes after Samuel or any of the other survivors."

"Thank you." I kissed him quickly and suited up.

I tried to wear something professional looking, something I've always seen Mannix and his people wearing. Black dress pants, black boots and black turtleneck. I strapped a gun on my right rear hip before leaving my bedroom. At my front door, Mannix handed me a black windbreaker with bold yellow lettering across the back that said 'VSPD — Arcane Division.'

"That gun is fine for tonight, but I'll have a department-issued sidearm delivered tomorrow. I pushed your paperwork through and was granted interim approval. You're good for twenty-four hours, but you'll need to sign all of the paperwork tomorrow. Don't kill anyone without me at your side, or this will turn into a fucking legal nightmare."

Cisco handed me a coffee to go and kissed my forehead. "Be careful."

"Go with Miguel, please. Make sure Samuel is okay. If he's taking a turn, call me."

"Don't worry, Ailis, we'll hold down the fort," Miguel said, jumping off the last few stairs, ready to go. "Go catch some bad guys."

"Let's go," Mannix said, heading out the door. I followed him to his black suburban and climbed in. He flicked on the lights and tore out of my driveway, spitting rocks on his way out.

"Tell me what happened," I said, holding onto the door to keep myself from sliding around on the leather seats.

"Not much to go on yet. Witnesses say a bomb went off in the middle of Rome's party," he answered. "Any issues while you were there? I was only there for a short time at the start of the night."

"I felt tensions rising but couldn't put my finger on why or who. There were too many powers in one room for me to get an idea."

He nodded. "The city is going to burn for this. Every higher-powered magic was there. We still don't know who lived and who will be the reason for war."

"How many are dead?"

"I don't know. Initial reports are saying a dozen, but we won't know the total until we know who succumbs to their injuries."

"What's on the agenda for us?" I asked. "Bag and tag? Witness reports?"

"We'll be conducting witness reports, reading auras of those being interviewed," he replied. "Those responsible are still there. The scene was locked down almost immediately by the survivors."

"Oh, Jesus. Reading the aura of someone who just went through trauma is going to be awful."

He nodded. "The worst part is that we're doing it on the scene, with bodies around us. We need to read their reactions."

I read the ID Mannix had tossed me. On the left, my recent driver's license photo. On the right, a shield with

the gates of hell in the background. *How artistic.*
"Specialist, Dr. Ailis Kyteler, Witch Practitioner. That's
a mouthful."

"We're not just called practitioners anymore. We
were granted special authority to do our jobs when the
red tape got in our way."

"I don't know what I'm doing."

"Think of it as any time you've been called in for a
consult. Own the scene, or the locals will walk all over
you."

The police radio buzzed to life with a report of a
second bomb going off in Point Grey, at the home of the
Master of the City, just moments ago. I pulled out my
phone and called Demetrius.

"Ailis!" Demetrius yelled into the phone over the
sirens. "Are you okay?"

"Yes, I left the party just after you did," I answered.
"I was calling to make sure you were okay. What
happened?"

"Someone tossed a bomb over our front gate, and it
went off. We have the two individuals responsible.
They are uninjured."

"What about your people? What about Webb?" I
asked.

"We heard about the bomb going off at Rome's party
and evacuated the house and our safe houses in case
they were targets," he said. "We were underground
when it went off. I just got up to street level. What do
you want us to do with the two women we caught?"

I looked to Mannix. "Demetrius caught the two
women who bombed his house."

"Tell him we have it all on security camera,"
Demetrius added. "I'll have a tape made for him."

"When the Arcane Bureau gets there, hand them over," Mannix said and smiled. "Tell him thank you."

"Will do," Demetrius replied before I parroted Mannix's words. "Keep safe, Ailis. I have to run. My people do not enjoy interacting with the authorities."

"Tell your people not to eat my people, and they'd probably have a different reaction," I said, and he laughed, ending the call.

"Do you want to tell me why you have the Master of the City on speed dial?"

"Remember that exchange student I told you about years ago, Demi Belov?" I asked, and he nodded. "That would be our new Master of the City, Demetrius. He said he has security footage of the bombing. He'll have a tape made."

"Demi, the exchange student is Demetrius? No fucking way." Mannix laughed. "You never mentioned he was a vampire."

"I didn't even know," I replied, making Mannix laugh harder. "Don't judge me. I was still pretty young and inexperienced."

"I'm not judging. It's just not often I hear of you being blindsided."

"Oh, it's happened plenty of times. But this one really bit my ass," I answered and left it at that.

Mannix took to the freeway on two wheels, lights flashing, and me gripping my seat as if I would fall out of the SUV. Shouts and orders played over the radio while Mannix gave me a quick rundown of what we were about to walk into. It was pure chaos. The main streets were bumper-to-bumper traffic with sirens blaring and lights flashing. It looked like every cop in town was on the job tonight. Mannix gave priority to ambulances and cut off anyone else foolish enough to tempt fate at intersections. I swallowed screams as he used his bumper to remind folks of why they were supposed to pull to the side of the road for emergency vehicles. When push came to shove, Mannix was a bull in a China shop.

"Idiots." Mannix nudged a small rusted car out of the way. The man in the car held his fist out of his window, receiving a middle finger from Mannix and a reason to need a new paint job.

We pulled off a main vein through the city into a residential neighborhood and parked two blocks from the cultural center. The street was lined with paramedics, fire and enough cops to make it look like the main dispatch had been relocated. The moment I opened the SUV door, I was bombarded with a hurricane of emotions. Terror and panic rended the air, mixing with smoke and blood. I pulled my shields closed, breathing through my mouth until the nausea faded. Mannix grabbed his bag from the backseat and took the lead. I followed him through the crowd of onlookers and gawkers. Why anyone would want to see the carnage was beyond me. I'd have been perfectly happy not having come at all. I had no interest in death and horror. People needed better hobbies, ones that didn't include someone else's final moments.

One glance up the road and my stomach flopped, making me stumble. Up ahead, where the hall once stood, was nothing more than half rubble and half burning building. I had never seen concrete burn before tonight. I couldn't imagine anyone surviving the kind of heat it would take to set stone on fire. The parking lot had been reduced to ruined vehicles, piles of concrete, burning wood, emergency personnel dragging bodies to the tents set up on the lawn, and random survivors wandering around in confusion. My eyes focused on small details, the kind that would find me in my dreams. Burned shoes, party decorations hooked on trees, a wine glass standing in the midst of the wreckage, and still-wrapped gifts. The scene was littered with destruction, and those willing to run into a burning building for those who may already be dead. A person's worst days were a fireman's every day, and tonight was an unfortunate example of their creed.

Screams of the injured, mixed with commands from firemen, filled my ears and pulled my attention in circles. Flashing red, white and blue, blazed in the otherwise pitch of the night, reducing the once peaceful street into nothing more than the stage of a tragic scene. The usual hush of a family neighborhood was now a canvas for the stench of death, cries of the dying, those seeing if their loved ones had made it out alive, and those responsible. There was no doubt in my mind, as I breathed in the auras of those still on the scene, that those who had created this nightmare were still here. I could feel it scratch at my brain like knowing a monster was under your bed.

No one would forget this night, including me. I stopped at the corner while Mannix spoke with the cops manning the police line. I glanced down the street to my left and groaned. A few blocks from here, in the park, was where the Witch's Market was held. The next time I went to the market, tonight would come to mind. Monsters ruined everything pretty. There wasn't a place in my life that wasn't affected in some heinous way by the cursed and the damned, human and creature alike. Even when the bad guys were caught, they still destroyed everything good they had touched.

"Detective Ashford," the cop at the police line said, extending his hand.

"Thomas, how's your sister? I was told she just had a baby?" Mannix replied.

"Almost nine pounds, if you can believe it. She's doing well, thank you for asking," Thomas answered, smiling. He eyed my badge and extended his hand to me, and I stared at it for a moment before shaking. It was unusual for people to be the first ones to offer their hand to me. It would take some getting used to. "Detective...Ket..."

"Kyteler, but Doc or Dr. K are fine if it's easier to remember," I said. "It's nice to meet you."

"I have a mind like a steel trap. I'll remember your name, Detective Kyteler." He twisted his fingers at the side of his head as though he were locking a door. "Your Captain is already on the scene. Good luck in there."

"Thanks, you take care." Mannix waved goodbye.

The tape lifted, and I followed Mannix into the scene. He pulled me up to his side. "Start remembering names, especially the full humans. When you meet them again, remind them in some way that you're not one of the monsters. It makes things go smoother. I make a point to find commonalities, something to remind others that I'm not the enemy."

"I'm used to being seen as a topside demon."

"You're not, and don't let anyone treat you as if you are," he answered. "If anyone out here behaves disrespectfully, let me or the captain know. We'll be a thorn in their sides until you receive an apology."

I nodded. "Thanks, Mannix."

"No one, shield or no shield, is treated like they are lesser, for any reason. It may happen elsewhere, but that shit doesn't slide with us." He paused, glancing around at what the night had in store for us. "I'm so sick of the way we all treat each other. Jesus, this world could be heaven if we all stopped shitting on each other."

I looked around the scene and almost laughed. "That's a mighty big dream, dear friend. This" —I motioned to the devastation—"is what we do to each other. We kill what we fear. We hate what we don't understand. Man discovered fire and used it to burn down their neighbor's house."

I followed Mannix onto the scene, feeling more and more queasy with each step forward. Four massive white canopies had been set up, tables and chairs set in the middle, food and supplies had already arrived. Groups of people were coming and going with a shuffle of mixed urgency and exhaustion. The faces of the emergency workers were grim with fatigue and agony of what they had witnessed. From what I could see, they were fighting a losing battle, trying to extinguish a fire that had more energy than they did while digging lifeless bodies from the rubble. Where the paramedics looked hopeless, the firefighters, as tired as they appeared, kept going back in, searching. I had yet to meet a hose jockey who didn't have the stamina of a demon and twice the determination. They'd work themselves to the bone and need to be dragged away, kicking and screaming, by their team. More than once, they had been quicker to arrive than the police and had helped me send a demon back to hell with nothing more than a hose, ax and more bravery than those trained to touch the pits. Hell was just another fire for them.

My new boss, Captain Troy Holland, jogged into the tent, covered in soot. His hands were black, and his clothes looked like he had crawled through the fire on his stomach. Holland was a big guy, towering over me and Mannix, and looked like he had retired from the army and never once missed his workout. He carried himself like he owned every room he stepped into, but his aura felt softer than my eyes told me. He was a dominating presence with a soul made for better things than nights like these.

"Ashford, Kyteler, I'm glad you're here," Holland said, cleaning the grime from his eyes with an already-blackened hankie. "I'm sorry this is your first day, Kyteler."

"What's the status, Captain?" Mannix asked, skipping the formalities. I took no insult. We didn't have time to shake hands and make small talk.

"Fucking ugly, that's what it is," he answered. "They're bringing in the dogs. We can hear people screaming in there, but there's too much rubble for us to see. We don't even know where to look."

"Waiting for the fire to die out for the dogs is going to cost a lot of lives." I dropped my bag onto the table and scanned the crowd. Not bothering to be asked for an opinion, I gave it anyway. "There are dozens of shifters here. Why not use what you have at your fingertips? Get them to help. They'll walk through fire for their people."

"And who the hell is going to ask them to track like a dog?" Mannix asked.

"I will," I replied when my eyes caught the attention of a few of the shifters I had met tonight. "The worst they can say is no."

"Do it," Holland answered. "The fire department is saying we have an hour, maybe less, before the rest of that building starts coming down."

I jogged to the last tent and found Rome's father sitting with a group of Rome's people. "Where is Rome?"

Calvin stood, bandages covering his face and arms. His pained face softened into a smile. "He's at Van General. He's injured, but he's okay."

I breathed a sigh of relief. "Mr. Bishop, we need your help."

"Of course. What do you need?"

I scrunched my nose and pursed my lips. "I don't know how to ask this, but we need a dozen shifters to track the scent of survivors. We don't have time to wait for the fire to go out for the hounds. The building is going to come down before that happens. We have, at most, an hour before those inside lose their chance of surviving."

Calvin chuckled until he realized I was serious. "You want to use shifters as dogs?"

"No," I said, then groaned. "Yes. I'm sorry, but people will die without your help. If asking makes me an asshole, so be it. I'd rather be an asshole, knowing we saved who we could, than be a coward who was too scared to ask for help."

"I'll do it." A young woman stood. She began pulling off her jacket. "I will need to shift. There are too many smells for my human nose, and I'm much stronger in my animal form."

Calvin looked back to the group. "Any other volunteers?"

Cole, the Mane from the werelion pride, stepped into the tent. "We will help. Point us to where you want us, and we've got this, Ailis."

"Thank you," I answered.

Mannix whistled, gaining Holland's attention. Holland was introduced to Cole, who would take the lead on the shifters tracking. Mannix and I went back to our tent and began setting up for the interviews. My stomach rolled, and my hands shook. I had interviewed survivors before and had sat in on magics accused of malfeasance. I had been there when witches were put to death and monsters needed to be hunted down. But tonight was different. Tonight, we stood in the middle of life and death, and every sound and smell reminded me of what was at stake. Unless we caught those killing the magics in our city, more would die.

Chapter Fourteen

I took a seat at one end of the tent, and Mannix sat at another. With my nervousness on high, it felt like we were a world apart, and I was on my own. I had conducted hundreds of interviews, but tonight, it felt different. I pulled out my notepad and pen and got to work immediately, noting all I had seen and done since getting to the site. Once I was ready, I gave Mannix a thumbs up. One by one, survivors were led into the tent. As soon as they sat across from me, I opened my shields just enough to feel the energy rolling off them, feel their emotions as I asked questions and provoked answers. Their answers were scattered, scared, fragmented and numb. They were all behaviors and emotions that I would expect from those who had just survived a direct attack on their lives. The majority of people weren't equipped to bounce back from life and death. Our souls weren't meant to suffer in such ways. My own soul hurt with each story told and terror I felt.

In between each disheveled victim, I took a few minutes to calm myself. Feeling their physical and emotional pain was almost too much for me. I kept having to remind myself that the grief I felt wasn't my own, but my soul hurt as though it were. Of the fifty people we questioned, those who had not been bussed out to the hospital, only two stood out. The second person I interviewed made my skin crawl. Such hate and joy mixed together, blending into something so intense that it turned my stomach. I couldn't figure out if her hate was directed at those around her or just me for being a witch. Each question I had asked her brought a new level of satisfaction that made me ball my hands. Mannix had flagged a young man for the same reasons. Both were held while the others were free to leave. They'd stay cuffed in the tents until they could be transported back to VSPD. Any survivors already at the hospital would be interviewed by the other members of Mannix's team, those who could smell a lie and those who could read souls with more ease than I could. I was glad we wouldn't be doing those interviews. Lowering my shields in a hospital would have left me a shambling, emotional mess.

I leaned against a police cruiser, drinking my third cup of coffee for the night, with Mannix at my side. It took nearly ten minutes before I had settled my soul enough to have anything to say that wasn't just a stream of swearing. Mannix was in the same boat, silent and hurting. My eyes scanned the crowd, picking up bits and pieces from each person. Exhaustion, anger, grief, utter revulsion, and a hint of contentment. The latter most likely came from the two cuffed in the tent. Under the waves of sadness, I could feel someone trying to contain their approval. It felt like Christmas morning and opening a gift you had been hoping for.

I leaned into Mannix. "The cop with the orange hair." I motioned with my head twenty feet to our right. The officer in question had eyes for the two we kept back. "He's hiding something. I don't know what it is, but his aura is all over the fucking map each time he looks at dumb and dumber in the tent."

"Everyone has eyes for the two responsible. It's not surprising that one of ours is thinking some nasty shit about our suspects. Even I've thought of unlocking them and letting the shifters deal with them." Mannix did a sweep of the crowd, his eyes landing on the man I was referring to. "Him? Branson is cheating on his wife with his patrol partner. His wife is on the scene. He's probably just shitting his pants that she'll find out."

"That's not it," I replied. "Cheaters feel like cheaters. They smell like sweat and lies. But with him, that's not what I'm picking up. There's too much going on inside his little head. There are flares of excitement, but under it all, I can feel uncertainty and anger, but it isn't the same as everyone else. I don't think he's pissed off that this happened. He's ticked that it wasn't worse."

"Are you sure?" Mannix asked.

I shrugged. "Every time Branson looks at the two that we tagged, his aura blazes. He's scared. Watch him while I go talk to the woman again. Pay attention to his aura and body language."

"I'm on it," he answered.

I went back to the woman, Cori Colins, handcuffed and under guard in the tent. With my notepad open, I took a seat. "Can I get you anything, Miss Colins?"

"Go fuck yourself," she said, glaring at me.

"Not tonight. As you can see, I'm pretty swamped." I smiled and jotted down her reply for my report later on. "I'm always surprised when offenders are dumb enough to stick around a crime scene."

"I don't know what you're talking about." She tugged at her cuffs, getting nowhere. "You have no right to hold me."

I tapped the badge hanging around my neck. "This little guy says I can."

"VSPD, what a joke. The Arcane Division has done nothing for this city." She rolled her eyes. "What do you want?"

"Why would you stay at the scene? The last group of you who were caught were killed by your own people. That should have been reason enough for you to blast and dash," I replied. "Imagine what would happen if we let you go. How long do you think you'd stay alive out there with your people hunting for you?"

"I don't know what you're talking about. I have no people."

"You have no people *now*. You're a dead woman walking." I corrected her. She smiled and huffed a laugh as if she didn't believe me. "I hope you're not counting on Officer Branson to save you. You're in VSPD custody now. He has zero pull in the Arcane Division."

Her eyes darted to the cop and back to me. "And?"

"That's all." I stood. "Thanks for your help."

"I didn't help you."

"Oh, but you did." I walked away back to Mannix. "She knows who Branson is. I didn't even have to point him out."

"His aura has been in flux since you sat down with her," Mannix said and motioned to the cop.

"It's still going wonky," I answered. "It's shimmering red with panic."

"He's going to run any second. I hate when they run from me." Mannix rolled his shoulders. Branson ran within seconds, and Mannix chased.

I whistled to the small group of shifters clustered close by as I started to run. "Grab the carrot top. But don't hurt him."

I booked it down the road, behind Mannix, who was much faster than I was. We weaved in and out of parked cars and crowds getting out of the way. The shifters flew past us, one by one, at a pace that ate up concrete in the blink of an eye. Branson was pushed down as they ran by him. He skipped across the road, leaving pieces of skin behind. I couldn't help but flinch at the sound of his body hitting the ground. Bones slamming into the pavement made my stomach turn.

"Why chase him down when you can have someone else do it for you?" I said to Mannix, coming to a stop beside him.

"Because they don't like me."

"We're scared of you," one of the shifters said, jogging back to us. I knew him from the university. He had attended night classes and a few seminars with his two younger sisters, who were earth witches. "Hey, Dr. K. You working with the coppers now? I got an email that your history class was canceled until further notice."

"Yes, I'm with VSPD now. They even gave me a shiny new badge," I answered. I felt no twinge of guilt over the canceled class. I thought I would feel embarrassed for losing my job, but I didn't. The only thing I felt was pride. I was attached to something that made a difference, however big or small. "I'll be teaching similar classes with the VSPD in the near future. I'll make sure I add your name to my mailing list so you and your sisters can attend."

"Walking into the cop shop without cuffs on my wrists, that'll be a nice change of pace," he joked.

"Thanks for your help, Paul," I replied.

"You have a weird life," Mannix said, standing over an unconscious Branson.

"It's why you wanted me on your team," I said, looking down at the crooked cop. "What do we do with him now?"

"Want us to eat him?" Came from the group.

"He'd probably taste like a rat," I said. "Can you carry him back for us?"

Paul picked up Branson and walked behind us as though Branson weighed no more than a sack of potatoes. A moment later, Mannix got a tap on the shoulder. A gun, two knives, and Branson's badge were handed over. "I took these off of him. I thought it best he didn't have them when he woke up. There's silver in that gun. I can smell it."

Mannix had Branson dropped at the feet of Holland. One look from Holland and I wondered if Branson would make it back to the station in one piece. Holland cuffed him and had him stuffed in the back of a suburban, out of his sight. None of us questioned if the unconscious man would receive medical attention. One glance around the scene and the destruction he had a hand in, and I didn't really care if Branson got a band-aid or not.

Holland gave us an update on the scene. The remaining parts of the building were starting to crumble, but the shifters were coming and going with survivors and bodies. Two dozen men and women had come to help, some in full shift and others still in human form, waiting outside the fire to carry those found back to safety. Those from various groups all worked together, and part of me was a little envious of their ability to put differences aside. Witches didn't do that, and neither did most humans.

Cori Colins still sat in the tent, unbothered by what had just unfolded. I paused as we walked back to the SUV. Cori was too calm, almost relieved. I'd have expected fear. It's what her counterpart had been oozing since being cuffed. Instead, she sat in her chair and smiled. There was no satisfaction for the dead, but there was something similar radiating from deep within. I doubled back to the tent and sat across from her. Her eyes met mine, and she sighed as though she knew I would be coming back.

"May I know the time, Detective Kyteler?" Cori asked.

No one got my name right on the first try. I frowned. "Why the sudden change in attitude? The last time I sat across from you, you told me off."

"The night is coming to an end, and I'm tired. May I know the exact time?"

I glanced at my watch. "Four twenty-seven."

She nodded. "It didn't take long, you know."

"For what?" I asked. "To kill and injure a few dozen people?"

"No. This was just the cost." Her smile widened when I motioned for her to continue. "It didn't take long to infiltrate Humans for Humans. Their desperation made them foolish and trusting. After Rome and his people came out of the shadows, they gave me the *in* I needed. I waved the secrets of werewolves under their noses, and they rolled out the red carpet for me."

I leaned forward. "What secrets?"

"Come now, Grimmwolf, we both know what I'm talking about," she replied, her lips curling into an uncomfortable grin. Her dark brown eyes gleamed with knowledge and power. Little sparks of energy filled the air around her. I could now feel the shields she held around her magic. "Secrets are worth more than money in this world, and it pays ten-fold to know them. Unfortunately, the Lycan secret was the only leverage I had that was of any use to me, but it's not *my* secret to keep. It's not like Pack has the power to knock on my door for telling their secrets, not unless my face was the last they wanted to see before their deaths."

"Why would you want to risk telling secrets you shouldn't know?"

"To stop Humans for Humans, of course." Her tone said I had asked a stupid question. "Did you really think Mrs. Davenport would stand by and watch?"

I groaned. "What does Mrs. Davenport have to do with this?"

"Everything," she replied. "HFH took my sister and her daughter, and now they will pay with their own lives. There is no place in this city where a man can hide. There is nowhere in this god-forsaken world that is out of our reach."

"Corali," I said as the first wave of her chaotic energy rolled out of her. Corali Davenport, the eldest daughter of Cordelia Davenport, sat before me. Her power was weaker than her mother's, but she had perfect control of her shields. One day, she'd follow in her mother's footsteps, if not rival them. I could feel the same edge of darkness in her that I had felt in her mother. Two Davenport witches would be hell on earth. "Necromancer."

"Good luck, detective. You're going to need it. Stay out of their way, and you may just live to see the sunrise. Don't say I didn't warn you."

I turned to call Mannix over, but was too late. The sky lit up like instant daylight in the distance. Radios on every hip and cop car started going off at the same time. Seconds later, Mannix began screaming at those around us, barking orders I knew would be useless. Nothing could stop what was coming. Mannix grabbed me from the tent, saying the Humans for Humans headquarters had been blown up, along with six houses and a few vehicles.

"It's the necromancer," I shouted to Mannix as we ran for the SUV. "The woman in the tent is Cordelia's daughter, Corali, the sister of the fourth vic. They're going after the HFH president. I thought Coven was in town to keep her shit from spilling out over the city? Didn't they have an eye on Corali?"

"They were, but Cordelia took it better than we thought she would. I told them to stick around? That Cordelia wouldn't show her cards until she knew she would win. They left, and now she's showing her hand. And the last I heard, Corali was still in Europe. Obviously, that intel was wrong." Mannix slid into his seat, started the vehicle, and reached for his radio, but whoever was on the other end had already found out what was coming their way.

"Fucking zombies!" Screamed over Mannix's radio. "There are zombies everywhere. Holy shit, there are dozens of them. They're coming from every direction."

I grabbed the radio. "Get out of their way! They're looking for Oliver Weiss, the president of Humans for Humans." The radio filled with screaming and cut out.

"How the hell do we stop zombies?" Mannix asked.

"You can't, not really. Cordelia is one of the strongest Necromancers in the country, if not the world," I replied. "Unless you burn them or kill Cordelia, those zombies aren't going back into the ground until their task is complete. Where is the ghoul squad? Ghouls are hunted in the same way as zombies."

"Most of them are training a team in Seattle," he replied. "There's only two in the city."

"Have them meet us at Weiss' house." I wondered if it was even worth the trouble. "Two ghoul hunters aren't going to make much of a difference, but it's better than nothing."

Mannix grabbed his radio and called in for backup. They were already suiting up, waiting on orders. "Fuck." Mannix slammed his hand on the steering wheel. "Do you have any spells that could work?"

"I don't know any that could best Cordelia's magic. She's more powerful than anything I could throw at her that isn't dark and straight out of the pits. Even both of us together, Mannix, we'll still come up short. Chaos witches like Cordelia are beyond level-three. They can use some of the darkest magics without taint or cost. They literally control the dead."

"Do you have any spells for fire? The ghoul team used flame throwers," he asked. "All I have is an inferno spell, *flamma*, but it's nothing more than a dime-sized ball of flame."

"*Flamma* calls forth a flame. That is why it is so small," I replied. "For a ball of fire, try *incoendo*. Then *ignis cinis*. It will command your flame to burn something to ash. Coat your hands in aura first, or you'll cook off your own flesh. *Incoendo* will create an apple-sized ball of fire in your hand. Once you throw it, focus your energy on the fire you've created and use *ignis cinis* to maintain the flames until only ash is remaining."

"What kind of taint does that carry?"

"None. You're not creating something out of nothing. Fire is a natural element and free for the taking, just like wind and water," I answered. "There's no taint for using it against zombies. They're already dead, so you're not killing anything. But, if the fire spreads and an innocent life is taken, the taint is as heavy as any other misfired spell resulting in a soul lost."

"How many balls of fire do you think you can muster?"

"A dozen, maybe?" I replied. "I wouldn't try for more than that. Not being on hallowed ground with a burned-away aura, no thank you. I'm not risking a demonic attack for the likes of Weiss."

"Two dozen balls of fire between the two of us isn't going to do a damn thing," he said, echoing my thoughts exactly.

I grabbed my cell phone and dialed Ziggy. "Let me check with Ziggy. If anyone would have a clue what to do, it would be him."

"Ailis," he answered on the third ring. "I do hope you're at home and not out chasing zombies."

"How did you know about them so quickly?" I asked.

"As I've said before, knowledge is power. Also, I just watched two dozen of them shuffle through Blood

Square. Three shifters are in rough shape after trying to stop them. I've been wondering how Cordelia would even the score."

"So have I," I replied. "But I was hoping it wouldn't be zombies."

"The daughter of a necromancer was murdered. What did you all think was going to happen? Cordelia is the closest thing to a demon with a soul we have on this side of the gates. Be thankful this is the only revenge she's cooked up."

I couldn't really argue that logic. I'd done some shady things for less. Had it been my child, I'd have opened the gates to hell in my grief and released every demon I could. Like Ziggy had said, we should probably be thankful all Cordelia was doing was raising a few graveyards. "Aside from killing the witch controlling them, is there a spell that will take them down?"

"Depends on how much you enjoy having a soul. To combat dark magic, you need to use dark magic. And the level of magic you'd need for the likes of Cordelia, would shave off your aura completely," he replied. "The only spells that would trump Davenport magic are black, unwritten, and carry enough taint to gain the notice of Coven. Not to mention, do you really want to be the one to stop her? Do you want her to have your name on her list? You just got the noose off your neck. Do you really want zombies knocking on your door next?"

"Not particularly."

"Perhaps this isn't a bad thing. The Davenports are doing us all a favor. It's a win-win for us all. Humans for Humans will be stopped, and Cordelia gets her revenge."

"And innocents will die in the crosshairs." I shook my head at his comment.

"No soul is truly innocent, Ailis," Ziggy said. My sigh was the only indication of my disagreement. Arguing semantics with a demon was a pointless pursuit. When it came to souls, we never saw eye to eye. Ziggy was one of the few who was more pragmatic than I was when it came to humanity. "If everyone stays out of their way, no one will be hurt except for those they have been summoned to kill."

"Since when do people stay out of the way?"

"This is true, but it doesn't change the fact that the only choice you have, knowing you're attached to that tattered thing you call a soul, is to stay out of their way. Once the risen have completed their task, they will return to their resting places. But, knowing your need to save the very rare and elusive innocent you speak of, understand that your circle of protection will not save you. Zombies are neither good nor bad. They're not evil or virtuous. Your circle will not recognize a zombie as it does a demon or any other form of magic, since you are not the one to summon them. The only way you can kill them is with fire, Cordelia's magic, Coven, or hell."

"That's not helpful," I answered. "There's got to be a spell I can use to protect myself and Mannix."

"Do you have hex bags? You can ward yourself and Mannix, making yourself unseen to all. This chaos will attract whatever demons are top-side at the moment, so it's not a bad idea to put them on regardless."

"What's the invocation to be unseen?"

"*Umbra*. It's more that you'll become a shadow, blending into your surroundings."

"What is the cost for that spell? How much taint?"

"Using natural elements has no cost. You are borrowing from the darkness. Since it is night, you're not needing to create it," Ziggy answered. "Just like with your fire spells. Now, if your darkness were to spread and something bad were to happen to someone, the taint would be the same as with any other life-ending spell."

"Thank you, Ziggy." I hung up before he could correct me. I knew he'd message me whatever his cost was for information. Nothing was free in this world.

"Did I hear that right?" Mannix asked, speeding through the residential streets. "Can hex bags hide us?"

"I don't know, but it's better than nothing. To be honest, I don't think we'll be able to do a damn thing. We may save a life or two, but we're no match for hordes of undead."

Thankfully, the traffic was next to nothing at half past four in the morning. But Mannix still took corners without slowing down. I closed my eyes and pursed my lips, doing everything I could to keep myself from screaming. When we slowed and my lungs filled with the stench of freshly dead and rotting corpses, I opened them to a nightmare. I had expected a few dozen, but was met with hundreds of decomposing bodies. The shambling dead filled a block of one of the more upscale neighborhoods in West Van. Cops were locked in their vehicles, and paramedics were dragging the injured off the roads. As long as they didn't get in the way, they were probably safe. Maybe. I hoped.

Shouting and sirens filled my ears. A woman stumbled by my window. She was elderly, with gray hair hanging in strands. Her once-dark complexion was rotting and hanging from her bones. She had been buried in her Sunday best, which now sunk into the parts of her that had started to fall apart. She was fresh enough for me to almost see what she would have looked like in life, but her squishy sounds reminded me of just how dead she really was. I turned away from my window and swallowed the vomit in my throat. Cordelia had the power to make zombies look as fresh as the day they had been put into the ground. That she released them all in their rotten state was a terrifying message.

"Oh, my god," I whispered, seeing the waves of death ahead of us.

"Oliver Weiss' house is at the end of the street." Mannix reached for his door.

I pulled him back. "Are you insane? There are hundreds of zombies with his name. What is your plan? How the hell do you suppose we save him?"

"We have to try," he replied.

"Try to do what? Me and you against what, a few hundred zombies? Have you seen what one undead can do? They will tear their way through a body, car, house, brick, or rock to get at those they were sent to kill. Nothing stands in their way. They feel no pain, no remorse, nothing but the drive to finish what they were sent for," I answered, motioning outside at the horde moving toward the house at the end of the block. "Cordelia wasn't fucking around, Mannix. She's out for blood, and I'm not going to let her have any of mine."

"So, we just sit here and do nothing?" he asked.

"No, we save those who have a hope in hell. I hate to break it to you, but Oliver isn't one of them. He was dead the moment he chose a Davenport to kill," I replied. "We save the innocents. It's all we can do."

"That's cold, even for you."

"No, it's just the truth. We can save who we can, or we can go down trying to save someone who will be dead before breakfast, with or without us," I answered. "There is no way we can save him, and I'm not dying to extend his life for a few extra minutes."

"We save the innocents. Stay on my six." He pushed his door open once the wave of dead had made their way past the SUV.

"Stay the hell out of their way. Shoot for the head, destroy whatever brain they have left." I dug into my backpack and pulled out two hex bags. I needle pricked my thumb and invocated the bags. Giving one to Mannix and hanging one over my head, I stuffed the rest in my pocket for the emergency personnel we'd find in the streets. I opened my door with a shaking hand and felt a wave of regret. "This is a bad idea."

Chapter Fifteen

My body trembled in tune with the graveyard army's march toward their prey. A symphony of steps and shuffles, each perfectly aligned with the one next to it, mixed with the terror-filled screams throughout the neighborhood. Even the most ignorant of souls, just waking up to the carnage, would know not to step outside. But people do stupid things every day that end their lives. Opening a door to a zombie wasn't that big of a stretch.

The stench that hung in the air rolled my stomach. It didn't match what I could see. It should have smelled like spring, wet grass and early-season flowers. Instead, it smelled like rotting meat and flesh, sludgy dirt and mold. My eyes watered, and my throat convulsed around my need to be sick. The once pristine neighborhood had become ground zero of everyone's worst nightmare, ones that would haunt us all. Gone was the sound of peace and tranquility that only old money could buy, replaced with the screams of those caught in the middle of a bloody war no one had seen coming. We should have seen it coming. The Davenports were the most feared witch family for a reason. Generations of Davenports had held their position at the top of the magical food chain. This shouldn't have come out of left field. Yet, here we were, out in left field.

Working as a team, we joined the emergency crews, pulling people off the road and filling vehicles with body after body, some alive and some missing too many parts and pieces to be put back together. Those who had left the safety of their homes were dead, dying, or frozen in fear. The upper crust of society rarely caught a glimpse of the world they really lived in and were sorely unprepared. Seeing the underbelly of what real magic could do was a once-in-a-lifetime event, and for some, it was the last thing they saw. For this little slice of the city, monsters didn't knock on the golden doors of the rich, not unless it was a demon who helped them build their fortunes. But even then, soul collectors rarely made such a ruckus.

"Cal! Jax!" Mannix called out over the whirlwind of sirens, screams and shambling grunts.

He motioned to two men jogging up the street, both carrying machetes and loaded with more weapons than I had ever seen one man carry. Anyone who needed that much firepower was doomed, in my opinion. I recognized the one man, Cal. Calvin Raynott was the nymph who'd interviewed me after I had killed the previous Master of the City's human servant, Elizabet. To this day, I didn't regret her death. The world was a better place without her. To his left was Jax, who I didn't know. The closer they got to me, the more familiar Jax's energy became. He was a shifter. The warmth pouring off him in waves reminded me of Cole, the werelion. I forced myself not to take a step back. Although he felt soft against my soul, under the calm, he was a raging inferno of emotions that grated along my aura.

"Two witches on site, and the neighborhood is still standing? You bring shame to the Sin Squad," Calvin said, coming to a stop beside me. With him, I stepped back when his power rolled over me. Unlike the first time we had met, he wasn't holding his energy back. Before I could introduce myself, he pointed at Oliver's house. "We just got word that Weiss is locked in his upstairs panic room. He has his grandkids here."

"Children? How many?" Mannix asked.

Jax nodded. "Three kids, all under ten. Holland sent us. His orders are to save the kids at all costs."

"Fuck," I groaned.

"Don't like kids?" Jax asked me, grinning.

"I don't like dying," I replied. "What about Wiess?"

Calvin shook his head. "There's no saving a man marked by a Davenport. There is nowhere in this world where he can hide, and Holland isn't going to risk the detachment by bringing him in."

"Am I the only one who thinks all lives have value?" Mannix asked.

"Yes," I said and Calvin and Jax echoed me.

Mannix rolled his eyes. "Where are the ghoul hunters?"

"Hospital," Jax replied. "They were taken out not but ten minutes onto the scene."

"Shit," Mannix groaned. "Are we the only team available?"

"Yes," Calvin answered. "It's fucking chaos there. The city is literally burning. HFH is out in full force, retaliating against the bombing of their headquarters."

"Against who?" Mannix asked. "They'll never touch a Davenport."

"Against every and any magic they can find," Jax said, sliding his duffle bag off and opening it up. "Time to suit up, witch."

"How can you tell I'm a witch? Do I smell like Mannix?" I asked.

"Because everyone knows who you are after your little run-in with those we shall not name. If I didn't know you, I'd have guessed you are a level-three witch or demon. I hate to say it, but you smell like hell and lightning. Mannix smells like an electrical fire. But you, you smell like a storm that'll burn down a village. What do I smell like to you?"

"I can't really sense through smell unless it's a familiar scent, but I can feel you. You feel like standing too close to an angry dog who has a history of mauling children. My brain is telling me to back up," I answered. "At first, you give off energy that is almost relaxing. But under it all, I don't think I'd want to piss you off."

He grinned. "The sharp edge of my emotions that you're feeling is because the full moon is in two days. I'm amped up and excited for the hunt. It brings my animal closer to the surface. Lions are predatory by nature, and the moon executes it."

"If you shift, what do you want me to do? Duck and cover? Keep moving forward?" I asked. "How long will it take for you to get your shit back together? Do you need me standing over you, protecting you until then?"

"That's cute, a witch protecting a shifter," he replied. "I'm an Alpha, just below our Mane. The shift will be quick, and I'll be ready within seconds. But I'd suggest you back up and be out of reach during the shift. While I have complete control of my claws, accidents happen, and I don't want to be the reason we're sitting under the full moon together if your holy water bath fails."

"Noted," I answered.

He handed me a machete and began strapping my thighs with weapons while Calvin and Mannix decided our best approach. Jax said very little while his eyes scanned the road and yards for possible threats. His nose twitched every now and again, scenting the risks around us. I had seen Miguel do this hundreds of times, long before I had even known he was Lycan. I had chalked it up to a keen sense of smell. Little did I know.

I dug out two hex bags from my pocket. I tossed one to Cal and handed one down to Jax. Jax put his in his pocket immediately, without even knowing what it had been. "This should keep you in the shadows. It'll help you go unnoticed until you make yourself a spotlight."

Cal put his hex bag around his neck without asking any questions either. Most people were overly cautious when a witch handed them something, but Calvin or Jax were obviously used to working with witches to have that level of faith.

"Thank you," Jax said. "I love when Mannix brings out the magic. It means I get to go home at the end of the night and not to the hospital."

"You're welcome." I checked out the new gear he had given me. "Thanks for the equipment."

"Can't have you dying on your first night," he joked. "The others would make fun of me."

"All right," Mannix called our attention to him. "We will make our way to Weiss' house in two groups.

Along the way, we save who we can. We help any innocents between here and the house of zombies."

"What's the drill when we get to Weiss' house?" I asked.

"Our only objective is the children. Anything more is gravy," he answered. "Jax and Doc, you two take the right. Me and Cal are on the left. Stay tight. Stay down."

I opened my hand, covered it in aura, and called a small ball of fire into my palm. Mannix mirrored me and took up position on the other side of the street with Calvin. With nods, we began our trek into the heart of Cordelia's revenge. I got behind Jax, to his right, and followed him up the block. He held a black, high-powered rifle with a scope mounted on the top, his finger a half inch from the trigger. He moved like every military man I had ever met. I didn't know if he had ever served, but everything about him had said he had the kind of training that killed those he set his sights on. His movements were silent, and every step had a purpose. His head moved side to side, keeping every inch of the block in full view. At his back, I held my handgun in one hand and a small ball of fire in the other. I felt sorely unprepared, like every innocent on this block.

We maneuvered around the emergency personnel who were moving in and out of the wreckage, dragging the injured to the side of the road. They were unarmed but still did all they could. I had a whole new level of respect for those who suited up even though the cards were stacked against them. Scared or not, they were here.

Twenty feet from our starting point, Jax lifted his hand, pausing us both. A burgundy-bricked house, at the end of a black paved drive, stood in complete darkness to our right. I lowered my shields just enough to sense why Jax had stopped us. Panic and fear filled my aura, and I slammed my shields back up. I didn't want to feel what was causing the terror, or worse, feel it all come to an end. Sensing someone's final moments scarred me in ways I never truly recovered from. Jax motioned to the house, and I cringed. I didn't want to go into that house, but I still followed him. Before we got to the front door, he pulled me to the side, behind the hedge-lined drive. Three zombies shuffled out of the house. All three were painted in the blood of the unfortunate occupants of the house.

"Too late," I whispered and felt for life beyond the walls of the dark house. "I don't feel any soul alive in there."

Jax nodded. "My guess is whoever lived here was tied to HFH."

"Do we let the zombies go or take them out?" I asked.

"They have a taste for blood now. They'll only pose a greater risk if we let them go," he replied. "I'll take them down. You burn them."

Jax fired three silent shots with expert precision. Following behind him, I dropped my ball of fire in the middle of them, and we left them to burn on the front lawn, continuing our way up the street without looking back. My flames would burn until there was nothing left to keep the fire going. Jax nudged me and pointed across the road. Mannix was motioning to the end of the street. Weiss' house sat behind what once was a massive black iron gate with six-foot-high brick walls. The gate was now sitting twisted on the ground, surrounded by shattered bricks scattered down the driveway. Between the children and us stood more undead than I could count, and each one was making their way into the house, hunting for one soul and killing those who got in their way. In the distance, pop shots echoed through the night.

"Let's hope your hex bags work," Jax said and proceeded forward.

"No pressure," I replied.

"I'll go in first. You stay at my rear. We clear each room together. Neither of us takes a room alone. Keep your head in the game and on nothing else. Mannix and Calvin will make their own way in. If one of them goes down, we keep moving forward. They have a partner to help them. We go in together, we leave together," he whispered. "Clear?"

"Crystal," I said. "Have you hunted zombies before?"

"Unfortunately, I have. You?"

"Enough times for me to not want to go into that house," I answered.

"In and out. We are here for three children, nothing more," he said. "Headshots, drag them outside and burn them if we have the chance. If we can't get them outside, we'll light the place up on our way out."

The hex bags held as we moved through those sent by Cordelia. Chunks of meat and other things clung to my clothes as we inched our way through. The sound of peeling flesh made my stomach climb into my throat. I held my breath until I had no choice but to breathe in or pass out. With my hand on Jax's shoulder, we cleared the front gate. Instead of going through the front door, Jax took us around the side of the house and pointed to a fire escape bolted to the side of the house, leading up to the third floor. I thanked the gods this house was up to code and had an alternative way in and out.

"This leads to the old maid's quarters, one floor above Weiss' safe room," Jax said, climbing the first few rungs of the ladder. "If we have to, we can go through the floor to get to Weiss' bedroom."

I gripped the ladder behind him and climbed. I didn't look down. I wasn't a fan of heights, or anything that risked my life. My nerves were far too shot to convince myself not to be scared, and I white-knuckled the ladder. Floor by floor, we made our way up and paused outside the maid's bedroom. Jax opened the window and went in first. A moment that felt like it had stretched into years went by before Jax held a thumbs up out of the window. I climbed the last few feet and pushed myself into the house. The smell was worse than I could have imagined, like stepping into a closed dumpster on a hot day. My eyes watered instantly.

"Dear god, I'm going to be sick," I said, tucking my nose and mouth into the crook of my arm.

"Puke later," he said and took a step to the door. "Mannix and Calvin are inside."

"How can you smell them through the stink of rot?" I asked.

He chuckled and pointed at his ear. "Radio. I can't smell shit in this hellhole."

Jax reached the door and slowly pulled it open a crack, peering into the hall. With one nod, he opened it and stepped out of the false safety of the maid's ignored room. With my pulse pounding in my ears, I tapped his shoulder and followed him into the house of horror. The smell intensified. Rotting meat and gasses of the dead. I swallowed my gag and tried to breathe through my mouth, making it worse. Tasting a zombie was no better than smelling one. Jax tilted his head and motioned to the stairs. We went down one set of stairs before we saw the masses in the hallway of the second floor.

Making our way through the hall felt like swimming against a current. It was shoulder to shoulder of death. Jax grabbed my arm and pulled me through the shambling dead, my feet squishing into the carpet. Ahead, I caught a glimpse of Mannix. Calvin was in front of him. The master bedroom was in view, and before I clutched a thread of hope, the house erupted in shouting and the ever-so-familiar sound of a shotgun. Weiss and his people were making a last stand. Jax pulled me to the side, against the wall and out of reach of the shotgun blasts. The jerk sent me to my knees, sliding in the goop of the dead. I stifled my scream when I felt Jax's hand slip from my grip.

"Go!" I yelled at him. "Get the kids. I'll meet you there."

"See you on the other side," he replied.

I clung to those passing by, pulling myself to my feet. I was covered in fluids, tissues and bits I didn't even want to look at. The mutterings of those without jaws and tongues were soon replaced with screaming and more gunshots. I gripped my gun and pushed my way down the hall, sliding between bodies and strong-arming my way to the bedroom. At the front of the line, Weiss was dead on the floor, a half dozen of his people at his side, long gone. The door to the safe room was demolished, warped and dented on the floor. Mannix and the team were in the corner of the room. Behind them, three bloody children. I hated scenes involving children.

"He's not dead," I said, pointing at Weiss. If he were, the zombies would be gone. Since no one here was going to finish the job, the only thing we could do was get the hell out of their way. "Go through the drywall," I screamed to Mannix, pointing at the wall to their right. "Get to the ladder."

"What about you?" he asked.

"I'm torching the place," I answered. "I'll be fine."

"We go in together, we leave together," Jax replied. "I'm with the witch. You two get the kids out. We'll meet you at the SUV."

Jax kicked the drywall until a hole opened up. He tore the remaining wall apart, kicking two studs out of their positions. Mannix picked up the two smallest children, and Calvin lifted the other into his arms. Once they stopped shooting at the undead, they surged forward, pushing me with them. I pocketed my gun and balled two fists of fire. I closed my eyes and whispered *ignis cinis,* throwing the flames into the middle of the horde.

"*Peruro,*" I said, setting the fire to scorch, burning everything it touched to ash. It spread like a hot summer day in a field of straw. I glanced at Jax, who had a surprised look on his face. "Move your ass! We're just as flammable in a fire like this as the dead are."

Jax snapped out of it, grabbed my hand, and half dragged me through the wall and up the stairs, the fire hot on our trail. We went out the same way we came in. At the bottom, the yard was already beginning to clear out. One look around told me Weiss was dead. Before we hit the driveway, the world around us popped in complete and bone-chilling silence. Ahead of us, zombies shuffled out of Oliver Weiss' yard through the torn-down gate. The undead who had been overcome by the flames didn't make it very far. They burned to ash on the lawn. Those who made it out of the fire marched back down the street, bothering no one, back to whatever hole they had crawled out of. I jogged beside Jax out of the yard while the house was engulfed in flames. We met Mannix and Calvin at the curb.

"Stay out of their way, and they'll return to their graves," Mannix said over his radio. "When it's safe, clear the scene and check on the occupants of the houses. Update the medical examiner. There's a few houses on the block with bodies."

We dropped the kids off with paramedics and walked down the middle of the road to the SUV. "What now?" I asked.

"Shower," Jax said, picking at his shirt. "Maybe two showers."

"Write my report, grab a few hours of sleep before we're back at it again," Calvin said, flicking remains off his hands. "But first, a shower."

At the SUV, Jax and Calvin gave me a fist bump before making their way to their vehicle a block down the road. I climbed into the SUV on legs that felt like they weighed a hundred pounds each. Mannix put the SUV in reverse. "Now, I drop you at the hospital. We don't do scene clean-up."

"I'm sorry we were too late to help everyone," I said as we turned around.

"We're always too late. Just once, I'd like to be on time."

"I can't count the number of times I've said those exact words," I replied.

"When you're at the hospital, if you pick up any weird vibes, call me," he said, turning his lights back on but keeping the siren off.

The drive to the hospital was quiet. I was tired, shaky from fried nerves, and wanted nothing more than to see my family and curl into their hugs. "Thanks, Mannix."

"You did great for your first night. Hopefully, your second night won't be so exciting. See you tomorrow. You now have a mountain of reports to do," he said. "And don't forget to sign your paperwork. Welcome to the Sin Squad."

I rolled my eyes, but the name was starting to grow on me.

Chapter Sixteen

With a badge around my neck and an official jacket on, no one stopped me when I walked through the hospital, even though I was covered in zombie parts. In the emergency room, Miguel found me first. He said he had smelled me pull up. The only news so far was that Samuel was in surgery. I did my best to clean myself, but I still stank like the inside of a year-old casket. I paced. I drank coffee. I made my notes for my report tomorrow. I paced some more. Mannix showed up to the hospital three hours later with my paperwork. I signed off on the documents. He said my official gun was sitting on my desk in the office across from his. He'd put my name on the door before heading over.

"It's not as fancy as your last office, but you're probably not going to need a window to chuck people out of." He laughed. "There's now a sign hanging at the start of our wing, the demon department, to make you feel more at home."

"Did you give up on the Sin Squad?" I asked.

"Oh, hell no. I'm going to make us special patches," he replied.

Rome limped into the waiting room, wearing a gown. "Any news on Samuel?"

Mairi stood first. "My dear, you shouldn't be out of bed."

"Give him a few hours, and he'll be fine," Cisco said, walking in behind him. "He got bored, so we went for a walk to the nurse's station."

"When Samuel felt something was wrong, he pulled me out of the way. I landed on Mairi," Rome replied, taking a seat beside her. "Samuel got on top of two kids to shield them. He took one hell of a blast."

Mannix took his leave, saying he had a few witnesses to follow up on in the intensive care unit. We all went back to waiting and watching videos Cisco pulled up on his cellphone. When the doors opened and a doctor came in, my stomach fell into my feet, and a small yelp escaped my lips. She looked as tired as I felt.

"I'm looking for Mr. Carmine's granddaughter, Ailis Kyteler," she said.

I stood. "I'm Ailis."

She smiled, and my legs gave out. Miguel caught me before I hit the floor. "He's going to be okay. The explosion caused significant damage to his kidneys and liver, but we got the bleeding under control. He should make a full recovery."

"When can I see him?" I asked.

"Only family for the next few days," she replied. "You and Mairi are listed as family on his documentation."

I grabbed Mairi's hand and followed the doctor to Samuel. I broke down crying the moment I saw him. I dropped to my knees beside his bed and bawled my eyes out, both sad and relieved at once. Mairi began spreading out stones and herbs, praying to her Gods, while I thanked every God I could think of for sparing Samuel. Eventually, Mairi pulled a chair to the bed and sat me in it, covering me with a blanket. I fell asleep and woke up in the same position, Samuel's hand in mine, my head on his legs, my arm draped over him.

"Ailis," Samuel whispered my name. "You smell horrendous."

I jerked awake. "Sam."

"You know I hate…"

"When I call you that," I answered for him. "Thank God."

"Go home, child, and wash the zombies off of you. I'm okay," he said and saw Mairi asleep on the small couch against the wall. A small smile formed on his face. "I'm in good hands."

"How long have you two been an item?" I asked.

"About ten years," he said.

"Why didn't you tell me?"

"Because you had just lost your parents. You needed me more than Mairi did," he answered.

I smiled. "You need Mairi more than I need you."

"We all need each other. That's what makes us family," Mairi said from the edge of the room. "We both love you dearly, Ailis, and we will always come when you need us."

"That's what family does," Samuel added. He tried twice to grab the badge hanging around my neck before giving up. He was still too weak. "The Arcane Division, it looks good on you."

"My first day was a little hairy," I replied.

"You were made for saving souls, Ailis. You've taught those you can. Now you'll save who the others can't." Samuel patted my hand. "You're so much like your mother. From your wild soul to your need to do what is right, no matter the cost. And like your father, you're not one to back down, no matter how scared you are."

My eyes watered, and my next words squeaked out. "Do you think they'd be proud of me, my parents?"

"Of course," he replied. "I am proud of you every day, just as they would be. When you stood up to Pack to save Rome, I knew you would be just fine out in the world. Sure, you'd need a bandage here and there, but I knew your soul would make it. And at the end of this all, that's all that matters."

"I love you," I said and gave him a gentle hug. I checked my watch. "I have to shower, change, and go to work."

"No rest for the wicked," he joked.

I hugged Mairi and left them to hug each other. Miguel drove me home, where I showered, took a power nap in the arms of someone I loved, and dressed for work. With my lunch in my hand and butterflies in my stomach, I walked into VSPD. I made my way through the lobby and scanned my ID at the rear door into the inner building. The door clicked, and I walked in. The first two officers who walked by me, nodded as though I had belonged there. It gave me the boost I didn't even know I needed. Mannix was heading my way with a stack of files before I cleared the inner lobby.

"Right on time," he said. "We have thirty minutes before we brief Captain Holland."

I followed him to the demon department and to my new desk across from Mannix. On the top sat a lock box with my gun. I holstered it and followed Mannix to

Holland's office, a floor up and through a maze of halls, desks and phones that didn't stop ringing.

Mannix knocked on the door and poked his head in. "Good time?"

"Come in, Ashford. Is Kyteler with you?" Captain Holland asked. His voice cut through the air like a knife to butter, but under the exhaustion, his energy felt kind.

Mannix pushed the door open, and we both went inside. He stood and offered his hand. A firm handshake and smile. "Since I wasn't able to officially welcome you last night, welcome to the team, Kyteler."

"It's a pleasure to meet you without bodies on the ground," I replied. I stared at our connected hands and the static running up my arm.

"Take a guess," he said and looked at Mannix. "No helping her."

I blurred my eyes and immediately sighed. His aura was pure, hopeful and protective. "I want to say you're a mystic, but you're much more than that, aren't you?"

"Yes."

I breathed him in and let my aura slide over his. In the back of my mind, I could see Holland in all his glory. I could feel his power, almost taste it. "I've only met one other like you in New York, and she was magnificent in every way. To stand near her felt like touching heaven. Your father was a warlock, but your mother was a mystic. You take after your mother, but you're one of the rare few who can use magic without earning taint."

He smiled. "You met my sister, then. She's an agent for the FBI out that way, in their Arcane Division."

"I did. I worked a case with her," I said.

"How'd you guess?" Mannix asked me. "I didn't."

"I wouldn't have guessed if it hadn't been for meeting his sister," I replied.

"Update on the bombings?" Holland said, taking a seat and getting straight to business.

"We received a package from the Davenports last night before the shambling dead did their bidding. It contained a thumb drive full of documents, surveillance, plans, videos, and admissions. We're still going through it all, but we've managed to snag seven members of Humans for Humans in the last few hours. Those files should bring the rest of the group to their knees," Mannix said. "The two cops associated are chatty Kathy's. Everyone is talking. I kicked them up to Richards. He'll be taking the lead with the Corruption Division. He can sort out who gets offered the deals. Cori Colins, AKA Corali Davenport, vanished from custody. Her cuffs were found on the floor of her open cage. Nothing on the cameras. I doubt we'll find her."

"No one has ever held a Davenport. Coven has been notified," Holland replied. "How many dead?"

"Twenty-one dead, and over forty injured at the community center," Mannix read from his file. "The undead killed seven people, one of which was Oliver Weiss. Three were his guards, and the rest were civilians. In the neighborhood, nineteen were injured, including two members of our ghoul squad."

"Have you read Kyteler in on all of our confidentials?" Holland asked, and from the confused look I knew I had plastered on my face, he didn't wait for the answer. "Ashford will read you in on confidential files containing magics unknown to the general public. Some you may already know of, some you may not. There's a world beneath the world you've grown to know and trust, with species living in the shadows."

"For example?" I asked, his comments piquing my curiosity.

"Top-side demons, daywalking vampires, and the elves aren't extinct. Those are just three of my open cases," Mannix replied. "There are a few binders on your desk. You'll find every known creature, species, magic and monster. You'll find every case file and report we've ever received on the Arcane system, as well. This afternoon, I'll read you in on the active cases we're still hunting."

I nodded slowly. "I knew about the top-side demons and elves, but daywalking vampires? That's a terrifying thought."

"A Dhampir," Mannix answered. "The child of a freshly made vampire and human. They're rare and are usually hunted down by the Elders, but every now and again, one goes unnoticed and becomes our problem."

"Sounds like a really big problem to have." I cringed at the thought of losing the sun as the only real protection against a vampire.

"Kyteler," Holland said, frowning. "You need a nickname. No one is going to remember how to pronounce your name. What does everyone else call you?"

"Dr. K. and Doc. My students butchered my name as well."

"All right, Doc it is. Where's your report?" Holland asked.

I pulled out my cell phone. "What's your email address? I wrote it while at the hospital. I assumed it would be the same format as when I consult?"

"I'll take that for now. Ashford will show you our systems. You can type them up on our forms moving forward," he replied. "There's an encrypted app for our systems that you can download if that's easier."

"I'll give her the grand tour and get her settled in today," Mannix said. "She's not on rotation until tomorrow night."

"Good, good," Holland said. "You still must complete boot camp, or our insurance won't cover you, but we'll figure it into your schedule. I hope you decide to stay longer than your probation. We can use all the help we can get."

I stood when Mannix did. "Thank you."

I followed Mannix to my office and touched the writing on my door. *Dr. Ailis Kyteler*. Mannix logged me into my computer and handed me a printout of my passwords. My first job was to change them all, since they'd expire in twenty-four hours and I'd be locked out. Thankfully, the system was straightforward, and everything was within one central database. Four white binders sat on my desk with hard copies of forms to use in the field.

"Can I bring some books in?" I asked.

"Of course. Bring in whatever you'd like," Mannix replied. "I'm sure you'll have better books than our library, anyway. I'd be interested in taking a look at whatever you've got."

Once I changed my passwords, I got the grand tour of the areas I hadn't seen the first time I had come, which were two floors, a smaller cafeteria, holdings, and interrogation. Rounding it off, Mannix introduced me to a few members of our team. A witch, a shifter, and a nymph. The rest of the team wasn't on shift until eight tonight.

"Everyone, this is Doc. Doc, this is everyone," Mannix said, leading me into the breakroom. "You've already met Cal, our resident mythology expert, and Jax, our cryptozoologist."

"I didn't think Mannix was telling the truth until I saw you kicking ass last night." Calvin stood. The energy pouring from him was as I had remembered. He held out his hand. "Welcome to the team, Doc. That's such an easier name to remember. When we met, I had to practice your name for five minutes, so I wouldn't screw it up and embarrass myself."

I laughed, shook his hand, and stared at my palm afterward. His energy felt unusual, almost prickly. I hadn't noticed it to this extent the first time we had met. Then again, I had just killed a human servant and wasn't as focused as I was today. "Nice to see you without bodies on the ground."

"I'm sure there will be plenty of bodies, but hopefully, you won't be the reason."

"I can't make any promises," I joked.

He leaned in. "You'll get used to my energy. I'm sorry, that's as dim as the power goes, I'm afraid."

"It's okay," I said, rubbing my hands down my arms. "It just feels like spiders on my skin."

"You wouldn't like it on full blast," Mannix said. "It feels like stabbing pain."

"Good defense mechanism," I replied.

"It's better than Mannix, whose defensive techniques are screaming and running," Calvin answered, elbowing Mannix and getting a round of laughs from the team.

"You scream like a girl once, and you never live it down," Mannix said and motioned to a grinning witch. "And this is Abi, our magiologist and magical historian. If you need to know anything about magic, spells, charms, and curses, she'll hunt it down for you."

"I'm Abigail Barker, but my friends call me Abi," she said with a thick English accent. The witch stepped between the men to shake my hand, smiling. I felt her magic the moment her skin touched mine. It was soft and earthy, and it felt like every worry I had could be solved in an afternoon in her presence. She was a healer first and a card-carrying witch second. She didn't pull her hand away or wipe it when she was done. Her face was glowing, and her smile was genuine. "I'm so happy to finally meet you. I've heard so much about you over the years. I took a few of your night classes when I first transferred here, and I was so disappointed to hear of you leaving the university. But this, you here with us, is brilliant. I'm so excited to be working with you. I can't tell you how pleased I was to hear of you coming onboard."

"Thank you. I look forward to working with you as well." I smiled and felt my face heat up. It was a rare occasion to be welcomed like this. "Barker, that's an old name. Any relation to the Massachusetts Barker family?"

Abi looked surprised. "Indeed, on my father's side. You know of them?"

"Hard not to," I answered. "They were one of the most prominent families to ever stand accused of witchcraft during the 1682 trials in Andover, Massachusetts. Members of the Barker family admitted to attending a meeting of one hundred witches in Salem Village, led by the devil himself. They were one of the first families I had learned about in school. To this day, the Barker family is part of every history syllabus on magic and witchcraft."

"We are the children of witches they didn't burn," she replied, a look of pride filling her eyes.

"They certainly tried to get all of us," I answered and glanced at the shifter, Jax. "Thank you for having my back. Not just last night, but for calling Mannix when I was in some pretty deep shit."

"It's the least I could do." Jax skipped the handshake and hugged me. "Rome is a friend of mine. I met him a few months after his attack. Thank you for what you did for him and his people."

I was surprised at how informal he was, but shifters were more touchy-feely than others. He gave me the kind of hug you saved for your friends and family. "You're welcome."

He set me down and finally extended his hand. "I'm Jackson Stoll, the team cryptozoologist and lion of the Dawnguard Pride. But please, call me Jax. You've met my Mane, Cole. He's spoken highly of you. I'm glad to see you made it out of your...recent issues alive."

"Recent issues," I scoffed. "Thank you. It's a pleasure to meet you."

"We were just talking about you, actually," he said, pushing out a chair for me.

"All good, I hope," I answered.

"We were wagering how long it would take before the rest of the world found out about Pack," Jax said, and I swallowed a rock in my throat. "Don't worry, the rest of these guys found out through government channels. Lycan isn't a new species. They're in the first draft edition of the Catalog."

I thought about what I could and couldn't say and went with saying as little as possible. I liked my head where it was, attached to my body. "If there are secrets to come to light, it won't take long. Nothing stays in the dark for good. The Davenports sold a lot of secrets to infiltrate HFH, including that one."

"You should see the news this afternoon," Jax replied. "Humans for Humans sent in a prerecorded tape with the late Oliver Wiess stirring the pot from beyond the grave."

"Of?" I asked.

"Lycan," he answered. "They responded to the accusations of them being responsible for the blast at the community center. Naturally, they didn't claim responsibility. They blamed infighting between shifter groups."

"Did anyone really expect them to own up to it?" I asked. "But what does that have to do with Lycan?"

"HFH blamed Pack for the atrocities. They outed Pack with the information provided by the Davenport girl. When Rome's tests went public, it traced back to original studies on other shifter groups. Corali provided them with photos, historical documents, studies, the works. Pack is out, and there's no going back."

My eyes widened. "Holy shit. They won't be too thrilled about this, I imagine. The Davenports pissed off the wrong people."

Jax shook his head. "I don't think Pack has a leg to stand on. The information provided can be found in textbooks and historical records. The Davenports didn't say anything that isn't already known if you know where to look, and the only information they turned over was found at the public library."

"It sounds a lot like this isn't my problem," I answered.

"Wise decision," he replied.

While they gossiped about the new werewolf species, I drank my coffee and was just thankful to have been included. Soon, we broke away to our offices with the promise that I'd grab a coffee at their desks soon. I followed Mannix back to our small chunk of space, smiling. I sat at my desk and stared at the walls. It wasn't as fancy as my last office, but being welcomed had made the place the pinnacle of luxury. Holland popped in once to make sure my introductions went well. Then, he proceeded to yell at Jax for not handing in his report. Every so often, someone would duck into my office to shake my hand and welcome me. Abi stopped in once with a plant from her office, with a small grow light poking out of the middle.

"Are you okay?" Mannix rolled into the hall on his chair.

I nodded. "It's just weird having colleagues who want to work with me, who look me in the eyes, who shake my hand and not clean their hand with bleach after."

"We're all monsters here." He winked. "Was it really that bad at the university?"

"It wasn't just there, but yes."

"It's not like that here. Captain Holland runs a tight ship. He boots any who are the wrong kind of problem. If you have any issues, he'll handle it on the DL," he answered. "So, how long have you known about Pack?"

"Since I went to Mexico. You?"

"Since I started working here. They're on the confidential list. Some secrets aren't worth telling, not when they end lives, so I kept it to myself."

"Come tomorrow, the entire world will know." My arms prickled in goosebumps. "I'd rather not see the fallout."

"I doubt there will be much of a fallout," he said, looking more confident than I was. "They've remained hidden for this long. I suspect they'll remain as such until the world forgets about them again."

"Or they'll be dragged into the light like the rest of us were," I replied. "Secrets don't last forever, no matter how hard we try."

I sighed. I was truly sad their secrets were out. I'd have given anything to be off the radar of mankind. But it wasn't my problem, and I couldn't let it become one. I wouldn't live through another fight for or against Pack. When neither of us had anything more to add, the conversation shifted to topics I could comment on and probably survive. Although the subject steered toward the current issues of demons hiding out in the city, eating local pets and the odd person, I preferred this topic over the noose I had just gotten off my neck. Mannix showed me a few documents he needed on the regular and gave me a quick rundown of the briefings he and his team did every morning, showing me what I needed to bring to the meetings and what information Holland would be looking for from Mannix.

At four, my day ended, and it came to a close with a smile. I locked up my office and was walked out by Abi, who was still as excited as when she had first met me. She was scattered, messy, blunt and everything you'd want in a new colleague. It felt nice to have someone want to walk by my side, want to talk to me, want to ask questions and not fear my response. With a wave, she went one way, and I went the other, with a promise to have coffee together in the morning. When I hit the parking lot, I grinned. Miguel was leaning against my car, waiting for me.

"How was your first day?" he asked, searching my face for signs that I hated it.

"It was amazing," I said and was surprised at how eager and excited my voice sounded. But I was genuinely happy. This was the first job I had where my coworkers had treated me like I was one of them and not just someone to tolerate. "Everyone, literally every person I met, wanted to shake my hand and actually talk to me. No one got out of my way or avoided me. Everyone on shift and on my floor made a point to stop by my desk to welcome me. It was good. Mannix wasn't lying when he said I'd fit right it. I did, and it felt so good to belong."

He hugged me. "You're worth knowing, Lish. I'm so glad it went well."

"Do you want to go for dinner to celebrate?" I asked.

"What were you thinking? Pizza at the hospital or Chinese food at the hospital?"

I hugged him harder for knowing I'd want to be at the hospital. "Samuel likes pizza most."

"We'll need a truckload. Cisco and Sofia are with Samuel."

I ordered a dozen pizzas and chicken wings for Cisco and Sofia. A small thank you for staying to watch over Samuel. On the way to the hospital, we talked about the news report and Pack being brought into the light. The entire world was soon to know about his people. He wasn't shocked, and, according to him, this wasn't the first time the world had run their hands down the furry backs of Pack. They had contingency plans for this, but I had a feeling those plans wouldn't be working now that werewolves were legal citizens, and so did Miguel. I felt guilty, but I also didn't care one way or the other. Pack was not my problem. The moment I started to care would be when I was back in hot water. I played a part in their outing, but I wasn't the one who opened my mouth. The Davenports did that all on their own. I understood why Cordelia had done what she did. I'd have done worse for revenge and utterly soul-stripping for an innocent. I'd have dragged a Pack member in front of a news camera and pulled their wolf to the surface to save a soul. And if I was ready and willing to burn to save one life, imagine what else I'd do to keep myself alive.

Sitting in Samuel's room, all of us laughing, Cisco and Sofia eating chicken wings at the window, was better than anything I could ask for, and I had asked the heavens for a lot lately. Too many close calls for us all. By the skin of my teeth, I made it through another knock on the door to hell. They say everything happens for a reason, but they also say that nothing on either side of the gates of hell was as capable of fury as a witch pissed off. Push me hard enough, and I'd show them why witches were burned.

My house felt empty again, with Pack missing, but I was still alive and could complain about it, so it was a fair trade. With Pack off my back and Miguel close to my heart, which was still in my chest, I'd say I came out of that mess on top, especially since I thought I'd be six feet under. We huddled a little closer for fear of being alone, the last month scarring us deeper than we wanted to admit. We hadn't picked a wedding date but agreed we'd marry in the city and honeymoon in Mexico. I wanted to do a drive-thru in Vegas but was voted down by Sofia, Cisco and Miguel, who all said it was tacky. *Please.* Getting hitched with Elvis would have been a hell of a lot more fun than a stuffy dress that scratched my skin with people I barely knew. I finally caved once we agreed we'd keep it small and only invite those we cared about.

Every now and again, I saw Demetrius do a drive-by. He and his people would keep patrolling until city tensions simmered. With Pack on the brink of discovery, Demetrius wasn't willing to take chances. All of the details naturally came from his partner, Webb. Webb made the perfect daytime lunch date, even though I knew he was watching out for me when the sun held Demetrius back. Webb was more excited about an upcoming wedding than I was, and begged me to hold the wedding at night and not in a church. I said I'd think about it. Like Demetrius, Webb had a seductive pull that everyone else seemed to lean into, but he was nothing more than a pretty face to me, and I didn't bend to any of his requests because of it. I don't know if he toned it down for me or if I was just used to playing in the deep end with bigger and badder monsters that he just wasn't monster enough for me to flinch. But that's how monsters win you over, isn't it? The innocent charm turned on level ten until they lured you into a basement. I wouldn't drop my guard around him, and until the other shoe dropped, I'd enjoy the gossip and stories from a time I only read in books.

Philip had Pack under control, or so said May, but it was still touch and go. Werewolves were out, and everyone knew where shifters came from. Now, the world was looking for the originals. Until Lycan were an official species, I'd keep looking over my shoulder, waiting for one of them to get bold enough to approach me. I was brave, but I didn't have a death wish, so I kept my head down. I'd keep an eye out for those still gunning for me, but I wouldn't take any more of their shit. I'd hate to curse their inner wolves, but I'd do worse to not see a pyre again. As a demon once said, just weeks ago, hell hath no fury like a witch scorned.

Sign up for our newsletter and find out about all our romance book releases, eBook sales and promotions, sneak peeks and FREE romance books!

Want to see more like this?
Here's a taster for you to enjoy!

Meridian: Book & Candle
Aurelia T. Evans

Excerpt

Violet didn't even smell the incense anymore. People walked in and wrinkled their noses from the strength of sandalwood, cinnamon, lavender, whatever happened to be burning that day. The smoke got into her clothes, her hair, her skin. It rose up through the building to permeate the apartment above. But she'd gone almost completely nose-blind to it by now. Every morning, before turning the 'Closed' sign to 'Open', she lit the incense, closed her eyes, lifted prayers and blessings to the pantheon, then sent a text to Clive to come down when he was done fiddling with the coffee machine.

Her loose sleeves brushed against inventory like fingertips as she inspected the merchandise, mentally determining what she needed Clive to pull out from storage and what she needed to replace. Some — like the *Blessed Be* keychains, her stock of incense and candles, as well as cheaper altars and common tools and ingredients for rituals — were regularly reordered through wholesale vendors. No one *needed* a hand-crafted altar or a knife plated with real sterling silver to celebrate their spirituality. She had products for all kinds of budgets.

But she had to keep an eye on the rarer and more esoteric products, and twice a week, Father Bryer reluctantly pulled up to the back door of Book & Candle to bless any new inventory that might benefit from such a blessing, as well as to replenish her stock of holy water. She couldn't trust her wholesale vendors, who'd tried sending her false holy water because they'd assumed she wouldn't be able to tell the difference.

The only reason she thought Father Bryer did her the courtesy was because the good stuff didn't melt her like rain to sugar and she was the one who knotted the prayer beads and crucifixes for the necklace rack, with nary a cross-shaped scar on her palm.

She and Clive also hand-carved vampire stakes from ash. Plenty of vampire hunters did their own rough carving, because a working stake didn't have to be fancy, but sometimes a demon hunter had to dispatch a surprise bloodsucker from his territory or a civilian learned that there were real monsters in the shadows. They'd creep furtively into her magic shop, hoping she had more than New Age crystals. And she did—a whole wall of weapons, in fact, with stakes and knives of varying degrees of artistry. Most hunters and civilians were strictly practical, but even veterans appreciated a little embellishment now and then. Or she'd get the odd tourist who liked the idea of displaying a pretty stake next to their collection of Monster High dolls.

She turned over the 'Open' sign before Clive made it down, because it was eight-fifteen, and she didn't like the idea of staying closed much longer after her posted hours. Granted, her more serious clientele usually called this hour bedtime, but walk-ins could happen at any moment, and tourists were sometimes early birds.

Clive finally turned the corner from the stairs as she took her place behind the counter. He handed her the latte he'd made for her, with extra foam as an apology.

"Late night?" she asked.

"Me and my insomnia." Clive settled next to the weapons display and the raw materials to make more. Customers loved watching a handsome man working with his hands.

"Did you try my tea?" Violet tried to keep her tone even, because this was far from the first time Clive had come downstairs with dark circles under his eyes.

"You know I don't like tea."

"Better than the five mugs of coffee you use to try to caffeinate your sleep deprivation into submission."

"I'm working on it."

Violet sipped her coffee. Milk foam didn't quite make up for the last four weeks of complaining about sleepless nights without doing anything about them, even though he knew anything she gave him would be more effective than over-the-counter pills, folk remedies, or sleep hygiene rituals. She'd heard the creak of his bedsprings deep into the night as he would toss and turn. She would then light an unscented candle to chase off the darkness and pray until the spring-creaking stopped and her chest ached like a heart attack.

The bells over the front door jingled. Two girls who Violet assumed were morning birds between their coffee and a yoga session entered the shop, followed by a meticulously styled woman who Violet knew wasn't as frivolous as her costume would suggest.

Someone might look at Cam Brumley and see only a pin-up girl at the end of a themed-diner shift—or perhaps from a classier strip joint—but Violet's shoulders immediately tensed. As Clive carved, he kept an eye on Brumley while she browsed with the civilians. She was silent, deceptively casual, as the other two girls chattered and picked up things to smell them, inspect the craftsmanship, or try them on.

Brumley moseyed to Clive's station to watch him sharpen the point at the end of the branch. Her lips were set in a smile, but she smiled like a predator, showing her teeth in an aggression display.

Brumley finally gathered a dozen practical stakes from the bins in front of his station and carried them with a small basket of holy water and two new crucifixes—one made with black onyx beads and the other in ruby—to the counter for Violet to ring up in a series of practiced codes. She had a spreadsheet somewhere for when Clive had to take the counter or she brought in her cousin's friend Claudia to cover for her during convention weekends, bead shows, and ingredient-purchasing trips, but she knew the codes by memory—not by heart, because her heart wasn't necessarily in the business, even though she was still damn good at it.

The vampire hunter handed Violet a hundred-dollar bill. Violet handed over her change. There were no words exchanged, because Brumley didn't like Violet and Violet didn't like Brumley. They tolerated each other strictly for business, because business didn't care about vendetta, blood or otherwise.

Taking her paper bag, Brumley smiled again, showing five hundred teeth between carefully applied red lipstick. Petticoats swishing, she sashayed back out of Book & Candle. The bells sang merrily behind her.

Both Violet and Clive sighed in relief, almost in cadence.

The other customers didn't notice. With suggestive grins and barely restrained giggles, they gathered in front of Clive's station to watch him lean between his spread legs while he sharpened a stake. Clive flexed his muscles, built from years of physical labor, and grinned winningly right back at them. Violet didn't recommend using the stakes as dildos — from either end, because even the less pointy end could splinter — but Clive sometimes inspired the odd adventurous woman to purchase one of the more decorative pieces.

These girls weren't that kind of adventurous. They meandered instead over to the crystal section and selected small amethyst crystal balls, larger clear quartz shards, and a grab-bag of smaller, tumbled stones — popular among young and old alike.

Violet didn't generally work with stones, other than clear quartz and the occasional carnelian or chalcedony, but there was no denying that they were pretty. She had a bowl in her apartment bedroom for her own collection of smooth stones through which she sometimes ran her fingers to ground her as effectively as touching grass. In the city, she sometimes felt so disconnected from nature. It didn't hurt to have an abundance of it within her place of business and her home above.

Violet slipped the girls a beginner's guide to crystal use — most of it useless to them, but in Violet's experience, crystals tended to end up on a shelf and made people feel better just to look at them, so no harm, no foul.

She'd always trod the line between fraud and folktale, because when civilians entered a place like this, it was usually for fun, only occasionally desperation. In the same way they consulted a priest or read their horoscope, they visited Book & Candle for one of her protection pamphlets and a blessed silver knife, or they sneaked in on Thursdays for Frida's fortune-telling gig next to the crystal corner. Frida was as much a psychic as Clive was a witch, but Book & Candle collected the table rental fee and people rarely stormed into the store to demand their money back, because Violet promised nothing to anyone who didn't have knives strapped in unexpected places. As far as civilians were concerned, Violet was just another novelty New Age occult granola tattooed hippie Wiccan who played with plants and rocks and called religion by another name.

But she wasn't. And the people who mattered knew it.

The real Wiccans and other Neopagans tended to look down their nose at her, but they still bought their accoutrements from Book & Candle because she was local, almost as cheap as online, offered the occasional hand-crafted piece people couldn't find anywhere else, and nurtured the coolest carnivorous plants. Also, she sometimes sold herbs that weren't strictly legal — for a price.

The hunters tolerated her, too, because she provided an endless reserve of spells and sharp objects they could use against the demons in their fair city, and she could guarantee valid blessings and spells upon them. Some of their patrons got them the good stuff, the really rare stuff, or made their own, dabbling in magic and alchemy as only the rich could afford to do. But some of those same patrons surreptitiously purchased those things from Book & Candle anyway.

The demons wanted to eat her heart, in the most flattering way, but they left her alone, too, because she sold them the same extralegal herbs, spells, and weapons of their own.

Book & Candle was neutral ground. By Meridian standards, Violet and Clive were diplomats —

untouchable. Everyone needed them as much as they resented them. At best, she balanced precariously on the fences between the factions, but as long as no one pushed her, she stayed out of everyone's way and let them have their war — somewhere else.

Perhaps she was simply an inevitability in a place like Meridian — a capitalist with a solid market grip on the guns and gauze, metaphysically speaking. If that were really the case, though, she'd probably be richer. As it was, Violet just felt fortunate that she could keep up with rent on the store and apartment and employ Clive full-time. She even had a nice little nest egg growing under the care of her financial planner, who'd been recommended to her by one of the demons who frequented the store. It was in that demon's best interest to keep her happy so she could keep him in secretly donated virgin blood, so Violet had taken the referral and hadn't yet been disappointed.

Her stretch of work hours saw another steady trickle of unpredictable customers, civilians rubbing shoulders with demons in disguise, angels sharing uncertain glances with hunters of every shape, size, and variety — and all of them wary of the witch with whom they did business. But in the end, money was exchanged and everyone left in better condition than they came, which was why Book & Candle had been able to operate smoothly for the last eight years.

Her parents had thought she was crazy to leave the mountains, the forest, the security and safety away from prying eyes. Crazy to leave family and venture out on her own with nothing but a spell, a prayer and a booth at several of the farmers' markets before putting six months' rent down on what had once been old tea shop in the downtown square — a relic of when downtown had still been a quiet little side town too far from I35 to garner much notice.

The historical downtown district had been the first place touched by Angela Cabrera's Gothic hand, the façades renovated to a haunted-house grime thoroughly taken advantage of for Halloween festivals and perfect for Violet's aesthetic. Sure, the store was, by generous description, cozy—and, by less generous description, cluttered—but it and the cramped two-bedroom upstairs did their duty.

She'd been alone at first, and that had been lonely and sometimes frightening, considering the element she and her store attracted. But after three years making it on her own, Clive had moved into the second bedroom. Both bedrooms could pretty much only hold a bed and a dresser each, but they liked having separate sleep space, even if they sometimes shared a bed.

She might have been the more powerful of the two, but hunters and priests could be a misogynistic lot, and having visible muscle nearby also dissuaded demons. So she'd effectively gained a bouncer, a good friend, and a portion of the rent covered in the bargain.

The city rang with cold stone and concrete and steel, but she heard birdsong here as well as home, she kept grass and earth in her shop and within walking distance, and she had easy access to the dead. She wasn't completely cut off, and the dark and light magic that threaded like lightning through each lodestone, cornerstone and headstone charged her almost as well as climbing trees, digging for earthworms by the pond bank, and cultivating her garden and greenhouse rows.

Because of Meridian's later nights and her most popular clientele's sleep schedule, she kept the shop open until nine in the evening—sometimes later, if she was working with a historically good customer on something custom.

Tonight, however, was relatively quiet. Clive had left his station to package dried herbs while she tended her indoor gardens ensconced under sun lamps on the other side of the room from the weapons. After she turned the sign to 'Closed', Clive held up an Indian food menu, which meant they'd have dinner together tonight instead of alone. She smiled, pointed to her favorites that he already knew then vacuumed the shop while he left out back to pick up the food.

It wasn't the most glamorous job in the world, and she and Clive didn't speak as much as they used to, especially back when they'd met each other through his stepbrother, a hunter.

More adjacent to her world than part of it back then, Clive had taken to her immediately, intrigued as soon as he saw her under the stained-glass lamps hanging above the counter. He'd said she looked like an angel, the golden and colored lights caught like fireflies in the halo of her curly hair and glittering in her dark brown eyes. His stepbrother had replied that she was no angel, and she'd concurred. Despite the warning in the hunter's voice, Clive had slipped her his number and hadn't had much contact with his stepbrother since. As far as that hunter was concerned, Clive had stepped over to the other side. Clive, however, could better tell the difference between what demons did and what she was. Magic flowed through her veins and seeped out of her skin, as incense seeped in, but it wasn't the same kind of magic as demons, any more than that of angels.

Violet checked the locks and wards, then headed upstairs to their shared living area, arranging the small coffee table with utensils and glasses. She started that evening's wine without him as she listened to her uncle's record collection and let the coil of her magic unwind, draping over her shoulders and curling through her hair like little serpents. Her magic never completely left her, but it needed to relax as much as she did. She wondered if she could convince Clive to use those well-worked muscles on her shoulders and back tonight—and maybe more, although she'd been sleeping solo for more months than she was used to since leaving home.

Clive re-entered through the back, set the security alarm—although her wards were more effective than any security system—and trod up the stairs with new smells much less familiar to her nose-blind senses and therefore welcome.

He kissed her hair as he set the bags on the coffee table. "So, how was your day?"

"Oh, you know, same shit. Wine?"

"I'll get it."

She unpacked everything and set out plates. Then she put another Billie Holliday in the player. She'd made no secret about the fact that she didn't like most technology. The security system was a requirement from their leasing company, but she'd never had a television, depended on an older code-based cashier machine, and merely tolerated telephones. She'd been pulled into the smartphone era kicking and screaming and ordered from her vendors online by necessity but refused to put her own store online, although Clive had offered to be in charge of it. One of these days, she might be desperate enough, but today was not that day.

She and Clive settled on the loveseat and said little, because they'd already shared their whole day. Violet didn't mind the quiet, and Clive seemed preoccupied as he ate. They finished with mango lassis, Violet reading a novel and Clive staring into nothing with whatever distracted him these nights. When he was done, he rested back on the cushion and rubbed at his face and eyes, stretching his back in the opposite direction he hunched during his work.

As much as she wanted him to give her the massage, she set down her book to crawl over and ease his fingers from where they dug at his eye sockets. She rubbed his temples, over his forehead, until his hands fell away from his face entirely and rested slack in his lap. She inhaled the mixed bouquet of garam masala with the spiciness of infused incense through the apartment and used the power of both to warm her fingers. If he wouldn't take the tea, maybe she could help him sleep in other ways.

Violet moved the massage to his scalp, lightly scratching through his feathery hair with her nails, then over the base of his skull, then down to the knotted muscles of his neck and shoulders. He groaned in a way that curled like candle smoke in her lower abdomen. When she pressed a kiss to his temple — feverish from her fingers — he leaned against it, then lifted his head to meet her lips, though he kept his eyes closed.

They weren't exactly a couple and never had been, unless Violet just hadn't known otherwise. They might have dated or might have just gone out. They'd had sex plenty of times, but neither of them discussed it, as though that would solidify the ghost of what was between them into something less mysterious and ethereal. Sometimes they fucked and sometimes they didn't, sometimes they went weeks without being seen together outside the apartment.

And now it had been over two months since they'd even kissed, and Violet hadn't known how thirsty she was until she drank from him. The whole point of whatever they were was that they'd never be alone when they didn't want to be, that they'd always have a friend or a lover or a partner on the other side of a wall or right next to them if they needed. But although their daily routine hadn't changed, she'd felt so alone at night. She didn't think she was supposed to, not in Meridian, which fairly seethed with ghosts and monsters and everything in between, and where someone or something was always watching. So why did she feel so unseen?

She'd just eaten, yet below her stomach, how she hungered. She framed his face between her hands, sending whispers of wish and suggestion, not to manipulate but because it was easier to make him feel what she wanted than to say it. And she was, in the end, a witch. If he'd wanted just a woman, he wouldn't have moved in with her.

He gathered her in his arms as she climbed over his legs, but although he was hard against her when she straddled him, he drank less and less from her, his kisses more passive, and his hands too gentle on her, as though running over the same paths again and again to only mimic desire. He wasn't there with her.

Violet sighed and sat back on his thighs.

"I'm sorry." Clive rested his head back on the cushions. "I want to. I'm just tired. The magic can help with a headache, but…"

"I'll put the tea on your nightstand this time," Violet said. "If you drink it with a straw, you barely have to taste it."

He managed a weary smile, kissed her back when she kissed him, but it wasn't the kiss of a lover.

As she climbed off him, they might as well have been on different sides of the same mountain on the loveseat. She didn't like it. Even during previous dry spells, they'd had companionship. Without the benefits, they'd still been friends. But every night he felt farther and farther away, and she didn't know what she was doing wrong.

Other men—good and evil—wanted her, for all kinds of reasons. She didn't know why the one she needed didn't want her anymore. But she couldn't say anything now, because they hadn't said anything from the start, and she knew better than to hold too hard, or else what was already slipping through her fingers wouldn't be there anymore at all. Whatever distracted him, he'd tell her about it in his own time, or he'd resolve it on his own.

They'd promised each other nothing. She couldn't expect more than his portion of the rent and what she employed him for, and he could leave at any time, although she dared him to find a better deal so close to the historic downtown, a stone's throw from the best of Meridian.

She made the chamomile and catnip tea and stirred turmeric, honey, cardamom and cream in with the straw. Then she laced it with an under-breath chant, *"May slumber strike soon and swiftly and as gentle as the stroke of a feather."*

Violet brought the drink to his nightstand, as promised, then made one of her own, without the catnip or chant. She stopped the record player, which left the apartment too quiet while the two inhabitants knocked about with their evening rituals.

She considered leaving the loneliness of her own home and going to one of the clubs. She was as untouchable there as in her store, but any antagonism toward her could be its own deterrent. It had an energy effect on the people around her, whether they knew why or not. She thought about visiting Cemetery Grove to commune with the graveyards, although the stone angels there refused to speak to her. Or maybe she could bring herself into the twentieth century only a few years too late and go see a movie.

Anything she thought of made her more exhausted than she already was, despite the nervous, horny energy she'd yet to exorcise.

After Clive finished in the bathroom, she took a long, hot shower, then lotioned herself slowly to rub against the muscles that he hadn't. She wasn't sure when she'd started to ache like this, joint and bone deep, untouchable by herb or incantation. Maybe there was a storm coming. Maybe she was more upset than she'd thought.

Or maybe it was just that she was older now — although far from old — and with wisdom came pain. She'd consult her grandmother's grimoire in the morning. If nothing else, Ethel Panabaker was no slouch when it came to her remedies, for anything from the sudden onset of a cold to the most violent heartbreak, sour stomach to lingering grief. Violet modeled her own grimoire on her grandmother's, wished she'd known her longer in life so she could seek advice more directly than through fading scribbles.

Violet uncapped her hair, then wrapped it up before taking the rest of her tea into her room, where she read until she couldn't keep her eyes open. Clive had already closed his bedroom door. He might as well have locked, bolted, and sealed himself away.

She needed to go to his door. She needed to knock. They needed to talk. It needed to happen, and soon. She needed to ask if their arrangement was no longer adequate, if there was anything she could do, or if what had brought them together had since frayed away, like a boat untethered. She needed to know if he still loved her as a friend, as something more. She needed to know if he wanted out, if he wanted to leave as her lover, as her friend, as her coworker. It would hurt to cut ties, but she hurt more not knowing whether she should reel him in or set him loose. It was time for a change, instead of this constant holding pattern, like a haunting — ghost ships passing in circles. Boundaries encouraged healthy growth, but once a plant outgrew its container, those borders could suffocate.

Violet reached up to stroke the shoots of the spider plant hanging above her bed as though to ask it what she should do, but plants didn't concern themselves with the doings of people, as long as the plants were fed, watered, and put in a place to soak up sun.

She tucked her book back in its nightstand drawer and switched off the lamp, sighing.

Just as she started drifting to sleep, she jolted awake as though falling.

At first, she didn't know what had brought her back, but then the creaking of mattress springs through the layers of dry wall between her and Clive's bed grounded her. Not the quick series of squeaks that meant he was restless in his inability to fall asleep, but the kind that meant he was either with someone or engaging in particularly enthusiastic masturbation.

Either one hurt her from chest to fingertips, because she'd been *right there*, and he'd told her he was tired. She hadn't heard any of the door alarms go off, any floorboard creaks on the way up the stairs. So he would rather jerk himself off than fuck her.

She was a goddamn folk witch of the Panabaker and Corinth lines, and even those who hated her watched the way her breasts moved under her dress when she chose not to wear a bra during summer, which in Texas lasted well more than half the year. Her body was wanted, whether whole or in parts, yet she was sexually frustrated in her bed while the man she'd thought still wanted her was roughly rubbing one off instead of knocking on her door.

Over and under the skin, her flesh tingled. She slipped her fingers beneath her sleep shirt to stroke over her abdomen but still resisted sliding her hand down. Her magic roiled inside her so deliciously that she would rather have someone to share it with.

Violet sighed, considering whether she should turn over and cover her head with the pillow to muffle the slow rise of his moans. It wasn't like he was going to take much longer, not at that pace and with that kind of insistence.

Instead, she released the pillow and raised herself up on her knees. She pulled her T-shirt over her head, leaving herself only in her underwear in the cool, air-conditioned room.

Then she lowered herself back down to sit between her heels, and she listened. Felt the vibration of the bed springs through her fingers. Found his rhythm. Imagined herself over him, imagined him inside her, imagined she was the one making him moan like that, imagined he was stroking over her instead of himself, imagined that when she shifted her hips up and down over nothing that she was taking him in. She rocked in her bed to the beat of his, biting her lip as her bed springs started to creak in time.

He wouldn't notice the sound, but maybe, just maybe, he would feel the tendrils of her magic within him. Arousal sang inside her, opened her like ferns unfurling toward the sun. The things she would do to have him beneath her. She'd knock his hands away from his cock and swallow him bare and straining down her throat, let him hold her head down. She'd moan and gulp and swallow and swallow until he knocked his head against the headboard and pushed up into her tightening mouth and let loose *that* sound, that one right there he made because he thought she was already asleep and couldn't hear him come without her.

Violet slumped, chin against her chest, turned on but a little nauseated.

Because his moan wasn't the only one she'd heard.

About the Author

L.A. Kennedy, beyond the story…

L.A. Kennedy is a Canadian born writer, living in the ever-growing city of Vancouver, Canada. Here, she spends her days getting lost in the beauty of reading and writing. L.A. Kennedy mainly writes fictional books. And can be found researching myth, folklore, and everything in between, with a special interest in edge-of-your-seat paranormal romance. L.A. Kennedy can be found behind a mountain of books, on any given Sunday.

L.A. Kennedy's writing credits include two hit series that mix mystery, horror, paranormal romance, fantasy, and intrigue.

L.A. Kennedy loves to hear from readers. You can find her contact information, website details and author profile page at https://www.firstforromance.com

ENTWINED PUBLISHING